Marcus Burke

TEAM SEVEN

Marcus Burke grew up in Milton, Massachusetts, just outside Boston. A standout athlete, he attended prep school at Brimmer and May and was recruited to play basketball at Susquehanna University, where he played varsity for all four years. A knee injury limited his playing time, so he took up fiction writing and was later accepted at the Iowa Writers Workshop, where he was awarded a grant in honor of James Alan McPherson from the University of Iowa MacArthur Foundation Fund. He lives in Iowa City, Iowa.

TEAM SEVEN

A NOVEL

Marcus Burke

Anchor Books
A Division of Random House LLC
New York

FIRST ANCHOR BOOKS EDITION, NOVEMBER 2014

The Library of Congress has cataloged the Doubleday edition
as follows:
Burke, Marcus.
Team seven / Marcus Burke. — First edition.
pages cm
1. African American teenagers—Fiction. 2. Drug traffic—Fiction.
3. City and town life—Massachusetts—Fiction. I. Title.
PS3602.U755245T43 2014
813'.6—dc23
2013032242

Anchor Books Trade Paperback ISBN: 978-0-345-80644-4
eBook ISBN: 978-0-385-53780-3

Book design by Michael Collica

www.anchorbooks.com

146122990

To my mother, my sisters, and Mary

In loving memory of my grandparents,
Lloyd and Ruby Sharp

Contents

TEAM SEVEN

1

Vitals

Pop and Uncle Elroy smoke the strangest cigarettes I've ever smelled. They smell sort of like skunk juice and gasoline mixed with the incense they burn at Nana and Papa Tanks's church, St. Paul's Episcopal. When Pop and Uncle Elroy are both home in the summertime they stay up late at night hanging out in the backyard, sitting below my bedroom window with the streetlights glowing on them from foot to midbelly. The rest of their bodies are hidden under the shadow of the oak trees in our backyard. They always sit facing away from our house toward the next yard over, blowing that smelly-smoke up into my window, and sometimes if I breathe it in long enough it makes me dizzy but in a giggly good way. I like it, it's nice.

I would ask Pop about his strange-smelling funny-cigarettes but I'm afraid to ask him questions anymore. He's always in a rush and never tells me where he's going when he leaves. Whenever I see him putting on his black Rasta cap, I find a reason to be near the door so I can try to stall him up and make him stay. I used to always ask him where he was going and most of the time he didn't hear me and he'd just leave. Other times he simply says, "Out," and forgets to say good-bye. But the last time he left, he yelled at me and this is why I don't ask him questions anymore and would rather spy.

I saw him in the living room putting on his Rasta cap and I

went into the hallway and opened up the closet near the front door where Ma keeps the extra soap, blankets, washcloths, towels, and toilet paper. When I opened the door a stack of washcloths fell from the top shelf. I caught them and looked up, and down came an avalanche of towels and blankets on my head. I didn't fall, but it dazed me. I heard Pop's footsteps coming and I shook the mess onto the floor. He was wearing his long black leather coat with his black sunglasses and Rasta cap. His shades were so dark I couldn't tell if he saw me or not.

"Where ya going, Pop?" I blurted out, loud, so he could hear me.

He grabbed the doorknob. "Out."

For some reason I was feeling brave and so I did something I'd never done before. I asked him again. A little louder, making sure he heard me this time.

"Out like where, Pop?" I said it loud but nicely. "It's so big outside. You could go anywhere." I smiled and he stopped and took his hand off the doorknob and turned to me.

"Out, I said!"

"I know." I put my hands in my pockets and rocked back onto my heels. "But like—"

"Andre! Don't ask me any goddamn questions." He clapped his hands together and squatted down. He pointed his hand in my face and then at the mess on the floor around me. "Clean. It. Up!"

I could hear the anger scraping through his closed teeth. He didn't understand my question but I didn't want to make him any angrier.

"Better be clean before I get back home!" He stood.

I was too scared to look at him so I looked at the scuffs on his boots and tried to keep my breath.

"Out of order questioning a grown man like you have no broughtupsy."

On the floor beneath us I could see his shadow shaking its head at me.

I focused harder on his boot scuffs trying to stay calm but my lip started shaking too bad and I couldn't breathe. I tried to gulp but whimpered instead and he heard me. He grabbed my shoulder and I dropped to the ground. It didn't hurt as much as it scared me, but I was down and he was standing over me. I hugged my head into my lap. He reached down and snatched me up by the side of the shirt and I hugged into myself as tight as I could.

"Get up and cut it out. Before I give you something to cry for."

He let me go, opened the door, and slammed it behind him.

I stayed on the floor crying in the blankets and towels until I felt stupid. I wiped my face with a washcloth and got off the floor and stomped to my room. I left those towels there because I didn't drop them, they fell on me and that's not my fault.

The only other place I'd ever smelled the smell of Pop and Uncle Elroy's cigarettes was once at Kelly Park. I was with Ma and it made her really angry. We'd parked up top of the hill at the track and Ma held my hand and we walked down to the basketball courts together. She was only coming down to see me make a lefty layup and then she was supposed to go back up and walk the track, but these older kids were hanging out, taking up half the court. Some of them were sitting around a picnic table playing cards and others were lying on the court and in the grass.

We stopped on the sideline and I recognized the older kids that hang on the other end of our block. I let go of Ma's hand and started dribbling my ball. I knew most of them only by face. They had a car parked at half court with its trunk open, blasting a Wu-Tang Clan song I'd never heard before. I knew I liked the song when my main man Ol' Dirty Bastard started singing and beat-boxing over the beat doing his ad libs. I couldn't understand what he was saying, but it sounded funny and I liked the beat.

Right before the beat drops it pauses and it gets quiet and then ODB yells, "You bitch-ass nigga!" And the song starts.

I started cracking up. Ol' Dirty Bastard's my favorite member in Wu-Tang Clan. His voice is so raspy and mousy he sounds like Mike Tyson with sand in his throat. As I laughed I looked up at Ma and her forehead wrinkled like a chewed Tootsie Roll. She folded her arms across her chest. I dribbled between my legs as we stood on the sideline watching the older boys swirl their clear plastic cups of what looked like the last couple sips of apple juice. They'd already played, most of them had taken off their shirts and changed out of sneakers into flip-flops. A few of them stood in a little circle and started smoking those cigarettes.

I recognized one of the guys smoking, it was Ma's friend Miss Myra's oldest son, Stanley. I see him around but I don't really know him. He pulled from the cigarette a few times and passed it to the guy on his left. After Ol' Dirty Bastard's ad libs, Stanley turned toward us and started bopping his shoulders and swaying to the music and all the guys started laughing and cheering him on. He was shimmying his way toward us. His eyes were dragon red and he slowly blew smoke out of his nose like an angry bull. When Ol' Dirty Bastard's verse came on, he closed his eyes and tossed his head back, waving his hands in the air like he was shooting pistols as he sang along with Ol' Dirty Bastard.

As high as Wu-Tang get,
Allah, allow us pop this shit
Just like black shoe fit
If you can't wear it, then don't fuck with it!

He jumped into a ghetto-girl pose, two feet on the ground, leaning hard to his left side, popping his hips, arms crossed like he was mocking Ma. He looked at us laughing. A guy passed him back the cigarette and this is when I first smelled that smell. I'd never smelled anything so strange, but I liked it. I nudged Ma's leg and she looked down at me.

"What's that they're smoking, that smells like that?" I whispered. "It's weird."

"Ayo, lil' man. Lemme get a shot. Lil' man!" I was glad Stanley didn't hear me.

I wound up to pass him my basketball when Ma reached down and wrestled it away from me.

"Andre, let's go." She tucked the ball under her arm and grabbed my hand pulling me back toward the track and we started walking.

I tried to wiggle away but her grip was too tight.

"But, Ma, I thought—" I whined but she wouldn't let go.

"Ayo, lil' man?" Stanley called, but we just kept walking.

We got to the top of the hill and Ma loosened her grip but didn't let go. She looked down at me.

"They aren't smoking cigarettes, Andre. They're frying their brains, they're foolish," Ma said.

She looked back down the hill at Stanley and yelled, "Kids have to play here too!"

Stanley and all his friends laughed and so did I. I thought she was kidding.

"Why would anyone want to fry their brain, Ma?" I asked her.

"Because they are foolish. You're not like them, you're a cut above the rest. Stay away from guys like them, Andre. They're no-good men."

I didn't understand but I said okay. For whatever reason Stanley and his friends brain-frying made Ma angry. It made her so mad I got stuck walking boring laps around the track with her, every now and again trying to get her to let go of my hand.

The second time I smelled that smell, it was midsummer and I was in bed. It came floating into my bedroom from outside, a little bit after Ma kissed me and Nina good night and tucked us in. I woke up to pee and when I went to lie back down I heard voices coming from out our backyard. I thought I smelled that smell but I wasn't sure, but after another gust of wind rattled my Reggie Lewis and Len Bias posters, I knew it was that same smell from the park. My heart started racing. I had to see who the brain-frying foolish-guys were making noise outside my window.

I snuck out of bed, pushed my toy chest up against the wall, climbed on top, and opened the window. I knelt down, leaning my face against the screen, breathing lightly so I could listen and see. My ears started to tingle and my cheeks got hot when I realized it was Pop and Uncle Elroy blowing that smelly-smoke into my room. I knew Pop was grumpy but I didn't know he was a bad man. I didn't think he was all that bad. I was confused.

If him and Uncle Elroy were foolish bad men then why did Ma and Aunty Diamond marry them? I wasn't sure what it was, but I got a feeling something strange was going on with Ma and Pop.

I could hear the nearby dance hall music so clear, but their voices seemed to only break through the songs in jumbles. Pop and Uncle Elroy both talked Jamaican, not all the time like Papa Tanks and Grampy Battel, they turned theirs on and off. When they hung out together they turned their Jamaican accents on, real thick. At first I couldn't understand what they were saying or talking about. So I started spying on them every night they were out there, and after listening to them a few weeks I started to understand a little bit. I learned that "Jah" has something to do with everything, and everything bad was somehow caused by "Babylon." Whenever they spoke, everything they said started with "I an' I" or "Brethren." I also learned that they call their weird-smelling cigarettes "vitals." After about three or four of those green-bottle sodas and two or three vitals apiece they'd go silent. Two red dots pulsing in the dark.

Every now and again the dance hall music would erupt into gunshots or police sirens and the whole song would flip into rewind and the DJ would scream out over the song. He'd yell Jamaican curses, there's a bunch of them and they all end in a clot: pussy-clot, blood-clot, bumba-rass-clot, anything ending in "clot," really. Or the DJ would say even more random stuff like "Bulla-Bread" or "To-Backfoot." He would shout three or four words tops, and nothing more. Pop and Uncle Elroy would say weird stuff too, like "Selassie-I" or "To-blouse an' skirt," and they'd laugh so hard. Half the time they said no more than one or two words to each other. It's like they didn't even need words to be friends. I'd kneel, watching them inhaling their vitals until I was dizzy with sleep or Pop said he was going to bed and I'd run back to mine.

Some nights Uncle Elroy wouldn't come back upstairs to Aunty Diamond. Instead he'd hop the fence and cut through our neighbors' yard heading toward the parkway. He wouldn't say bye to Pop either, he'd just laugh and say, "Riddim and Spice," and hop the fence. Pop would chuckle and call back, "N'everyt'ing nice." Some nights after Uncle Elroy left, Pop would get up and hop the fence too. Sometimes he'd be home the next morning. Sometimes he'd be gone for days, sometimes weeks.

When he left, I just hoped it wouldn't be for months like Uncle Elroy.

On the nights he stayed, I liked it better that way, but I couldn't ever tell if he did. He'd just sit there all alone in the shadows. Without Uncle Elroy he didn't listen to the radio. He'd sit in quiet, with one leg on the ground and one on the edge of his chair, rocking himself side to side, muttering to himself. I always tried but I could never quite hear him. Every once in a while he'd sigh real deep to himself, blowing smoke into the shadowy darkness. One hand holding a green-bottle soda and the other a burning vital.

As much as I spied on him, the one thing I never got to see was what was on his mind. What was out there for him in the streets on the nights he stayed away? When he was gone, I wondered if he was out looking for Uncle Elroy or off doing his own thing.

On the nights he stayed, I'd watch him sitting out there all alone and I don't know why he always seemed so sad but I could just tell. I wondered if he wanted company. If I went out there and sat with him, would it cheer him up?

I wanted to go out there and sit next to him. Maybe rest my

head on his shoulder. I'd tell him that I liked the smell of his vitals. I'd ask him why that smell makes me dizzy and sleepy after a while. I'd ask him why he wanted to fry his brain, and if he knew that Ma thought he was a foolish and bad man. More than anything I wanted to know why he got so mad when I asked him questions and why he never took me out with him.

The nights he stayed I watched him until he'd yawn and stand up muttering, and I'd hop off my toy chest so he didn't see me when he turned around and faced the house. I'd sit in front of my bed, waiting, listening, nervous that he might still change his mind, hop the fence, head toward the parkway and leave. Sometimes he would. Sometimes he wouldn't. It wasn't until I'd hear him rattling through the basement door that I'd smile and get in bed, happy and ready to sleep, wondering what made him stay.

2

Breakfast of Champions

Gemini stomped his feet on the platform, marching in place, pounding his chest as the crowd cheered. The camera zoomed in on his face and his bushy mustache stretched thin and he growled at the crowd and strapped on his headgear. He adjusted his elbow pads and locked his fingers, stretching his arms out and cracking his knuckles and bouncing his pecs. The camera moved to the other platform where the contender stood. Patrick Sullivan, a redheaded computer programmer from Los Angeles, California. He played wide receiver in high school and club dodgeball in college.

The American Gladiators logo floated across the screen and the picture zoomed in on Patrick's freckled cheeks. He flashed a gap-toothed smile at the camera and scrunched his nose trying to look meaner as he pumped his bony arm at the crowd and the platforms began lifting him and Gemini up into the air.

"A' joke t'ing dat." Papa Tanks stood in the doorway of the den pointing at the TV, waving his fork back and forth. "Look 'pon the broad-back black man, he a'go kill him. Look how him scream up the place like a'leggo beast."

"Who? Gemini? He's my favorite Gladiator on the show. He beats everyone, Pa-Paw," I said.

"Don't correct me." He pointed the fork in my direction. "No matter, whoever him is he wouldn't beat me. He facing off against a pink-skin mawga-dog. Him nah' prove nothing, mashing up a lickle man."

"But, Grampy, Gemini's the man!" I crossed my arms and turned away from him. The announcers started explaining the rules, basically they're jousting with each other using what look like giant Q-tips. First one to fall off their platform loses.

"Wha' ya say? Him a'who? You na' know him, wha' mek him a man? I bet him couldn't even cook a one blinking dumpling fi himself. How him a man if him na' cook? Muscles na' mek you a man. See, I am a man, the man of dis house. Me handle me business, protect me yawd, and na' tek bright from no one."

Papa Tanks grinned at me and turned his body to the side, flexing his biceps. His rubbery skin stretched tight, puffing out a maze of veins up and down his arms.

The referee walked into the arena and stood on the red bouncy pad below the platforms. He slipped his whistle in the side of his mouth and looked up at Gemini and raised an arm in the air.

"Gladiator, readaaay!!" Gemini rocked side to side, knees bent, slowly nodding yes.

The referee raised his other arm up and looked up at Patrick.

"Contender, readaaay!!"

Patrick snapped his head side to side and gave a thumbs-up. The referee leaned back with his hands above his head and right as he went to blow the whistle the theme music came on and it cut to commercial. Papa Tanks went walking into the kitchen shaking his head as he flipped the plantain frying on the stove. We watch *American Gladiators* every morning and every morning he stands in the doorway keeping an eye on his breakfast cooking on the stove, and I sit on the couch in the front den eating my bowl of Honey Nut Cheerios. Each day he tells me about a new person he remembers from back home in Limón, Costa Rica. He says he and the rest of the Jamaicans that came over to work the fields were built like oxen.

He cooks breakfast for himself and Nana Tanks, because she's got a cold in her knees and some mornings she can't come into the kitchen because it hurts to stand up too long, so she stays in bed watching reruns of *Bonanza*. Papa Tanks always fries some ripe plantain and cuts up some hot dogs, onions, and tomatoes and makes an egg mix-up.

"You think you could beat Gemini, Pa-Paw?" I called into the kitchen.

He walked back over from the stove.

"Champion, you mad or wha'? A'dat you know!" I like it when Papa Tanks talks about how tough he is and flexes his muscles. Sometimes he even does push-ups in the doorway as we watch. "Me a'give him one rattid box in'a him head. Mek him drop like bird out'a sky. From you see how dem size nah match up, you know dem a'bad mind the lickle red hair bump-face boy."

The show came back from commercial and the theme music played as the referee blew his whistle, and a blast of smoke blew up between Gemini and Patrick. When the smoke cleared, Patrick wagged his stick at his waist like he was rowing a boat. He leaned down pretty low and swung a few times at Gemini's legs. Gemini's eyes locked in on Patrick and he whacked him a few times until Patrick looked stunned and Gemini wound the jousting stick above his head like an ax.

He chopped down and Patrick dodged the strike.

Gemini lost his balance and swung the stick back trying to regain his footing, and Patrick jabbed his stick into Gemini's ribs, and Gemini jerked to the side, dropping his jousting stick. Before he fell off the platform he turned and caught the side of Patrick's next strike and bear-hugged the padded end of the stick and pulled them both to the ground. It was unreal. I'd never seen anyone beat Gemini. Gemini roared out as they fell to the pad. When his body hit first, before Patrick's, I got a jolt in my knees. I didn't think about it, I just jumped up out of my seat and roared like I was Gemini myself, but instead of me hitting a bouncy pad, milk and Honey Nut Cheerios splashed up in the air and flew everywhere.

"Woi! Boychild, look how you bright up yourself, wha' sweet you?"

"I forgot that my bowl was on my lap, Pa-Paw, but Gemini lost." I looked down at the Cheerios stuck to my legs and the milk at my feet. "I just jumped. I'm sorry, Pa-Paw." I felt my face getting hot.

"Mmm hhhmm." He turned his head, gazed down at me sideways, folded his arms, and smirked.

"I is da real champion—in'a these parts." He flexed his arm at me and we laughed. I looked up at him and he smiled at me and his new dentures gleamed. "I know, Pa-Paw, I know."

He came over and put his hand on my shoulder. "You lucky Nana in'a she room this morning, eeh?" He rubbed the top of my head and patted my back a few times. "Come on, get a rag and clean up and pour a next bowl for yourself."

I shook my head. "There's no more cereal, Pa-Paw, and I only had two bites before I dropped it." I sniffled and looked away.

"Ay, don't cry, my yout', you alright. We a'mek you some breakfast, eeh?"

He clicked off the TV and we walked into the kitchen and I got a rag and started wiping up the milk. He took the plantain off the stove and walked the plate in to Nana Tanks.

He came back into the kitchen with a footstool and set it down next to himself.

"Boychild, come here." I walked over to him and stepped up onto the stool next to him. On the counter in front of me, he put a bowl with two eggs in it and a plate with a short butter knife and a hot dog. He had the same setup in front of himself except he had small pieces of tomato and onion on his plate.

"Hold your knife in your right hand and hold the hot dog steady with your left, and cut it into eight pieces."

I cut the hot dog down into eight little pink nuggets and looked over at Papa Tanks.

"What now?"

"Crack the eggs. Watch me." He took an egg and knocked it on the counter until its shell cracked and he pulled it open and the egg dropped into the bowl. "Now you try," he said.

I picked up the egg and cracked it on the edge of the counter, pulled the shell and the egg fell in the bowl, but some of the clear part got on me and it felt nasty. I dropped my fork and stepped off the stool, wiped my hand on my shorts. I looked at Papa Tanks. "I don't wanna cook, Pa-Paw, the egg juice got on my hands." I looked up into the bluish-gray rims around his sagging brown eyes, and he scratched the bald spot on top of his head. He put his hand on my shoulder and looked at me and the wrinkles on his face hung smooth and I could tell he was about to tell me something serious.

"You must learn to cook. Man is only to need a woman for love. If your wife run off and leave you, you na' go' dead. Champion, get ya backside back up here."

I could tell what he said was important, even though I didn't understand what he was talking about exactly. I hopped back up on the stool and cracked my other egg into the bowl. Papa Tanks looked over and tipped my bowl toward him, and smiled. I watched Papa Tanks cracking eggs for Nana Tanks's breakfast too, only he took the yellow parts out of the bowl with a spoon and tossed them in the sink.

"Why'd you take the yellow parts out, Pa-Paw?"

"Them is called the yolk. I take it out 'cause Nana has high salt and too much weight squeezing at she heart. She even take pills to equal herself out. Pick up the fork and pop the yolks."

I poked my fork into the yolk and watched the yellow ooze out. Papa Tanks splashed some milk into my bowl.

"Now stir them up," he said as he mixed the eggs in his bowl.

Once the eggs were creamy yellow, Papa Tanks told me to hop down and he picked up the stool and walked it over to the stove and set it down next to himself. He turned on the fire and we sat at the kitchen table. I looked at the sales flyers for the supermarket and Papa Tanks read the newspaper until the oil heated up and I could see the air rippling over the frying pan.

"Come on." Papa Tanks turned back to the counter and got both our plates. He handed me my plate of hot dog bits. "Here, drop them in the pan."

I stepped up onto the stool and the oil swirled around in the frying pan. I forked the hot dogs into the oil. The oil splashed up and a haze of smoke started filling the kitchen. I jumped back off the stool again and almost fell, and Papa Tanks leaned back against the counter holding his sides trying not to laugh at me. I could tell he was laughing, so I crossed my arms and headed for the front den, but his big hand wrapped around my shoulder. "Where you running off to?"

I thought he was mad but when I looked up he was smirking at me. "Lesson you a'go learn today. Step up, champion."

He held his hand out and I grabbed on and he helped me back up onto the stool as the hot dogs sizzled and the oil bubbled and the smoke died down. He handed me the bowl with the eggs in it.

"Pour it in the pan."

I poured the eggs into the pan and they sizzled.

"Take this." He handed me an oven mitt and a spatula. I put on the oven mitt and he said, "A man mustn't fear the heat, boychild."

He walked behind me, leaned over my shoulder, and held my hand, gripping his hand over the oven mitt and spatula, and we stirred the eggs together. "You just have to know when to turn the gas down." We kept stirring until the eggs got thicker and started to clump, his arm tracing over mine. He stepped back and loosed his grip. "Now keep stirring until the hot dogs get brown."

He walked to the cabinet and got me a plate. "Good job, boychild. Dem cook up nice, step down."

I hopped off the stool and he walked up to the stove and poured the egg mix-up into the plate and walked it over to the table, where he poured me a Dixie cup of coffee mixed with hot chocolate. He poured a cup for himself and opened a pink packet and poured it into his coffee.

"What's that?" I asked.

"It's sugar for people who got high sugar, like me. I eat too many sweets when I was a young man and too much sweets nah good fi de blood."

I nodded okay, not really knowing what was in the packet or what he was talking about. I ate my plate as he cooked eggs for him and Nana Tanks. After he walked Nana Tanks's plate into their room for her, he came to sit down next to me right when I was on my last bite. He put his plate down, poured us more coffee, and he ate as I sipped my coffee. We didn't say anything to each other but we'd glance and nod our heads every now and again. I finished my third Dixie cup of coffee and stood up. Papa Tanks looked over his shoulder at me and chuckled a bit.

"Eat and go 'way, huh?"

I smiled at him. "Thanks for breakfast, Pa-Paw."

"You get enough to eat?"

"Yes."

I flexed my arm muscles at him and he squinted and patted at the little bulge in my bicep.

"You a grown man now, eeh?" I nodded and he rustled my hair and pulled me into his side and nuzzled his head against mine. He let go of me and said, "Not quite a man yet, but you getting close. You still need to grow some whiskers, soon enough though, my yout'."

I glanced at the clock in the den. *Captain Planet* was about to come on. Papa Tanks slapped his hand on the table and I flinched.

"Ay, boy, you listening to me? You'll never starve 'cause you know how to cook, I say."

He squinted at me, lowered his shoulders to my level from his chair, and poked me in the belly and tickled my sides, and we both laughed and I squirmed until he let me go.

"Alright, now run along, go watch the TV."

"Okay, Pa-Paw," I said and ran into the front den.

I clicked on the TV just as the theme song was playing and I sang along, "Captain Planet, he's a hero—"

"Bobby-sock, I am the hero!" Papa Tanks called to me from the kitchen.

He let out a big belly laugh and I laughed too.

3

Team Seven

Ruby Battel

It was Christmas Eve and we had just got back from Star Market. I sat down at the kitchen table to sort through the mail as the kids zoomed around the kitchen putting away the groceries all giddy and excited for the night I'd planned. We always do a fish fry and then make Christmas cookies. Eddy and I started doing that when we first got married and the tradition stuck around way longer than he did. A letter had come for Eddy from the Norfolk County Child Support Enforcement Bureau. A woman named Iris K. Patton was filing a grievance for unpaid child support for their son Eddy Battel, Jr. I read on. The letter said his extracurricular bastard child was nine years old too. That little out-of-wedlock thing is only one year younger than my baby Andre.

The news lodged a hot piece of coal in my chest and wrapped me in a straitjacket. I couldn't just take the kids and leave. Where would we go? We live in the apartment downstairs from my parents in their two-family house and we don't hardly pay the rent on time. He didn't come home last night. He's like a cat, he comes and goes on his own terms. He left yesterday while I was at work and all he told Andre and Nina was that he'd be back with us tonight to bake cookies.

"You ready, Ma?"

I looked up from the letter. Nina was holding our big silver mixing bowl and a wooden spoon. The smile on her face melted a fake one into mine. Christmas was always about the kids. Every year we put on the Nat King Cole Christmas album and stay in the house together to bake sugar cookies as a family. At midnight we all go upstairs to my parents' apartment, and Nina and Andre open up the presents from my parents. Then they go to sleep and wake up and unwrap what I got for them.

The doorbell rings and I know it's my younger sister Diamond with her new snap-turtle-looking boyfriend, Lex, with his bald water-baby head, and his no job. My eyes watered up and my insides started to twist. I wanted to run to the door and collapse. Drag Diamond by the arm into my room and just melt down. But no. This is my life, and Diamond, she never liked Eddy. I give her five minutes of milling around the apartment before she gets around to asking, "So how's Eddy?" She'll look concerned, put her hand across her mouth and follow me around the room with her eager eyes. Ever since she divorced her ex-husband Elroy and got him deported back to Jamaica, she thinks she's better than somebody. She'd know Eddy's truck wasn't out front but she just liked to hear me say it. She gets a kick out of the whole exchange. So she could hold a deep stare over my shoulder and shake her head, searching and waiting, like I owed her an explanation.

He's a wayward bastard and that's been established, but he is my husband and the father of my children. He at least makes it home for the holidays. I swallowed and tucked that letter in my back pocket along with all my good emotions. I opened the front door and told Diamond that Eddy was getting off of work late and that we could go ahead and start baking without him. The night rocked along slow. The kids were enjoying themselves but I was losing faith.

Around ten thirty his Bronco rattled up outside. He blew inside, stumbling, and smelling like the bar he'd probably been slumped in all night. From the minute that man stepped his feet in the house he was all jumpy and twitching around like he had lightning in his veins, eyeing the clock like he was already trying to leave again. His jaw was chattering and I knew he was high on something. I just hoped I was the only one who noticed it 'cause tonight was not about him.

I've always tried to live the way my mother says: "Never let your life show." I stretch out my pockets so the kids can have a few things to show their friends when they get back to school after vacation. I supported Eddy when he began to struggle, same way he continues to struggle, all in the name of getting his reggae career off the ground. I even sign the kids' presents: "From Mommy and Daddy." All I asked is that he just be around to spend time with his kids. He checked out of our marriage in terms of a relationship a long while ago. But the papers aren't signed yet. And I'm still the wife of Eddy "E-Bone" Battel.

"Pop!"

The kids screamed in unison and ran up the hallway, draping off of him like he was a walking coatrack. They almost knocked him over. We were making the frosting for the sugar cookies; Diamond snorted and flashed a look across the table at Lex. They both stood up and walked through the back door up to my parents' apartment. I was slow simmering with that envelope in my back pocket, pretending like I wasn't hurt. I couldn't even look at him. He didn't say a word to me either. He ain't come home last night, he knew just what was on my mind. He knows I don't like going through it in front of the kids, and with that stupid smirk on his face he thinks he is safe.

As soon as Eddy took his coat off Andre was his shadow. Andre sat next to the head of the table with his father and Nina was down the other end with me. Every time Andre cut out a cookie he stared at Eddy and waited until he'd smile or nod. Nina just sat with me and smiled. She always liked when we were all together, but she's shy. She'd just sit there and admire Eddy from afar. Every five seconds Eddy was glancing at the clock or checking his pager. I knew he was looking for an out, and he sure pounced on it when it came.

After we took the cookies out of the oven to cool, we all went into the living room to put more candy canes on the Christmas tree. I sent Andre into the kitchen to check if the cookies had cooled so we could frost them. The boy wasn't in there more than a minute before it sounded like he'd turned over the whole tray of cookies. I was sitting down on the couch watching Eddy and Nina under the Christmas tree when Andre ran into the room, out of breath with frosting all over himself. Nina laughed.

"It's not funny," Andre cried. "A mouse jumped out at me from under the stove and ran over my feet."

Eddy laughed and patted Andre on the head as he walked past him into the kitchen. "Goddamn it, Andre!" he roared into the room. I looked in the doorway and he was standing there with his leather coat in his hand. Andre had knocked over the whole bowl of frosting and it had spilled down the inside of Eddy's leather jacket. He stood there and stared at Andre, then he took three big steps into the living room toward him, Andre's eyes looked like two full moons, the boy didn't even have any slippers on.

"It ran up over my feet, Dad," Andre said as Eddy shook out his coat. Andre was damn near hyperventilating. "I'm sorry," he squeaked. "I didn't mean it."

"Don't be sorry. Be careful! Running from a god-blasted mouse!" Eddy yelled.

Andre jumped and ran out of the room.

I couldn't deal with him anymore. "Jesus, Eddy!" I said, "You need to calm your black ass down. It's a coat. That's your son."

He ignored me, staring into the hallway like Andre was still there. Then Eddy slid his coat on and just like that he walked out. I heard our front door slam and it was on. I couldn't even see straight. If I can't leave, then neither can he. He walked out that door and I was five steps behind him.

Reggie Graham

Christmas Eve the Squad Six way. All of us—me, D-roc, Buggy, Sticks, Claude, and my cousin Tony—huddled up on the corner of Lothrop, hugging the block to stay warm. Sipping Hennessy and Alizé posting up on the wall in front of Sticks's crib, getting them bags off. It was our version of spreading the Christmas cheer 'cause that's what us Squad Six boys do: we get money. It wasn't too late night, something like eleven o'clock, when E-Bone Battel exploded out his crib spittin' flames. No more than two steps behind him was Miss Ruby. She was tight too. Eddy got right about to his truck when Miss Ruby jumped in front of the driver's-side door of his beat-ass blue Bronco.

We couldn't call it, but they were blowing hella hard. Then Miss Ruby stopped yelling. She just stood there in front of the truck with her hand fixed high on her hip, dangling a piece of paper in his face. He bucked up and snatched it out of her hand. She stood there, arms folded. He paced back and forth in front of her, still snapping. I couldn't make out all the bullshit he was popping off, but I caught this much through his bootleg Jamaican accent, "You think me and you are of size, huh? Woman, keep on tonight and see what takes place in these streets!"

We'd played our position from the sideline long enough, but talking all silly like that wasn't about to work out for nobody. We broke toward them before someone hit up the jakes and we all got in hot water.

"Ayo, E-Bone, why don't you just be out fam?" my right-hand homie Sticks yelled up the street as we strolled toward them. Buggy and his twin brother D-roc raced out a few steps ahead of the rest of us. Them two wild-ass Dominicans live across the street from me and Tony on Verndale Road, there's no kill switch between the two of them, once one of them bucks ain't no point in trying to stop them. But E-Bone's a loyal customer. When he's around the way he come to me for his bud, sometimes a little soft white, never gives me any trouble and I wasn't really trying to fuck that up, but he was so caught up beef'n he didn't even respond.

When we got over to their driveway I flexed up and stepped between them. E-Bone looked me in the eyes like he wanted to box. He knew better. I'da beat the brakes off his punk ass right then and there. From the yellowish-red tint in his eyes I could tell he'd been fucked up sniffing the white girl and some other shit. He stared at Miss Ruby and crumpled up the paper, then said, "Cool," and for a second they both lowered their voices. I looked at the boys and with a few nods of the head it seemed like our business was settled. I didn't like that look E-Bone had in his eye, but we began to roll back over to our corner anyway. We turned and I heard a loud crunch and a dense thud and I knew what was poppin'. In the corner of my eye, I saw Miss Ruby's long brown extensions fly up in the air under the streetlights. By the time I turned fully, E-Bone was on his tippy toes with Miss Ruby yoked up on his truck. We all doubled back. Before we could get there, he landed a big-boy combo on her jaw.

"Fuck is wrong with you, nigga!" D-roc growled and then speared him from the side onto the wet concrete. "So what happens when everyone gets bagged 'cause you on some hot-boy bullshit!"

Buggy spat in his face and then slid a hook across his jaw. Them two could have handled him but we all pummeled. We were really total-packaging the fool too, until I started to hear the slow rattle of wind chimes and the squeaky swings of screen doors opening. I stopped and looked around to see the neighborhood slowly waking up. By the time we composed ourselves and wrestled him away from Miss Ruby, I could already hear the howl of the jakes racing up Blue Hills Park-way. We dipped up the block and stashed off all the product. By the time we made it back, the neighborhood was already buzzing with gossip as the blue and red lights strobed around the block.

Through all the commotion, I looked up at Miss Ruby's house and saw little Andre and Nina's tear-swollen eyes look-ing out through the shades in their front window. A little far-ther up the way was Vernice Taft, the ringleader of the suntan ladies, standing in her driveway. Her and all her followers outside in their bathrobes and slippers, deep in a coffee klatch, all of them rocking curlers under their head wraps, weird-colored night crèmes dotted around their faces, smoking Vir-ginia Slims, and generating rumors about the "Christmas Eve disturbance" courtesy of the Squad Six crew.

These suburban broads love to hate and call the jakes on niggas, they think they're the neighborhood watch but they're really the peanut-gallery-of-insignificant-opinions, that's all. Ain't nobody on the block two-faced like them hypocritical bitches. They hate on us from afar, but their thoughts and judgments don't make or slow up my money none. We sit on the corner and in the summer they tan outside Vernice Taft's house and because they've lived here longer than us, they think they got the right to talk shit all day. What them broads need is some hobbies and jobs. I mean, shit. We use brown paper bags. They use coffee mugs. They ain't no better.

As the jakes were talking to E-Bone and Ruby, we all slowly slithered back to the corner and chilly-pimp'd it, panning the crowd. You always gotta be careful when folks get into little crowds. That's when people start to drink their I-can-fuck-with-them juice. So we posted up and had our eyes lurking. I could see all the old folks leaning over their porch railings looking down to see what was going on. Nosy-ass people. Every window on the block was lit up with little dark figures peeking their heads out.

At the very top of the street, I could see Smoke and his boys standing on the high porch of his crib, a glowing doorway behind them, none of them wearing coats, shivering and fumbling all over each other, looking down the block like the pack of corny-ass classroom niggas they are. I used to go to school with them niggas, they some diet-thugs for real, Smoke's the only one in their little crew with heart, the rest of them cats are straight pussy.

See, me and Smoke, we were cool at one point. More like business partners. Long story short: we decided to pursue our local hood pharmaceutical endeavors on different ends of the street. Lothrop Ave. and Verndale Road, that's me and mine's, it ain't much but I eat good over here. Smoke, he can have all the bullshit up the block on Lothrop and Decker Street.

We had some serious conflicts in morals, which is really what caused us to have to just walk our separate paths. I guess I'm more like a Robin-Hood-X-type brother. I do what I do to get by in the hustle game, but I look out for my peoples. I ride for mine's. Smoke's the type of nigga that'll steal your wallet and help you look for the shit. Only looks out for himself, if your money's green, he's got what you need, no questions asked. The other day I saw him serve some young bucks that looked about his little brother Beezy's age. Them little cats couldn't be no older than ten or eleven like Andre and that's a damn shame.

I heard the buzz of the crowd muffle down and I refocused on them. I saw the pigs cuffing E-Bone as he yelled out at everyone, "Y'all can go back inside now. Show's over!"

The swine tussled him toward the car, then like a little beam of light Andre ran out of the house barefooted, wearing an old ratty oversized T-shirt. He stopped a few feet away from the cruiser and sounded off like a big dog, through the whimpers of his cries, "Pop, I hate you! You just gon' leave us on Christmas, huh? Go 'head! Just leave! Don't you ever come back!"

Papa Tanks grabbed Andre, hugging him tight and rubbing his head as he sobbed into his stomach. Nana Tanks consoled Ruby as she wept, while Nina stood arms folded next to her aunt Diamond, Miss Ruby's younger sister. They all watched from the walkway behind their fence.

Nina looked up at Papa Tanks and asked, "So, what are we going to do now?"

He looked up the street at the jakes. "You mustn't get involved in the grown business of a man and his woman, you understand me?"

She looked confused but nodded yes anyway.

When I heard Andre snapping, I felt them words. Way back when, I cried some tears like those too. Back when my mother told me I was going to have a sleepover with cousin Tony over at Aunty Gladys's crib, but when she tossed me a duffel bag full of clothes, said, "Have fun," and didn't even walk me up onto the porch, I knew she wasn't coming back. It wasn't the first time she'd disappeared in the streets.

I used to live over in Dorchester on Dakota Street, at my grandmother's. My mother came around sometimes, but she had a real bad thing for the needle and anyone who could help her fill it. She was one of my father's favorite hoes, but he cut her loose when she got too fiended-out, stopped following orders, and started messing up his money. He had a reputation for having a stable of the best-looking broads around and she was fucking up his image. Once she popped up pregnant with me and wouldn't stop using, he stopped dealing with her.

I was born flagpole-high, premature, and super dependent on whatever my mother was using while I was inside of her. Once I stabilized, the social workers released me to my grandmother's care. My mother was always in and out of rehab or drifting around the city. My grandmother never lied to me about who my parents were. She was the first to tell me my mother was never quite right. She ain't have to say much about my father because his name rang bells in my neighborhood anyway. He started out just a rip-and-run stickup kid and that's how he got his nickname "Dicey," he liked to rob back-alley dice games when he was younger. That's before he started pimpin'.

I heard a lot of stories about him from the old heads on the block, about the endless niggas he'd disappeared or broke bones on, for fucking around on his ho-stroll over in Codman

Square. He was known for driving an all-black tinted-out Buick Electra, the old-timers called it a "Deuce and a Quarter," his always had hundred-spoke gold rims and whitewall tires. The old-timers would tell me that I looked just like him all the time. It's hard to say, I've never met him face-to-face. He sent money and toys to my grandmother's house when I was younger. She's the one who really raised me until she took sick when I was five while still my mother was gone chasing the high.

I saw my father's Deuce and a Quarter cruise past me a few times but I couldn't see through those night-black tints on his windows. I sort of knew his face from the pictures of him on my mother's dresser, with him and her in front of his car, her poking her ass out, him gripping it, and a gang of his tricks lining both sides of them.

I think I saw him one time in the flesh while I was taking the bus home from school. He was walking out of a bodega on Blue Hill Avenue. His black Deuce and a Quarter was parked a block up the way and two tall skinny brown-skin cats with long wavy perms and three-piece suits were strolling toward it, they both looked alike, one must've been him and the other was probably one of my uncles, but who can tell? The bus turned and I lost sight of them.

He stopped sending money and presents and disappeared completely when I was six. This was around when my grandmother died and my mother finally came back home. Word on the streets was that he got caught up with some cats from over in Roxbury and he took a few hoes and dipped off somewhere down south, to hide out. After my grandmother died, my mother got clean for a little bit. Her Narcotics Anonymous sponsor encouraged her to go to church and she became a church lady, but I never trusted that shit.

We heard no word from my father for two years, and then randomly he started sending us envelopes with money stuffed inside a card with a picture of two dice. No words. No return address.

It was clear as day, he wasn't really fuckin' with us, but my mother started praying about him and meanwhile worshipped his memory. She kept all of the cards in a neat stack on the nightstand beside her bed. Every morning when she got dressed, she'd put on a couple dabs of the big bottle of Brut aftershave she had, she said she had it in her purse when he kicked her to the curb.

She took the money and the envelopes as a sign that he still loved her and that maybe he'd come back. She was a pathetic sight to see in those days. The way she'd talk about him like he'd just been over to our apartment or something. She told me she got clean just for him and for two years she stayed clean, wishing on a star. Rumors started up when I was nine that he was back in town but I never saw him or his car around. The envelopes stopped coming when I was ten and the word on the streets was that old beef had caught up to him and someone shot him while he was sitting in his Deuce and a Quarter, outside Brother's, over in Mattapan Square. He was eating a breakfast plate. Caught slipping, should've known the sitting duck always gets fucked.

My mother didn't want to believe it until she read it for herself, it made big headlines, "Notorious Gangster Remington 'Dicey' Graham Murdered Execution Style in Broad Daylight Outside Eatery in Mattapan Square."

My mother was always weak, but I never knew a person could implode and crumble so fast. It's like my mother went from marble to dust. She stayed in her room for a few days blasting Curtis Mayfield's *Super Fly* record, crying, screaming, and cursing at God. On the fourth day she took me over to my aunt Gladys's crib in mild-ass Milton and I been out here ever since.

Sometimes life just ain't 'bout shit. I know what it's going to be like for Andre to grow up on the west side of Milton around these fake-ass people, being that kid from the broken home. All of us Squad Six boys know that struggle, being a have-not in the land of good and plenty. The object of scorn, judgment, and pity.

I heard the jakes slam their doors and they stopped flickering the red and blues as I watched Papa Tanks walk Andre back inside the house. Once the cruiser topped the hill the neighborhood slowly went back to sleep.

The next morning I woke up early and decided to spread the Christmas spirit. Since I live on the corner of Verndale Road and little Andre lives on the corner of Lothrop, we're basically neighbors. I walked over to his spot to see how Miss Ruby was doing. I knocked and Miss Ruby answered the door, her left eye puffed out like a dragonfly, her lips swollen a deep reddish purple. She half smiled.

"Look, Reggie, you didn't have to get all up in it last night. But thank you. I hate when he comes up in here acting like that in front of the kids, especially around the holidays. It's just so hard sometimes, ya know? Sometimes a sister just feels like giving up."

Her eyes began to get watery, and I wasn't trying to get her all upset. I let her know it wasn't a problem and that I was happy she was okay. Honestly, I wish someone had helped my mother. Maybe she would still be here. Before I left, she gave me a hug and held on tight. I reached in my pocket and whispered in her ear, "I'm glad to see you're getting along fine on Christmas. Hope y'all have a good one." Then I slid her a stack.

Immediately she gave me the screw face. "Reggie, do you know how much money you just gave me?" She shuffled the bills and looked up at me. "This is ten hundred-dollar bills."

I almost laughed. "Miss Ruby, trust. I *always* count my money. I know Pa's gone on that iron-lock vacation for a bit. Just hold down your household. I see you grinding out here on some legal shit and I tip my hat to ya. If you or your youngins need anything, holla."

I breezed back to my corner.

Andre Battel

After New Year's Day passes, Nana Tanks's baking cycle is complete, and on the second day of the year, her and Nina begin the preparations for next year's batch of her famous Christmas Black Cake. By the time I make it upstairs to watch *Gladiators,* they're already sitting at the kitchen table listening to some old-school calypso, Nana Tanks chopping up a big pile of dried dates, raisins, and prunes, Nina sitting beside her carefully gathering all the cuttings and tossing them into Nana Tanks's tall silver Dutch pot.

I don't go and sit by them while they're chopping because Nana Tanks says she's suspicious of any boy who'd rather stay up under the women cooking in the kitchen rather than going outside to play. It's more their thing, they got a little ritual and everything. After all the cutting is done they stand over the nearly full pot of raisins, dates, and prunes, looking down into it like an open grave. Nana Tanks holds the lid as Nina tosses in the last couple of cinnamon sticks and balls of nutmeg right before Nana Tanks douses it all in a mixture of rum, wine, and brandy and closes the lid.

They both take it very seriously. Once the Dutch pot is closed, Nana Tanks wants it to stay that way. She's made it very clear to me and Nina that us "curious and confounded picknies" are not to "trouble she pots." Throughout the year she adds a couple of containers of mincemeat and some extra rum to the mixture and closes the pot back.

Sometimes in the afternoons when she's in her bedroom watching *The Young and the Restless* I like to open the lid a crack and stick my nose into the pot and take big whiffs of that dank vinegary fruit smell rising out of the pot like a hot steam burning my nostrils, making me dizzy, almost like the summer nights when I'd inhale too much of Pop's vital smoke.

The smell only gets stronger and stronger too, until around Christmastime when Nana Tanks empties the mixture in a huge glass mixing bowl and Black Cake Baking Day begins and shuts down the entire house. Both kitchens and both stoves. The whole house reeks of hot molasses, rum, and burnt brown sugar. By the end of the day the sound of the stand mixer is like a woodpecker pecking at my brain. It's a good day to be up the street playing over at Chucky or Beezy's crib.

It always looks like they bake hundreds of Black Cakes, some with frosting, others without. I ride in the car with Papa Tanks and we deliver plastic-wrapped bundles of Black Cake to every West Indian family or person that Nana and Papa Tanks knows in the city of Boston.

After New Year's passes there's always extra Black Cakes sitting around the house to get rid of, and on the first day school resumed from winter break I woke up to a note on the whiteboard in the kitchen from Ma telling me to take two Black

Cakes over to Reggie's place when I got home from school, one for Reggie and Tony, the other for his aunty Gladys. I sat down and my insides slowly began curling. I just showered, got dressed, and couldn't even eat breakfast. I hadn't seen any of them Squad Six boys since the day I stuck my basketball in the middle of their business when that brawl broke out.

Before the day of the brawl I didn't think they knew who I was. When I passed them on the corner they'd say, "What up, lil' man?" or nod their heads, but I never stopped and talked to any of them. Since Pop and Uncle Elroy ain't around much anymore, them Squad Six boys are my new favorite group to spy on. It's a lot easier than peeping on Pop and Uncle Elroy too. I don't have to crouch down staying still and quiet in an uncomfortable position.

Unlike Pop and Uncle Elroy the Squad Six boys hang out in the daytime too. When I get home from school, they're always holding court on the corner. I toss my backpack on the porch, pull my Red Sox cap low, up my hoodie's hood and that's all the disguise I need to watch and listen to the corner comfortably as I dribble my basketball up and down our walkway.

Monday though Thursday, Reggie, D-roc, Buggy, and Sticks are always out there, while big Haitian Claude and Tony are still in high school. Friday through Sunday all the Squad Six boys are chilling on the corner, freestyling, talking shit, blasting music. They smoke vitals like Pop and Uncle Elroy. I smell the smoke drifting off the corner, but their vitals look different. They're not skinny and white, they're thick as a finger and brown, sometimes green. They call them blunts. Ma calls it frying their brains, they call it getting high. It sounds better.

Ever since Christmas morning when Reggie came over to wish Ma a merry Christmas, she seems to be okay with the Squad Six boys. She used to evil-eye them as they'd wave to us as we drove past, but now she waves back, sometimes even smiles. I know all their names from hearing them on the corner. I've always been curious about them, and a little scared of them too. I saw what they did to Pop on Christmas Eve, he shouldn't have hit Ma, they weren't wrong, but they still made me sort of nervous. Sticks lives in the house on the corner. It's built up high, his front yard elevated by the wall that wraps around the corner. That's where they all chill, it has Squad Six spray painted all over it.

I think Sticks was the reason Ma started not liking them in the first place. Sticks is the quietest one in the Squad and besides Reggie he's by far the craziest. The first time I ever saw Sticks in action I was walking home from Mattapan station with Ma. As we rounded the corner of Verndale onto Lothrop, all the Squad Six boys were outside, shirts off and ready to fight a bunch of guys from another neighborhood.

Ma grabbed my arm and we crossed the street and kept walking toward our house. I heard some yelling and stomping up on Sticks's front porch, and the guys I didn't recognize started scattering away from the corner. I looked up and saw Sticks with a big butcher knife in his hand and big Haitian Claude standing in front of him holding him back. I paused to look at the commotion.

"Let's go!" Ma tugged my shirt toward our house, my neck twisted around like an owl trying to see.

When we got to our gate Ma squeezed the back of my neck and pinched me as she brushed past walking up to the front porch.

"Bring yourself on! Ain't nothing over there to see. What, you think them boys are cool or something? They're fools, you're a cut above the rest. Boy, you better get with it."

I didn't answer her. She held the front door open for me as I slowly walked up the walkway trying to sneak some glances at the corner.

"Get in the damn house. Now, Andre!"

Ma looked at me like I'd pulled a knife on her as I slowly slinked up onto the porch. She grabbed my shirt and pushed me through the doorway, stepped inside behind me and slammed the door.

The best days to watch the corner were the days when a free-style battle broke out. All of them Squad Six boys could rap but only D-roc and Reggie could compete verbally; the rest of the crew didn't seem to take it as seriously. Them two are the only ones that freestyle off the top of the dome. The next best thing to watching them battle is hearing them do verbal exercises. Buggy or Claude point to things around the way or say random words and Reggie and D-roc weave the words or things into their rap without skipping a beat, almost like it's scripted.

Watching them battle freestyle was like being on the blacktop playing a pickup game at Kelly Park, it didn't matter who was who and from where, reputation, pride, and ego were always on the line. Reggie's better at freestyling than D-roc. D-roc's voice is deep, and he got a wild style like Busta Rhymes, but his delivery is more like ODB with the voice of DMX, and sometimes I don't know what the hell he's saying but it goes along with the beat good. Reggie doesn't have to do all that, he's smoother, raps slower, hardly ever loses the beat. He don't come off as the book-reading type, but I can tell he's the smartest one in the crew. When he battles, he uses every and anything within his eyeshot as material to use against his opponent.

Last time I saw Reggie battle-rap was a couple weeks before Christmas when he destroyed some older dude I'd never seen before. The dude pulled up on the corner in a white Honda Accord, bass vibrating all through his trunk as he blasted his new single, he was hype on it too. He hopped out of the car smiling.

"Check my new single," he crowed as he paced back and forth in front of all of them, "Tell me my shit ain't hot." He bounced his shoulders and kept saying, "My shit's so dope. Hate if ya want to. My shit's dope."

He was yelling it over the music, looking for someone to agree with him, but they wouldn't. They wouldn't even look him in the face. They all looked around the block like he wasn't even there, but if I could hear him, they could too. No one responded until Reggie ashed his Newport and flicked it on the hood of the dude's car and said, "Man, turn this bullshit off. Polluting the good air on a Friday and shit. Scram with that bullshit, go 'head, man."

Reggie waved, abruptly dismissing the dude and his new single.

All them Squad Six boys busted out laughing, they howled so loud I couldn't hear what was being said, but the dude was moving his hands fast as he spoke to Reggie and Reggie waved his hands around in the dude's face a lot faster. They stopped arguing and the Squad Six boys circled up around the two of them and I knew it was officially battle time. Reggie versus White Honda Guy. Sticks started beat-boxing, and I stopped bouncing my basketball so I could hear them better.

From the jump it was clear, White Honda Guy was spitting

written raps, none of the stuff he was saying had anything to do with Reggie. He kept talking about the same things, how he had money, how all the bitches loved him, how many guns he owned, and all the ways he knew how to kill niggas. It was a bunch of recycled garbage, a nigga trying to sound like the niggas already on the radio.

Reggie turned his back on White Honda Guy while he was rapping. Once the dude finished, Reggie turned back around and started frying him, they went three rounds and Reggie won them all. In the middle of Reggie's last rap Sticks said, "Finish him."

Like the voice in *Mortal Kombat* just before you win and the competitor's standing helplessly beaten into a trance, Reggie's last couple bars were the fatality. He pointed at the dude and said,

> Pull up on the block looking like a fake thug,
> Fat gorilla-black nigga, rocking fake Lugz,
> Dirty-ass hoodie, oh boy, yous a scrub!
> You can fool Milton, niggas, but you can't fool us
> Said your single's trash, now your face screwed up
> Yup, ya hubcaps they got rust, and you shoulda
>   been known: no one's fuckin' wit' us.

Reggie laughed and paused to take the last drag from his Newport and he flicked that one on the hood of the dude's car too. They stood there looking at the two cigarette butts on the hood of the car, and then Reggie started back in on him.

> You still here, you silly-bitch?
> Take yo ass home and go write some new shit.
> Get gone, playa.

Sticks started waving his arms back and forth. "It's over." He laughed, pleading with White Honda Guy, "No more, please, it's over. It's only gonna get worse for you."

Sticks held his sides laughing, and big Haitian Claude agreed. "Is ova, mehn, is ova, mehn," he said through his thick accent.

I watched from the walkway inside of the fence, dying laughing too. White Honda Guy was tall and stocky, his skin was shiny jet black, but by the end of the battle he looked about four inches shorter, a couple shades lighter, with his big muscles deflated. He stomped into his car, slammed the door, and yelled, "Y'all got jokes? I'ma see y'all niggas." He turned up his single and burned rubber as he peeled off.

Reggie yelled back, "Yeah, 'ight! Fuck outta here, nigga, we'll see you first. Niggas ain't hard to find."

They all kept laughing. I didn't think much of it, wasn't the first battle I saw a dude storm off the block all salty because Reggie chewed him up. Them Squad Six boys didn't seem worried about it either. I remember as soon as the dude pulled off they jumped right back into arguing about whether or not America will ever have a black president. Reggie, Tony, and Sticks think it just won't happen, D-roc, Buggy, and Claude think it will, just not while they're alive.

Them Squad Six boys argue about almost everything, it's just how they are, sometimes they argue just to realize they're all saying the same things. They're always cracking jokes on each other, they're like brothers. They grumble, fuss, fight, and cuss each other out but at the end of the day, when shit gets real, they're down for the cause like four flat tires.

———

A week passed and I was dribbling my basketball in our walk-way after school as the sky began graying over, clearing out the blue, making room for the moon. We hadn't had our first snow of the year yet, but it was still wear-your-long-johns cold outside. I could hardly feel my fingers dribbling the ball. The only reason I stayed out there was because Reggie and D-roc were trying to get big Haitian Claude to freestyle and I really wanted to hear it, but it all got put on hold when that same white Honda Accord pulled up to the corner, with that same big blue-black ogre-looking dude driving. A black Honda Pre-lude trailed behind him too. They were five-deep in each car, all hoodied up, rocking black skullcaps.

They sped up to the block and tossed the cars in park right in front of the green mailbox where them Squad Six boys were posting on the wall. No words were exchanged. The car doors flew open, and Reggie, Tony, and Claude rushed the white Accord and D-roc, Buggy, and Sticks broke toward the black Prelude. Them Squad Six boys were outnumbered by two at each car, but D-roc, Buggy, and Sticks didn't even let all of the dudes get out of the car. Sticks kicked off his Timberlands and started beating the skinny Spanish-looking cat that drove over the head with his boot as he tried to get out of the car. The dude fell back and Sticks pulled his shirt over his head, snatched him to his feet, and gave him one more boot-bash and he dropped back, arms out like he was being baptized at church. D-roc and Buggy handled the other four dudes in the car. They're twins, they were the stars of the football team at Milton High. I used to go to their games and they love to fight. Everyone thought they were going to get full rides to play in college but for whatever reason they didn't. Same way Reggie never went off to play college basketball. Anyway,

Buggy was knocking one dude's head off the trunk of the car as he yelled, "Y'all just gon' run up on our block like niggas is bitches? You think shit's sweet?" He was like a mother giving an ass whooping, yelling "Huh?" every time he hit somebody.

D-roc was tap-dancing on a guy he'd floored on the other side of the Prelude. Them Squad Six boys weren't as big as the dudes that came in the cars, they just seemed way more pissed off that these cats had the nerve to try and ambush our block. D-roc, Buggy, and Sticks whooped them dudes until the driver stood up and limped back into the car with blood running from his nose. The dude that came in the passenger seat was still inside, two of the three from the backseat were back in the car too. The driver started it up, and the last guy broke away from D-roc and Buggy and hopped into the door of the car, legs dangling out of the Prelude as it sped off, almost crashing into a parked car and a telephone pole, leaving the white Honda crew stranded in enemy territory.

Buggy and D-roc chased after the Prelude as it swerved down Verndale Road. Sticks started running up the block, away from my crib toward Churchill Street, where Reggie, Tony, and big Haitian Claude were brawling. Reggie and White Honda Guy were tangled up, seesawing back and forth. Reggie shifted and snatched him into a headlock and started hammering his fist into the side of dude's head like he was playing the bongo. Claude and Tony were holding their own against the other four dudes until Sticks ran up and started swinging his Timberland again, clearing out the scene.

Reggie lost his balance right as Buggy and D-roc came jogging back around the corner onto Lothrop. Reggie yelled "Oww!" and his broad tree-trunk legs went up in the air and his body followed as the dude slammed him into Mrs. Unger's ornate bushes. White Honda Guy started sprinting up the street right toward where I stood in my walkway.

Reggie was on the ground holding his crotch. He yelled, "Faggot-ass nigga, squeezed my nuts."

Tony, Claude, Sticks, and D-roc were a couple steps behind him.

I clutched my basketball, watching White Honda Guy sprinting right in my direction, getting closer and closer, eyes wide open, arms pumping, beating his feet.

"Get that motherfucker," Reggie roared as he stood up.

White Honda Guy was closing in on me, I tossed my leg up in the air and slowly leaned back like a pitcher on the mound and launched my basketball at his face. I didn't even think, and before I could stop myself the basketball was gone, sailing over our fence. The ball connected perfectly with his nose, it sounded like a bug splatting on a windshield. Stunned out of his run, he grabbed his head and staggered a few steps to the left. Tony charged in with a running fist that spun his body to the side as Claude and Sticks tackled him to the ground.

They swarmed him, boxing each other out to try to get a kick or a punch in as the brawling reignited for round two. Reggie jogged past me standing in the gate as he caught up with the pack. We made eye contact for a quick second and he tugged at his waistband. My heart hiccupped a few times as I saw the silver gleam of Reggie's shank as he snatched it open and started running faster. His cousin Tony yelled, "Nigga, chill, we got 'em. You don't need another case."

It felt like my body floated up onto the porch. I locked our front door, too scared to see what was about to go down.

I sat at the kitchen table winded, thinking, What if White Honda Guy remembers my face? I didn't even think to go get my basketball and I really didn't want to go back out there, but I had to. It was my only good basketball. I heard a lot of yelling, an engine rev and tires squeal, but no sirens. I sat for a whole fifteen minutes and then opened the front door and peeked my head outside.

They were all gone. The block was quiet like it was before.

My basketball was sitting on our doormat.

That afternoon, when school started back up after winter break, I walked the Black Cakes halfway down the side alley running alongside Reggie and Tony's crib leading over to Verndale Road. Them Squad Six boys post up there when it's too cold to be outside for too long. Sometimes I watch them go in and out from the bathroom window in our shower, but it gets boring after a while. Anyway, I stopped in front of the little wooden door, I could feel the bass through the door knocker. I knocked and the music paused.

"Who?" I heard Reggie call.

"It's Andre, from next door."

I heard his feet creak up the stairs. The door swung open and a gust of smoke rushed out the door. Reggie stepped through the cloud smiling, smelling like a bomb of Pop's vitals. He had a pair of red biker goggles around his forehead, a white T-shirt on under his blue and white Avirex leather coat with Chief Joseph on the back, Adidas basketball shorts, and some gray Timberlands. I held the Black Cakes in my hands ready to drop them and run. He grinned at me.

"Good aim the other day, lil' nig. Whatcha got there?"

"My mother wanted me to bring over two of Nana Tanks's Black Cakes. One for you and Tony, one for Miss Gladys." I handed him the cakes.

Reggie took them and started digging around in his pocket.

"Check it, good lookin' out for the cakes but niggas still need some cookies, chips, soda, and shit. If I give you some dollars you'll run to the store for me?"

It was an offer I couldn't refuse. Other than that ten-dollar bill I found on the walk to school a few months back and hid under my bed, I never have any money of my own. Even when I'd get a big bill inside my birthday cards, I had to give the money to Ma for her to "put away" for me and I'd never see it again. They sent me to the store to get four Arizona Sweet Teas, a two-liter of Sprite, six honey buns, a big bag of ketchup chips and cheddar fries, plus three king-sized bags of Skittles and Starbursts. The whole walk home the idea was unreal to me, all I had to do was walk down to Tedeschi's and they'd pay me for it. I started wondering how much Reggie was going to give me, not that it really mattered, I was more excited just to have some money all my own.

I got back and knocked on the basement door, ready to give Reggie the snacks, take the cash, and leave. He opened the door and this time he had on a dark pair of sunglasses. Reggie took the bags and reached into his coat and took out a wad of cash, peeled off a few bills, and stuffed them in my hand. I glanced down at my hand quick and saw he'd given me two twenties. My whole body broke out with goose bumps. I didn't even know what to do with that much money. I looked up at Reggie, trying not to smile too hard, said thanks, and turned to walk back home, but he tapped my shoulder.

"I'm saying, what you 'bout to get into? I put a lil' something extra in there for you. Niggas got a good laugh outta that shit you did, 'preciate it, for real. You should come through and say what's up to niggas. We just kickin' it."

I put my hand in my pocket and felt the bills, almost afraid they wouldn't still be there. I looked down past Reggie into the dark shadowy basement and I couldn't resist, I said, "Cool," and followed him down the creaky steps into the basement. The second Reggie opened the door from the hallway to the main room the blunt smoke drop-kicked me in the chest. I coughed a few times but held it in as best I could. Reggie pointed at me and said, "This here's lil' Andre, wit' the good aim." They all sort of chuckled.

D-roc and Buggy were over in the corner near the big-screen TV, sitting on a weight bench watching ESPN, lifting cement buckets full of water like they were dumbbells, both of them tossed me the peace sign. Sticks was on the other end of the basement with boxing gloves on, punching a dirty old heavy bag. He pumped a fist at me and nodded his head. I followed Reggie over to the big card table in the middle of the basement, where Claude and Tony were sitting. The Lox's new album, *Money, Power & Respect,* was banging from the two subwoofers on both sides of the table. I coughed a few more times as I pulled up a chair and sat down.

Tony looked at me and said, "Well, if this ain't the most dribblingest, throwingest nigga I ever done seen. Wat's good, lil' homie?"

He threw me a dap and I reached across the table and it felt like I'd stuck my finger in a socket. He gripped my hand so hard that he shook my whole body, nearly pulling me out of the chair.

"That was good shit, son," he wiggled his eyebrows.

Claude nodded and tossed me dap. Then he too strong-armed me like he wanted to dislocate my shoulder.

"Yeah, goo' shee-t," he said.

I didn't really know what to say so I just nodded back and said, "Yeah," under my breath.

There was a bunch of dried-out grape-sized flower buds on the table everywhere, some loose, some still on the branches. I knew it was weed from the smell, it reeked sort of like moth-balls and fresh-cut grass. Tony and Reggie were smoking small blunts while they snapped the buds apart, stuffing them into mini baggies. Claude grabbed a cigar from a brownish-colored pouch whose label read "Backwoods" in red letters. He slobbered all over it and then slowly unraveled its skin and tossed out the tobacco. Then he sprinkled some of the crushed buds inside and started rerolling it.

He finished rolling the first one and Reggie and Tony stopped what they were doing and Tony said, "Session; two-minute warning," and all the guys slowly started making their way to the table. I looked around at them as they settled in, they all looked so tired, with bloodshot eyes and moving slow. Claude lit the cigar and started smoking it. He blew a thick stream of smoke across the table at me and passed the blunt to Reggie. Reggie took a couple puffs and they kept this rhythm up until D-roc let the blunt linger in his hand and Buggy punched him in the arm and said, "Pass the blunt, nigga," and snatched it from him. I grinned but no one else started laughing so I held it in. Claude took out another Back-wood and started rolling another. The music pulsed through my whole body as I sat, feeling like I'd been inside a steam room too long. The air was foggy and thick, and my head felt loopy and light. I looked around at all the guys, they were laughing and smoking, but I didn't know what they were laughing at. I saw their smiling faces and felt like maybe they were laughing at me and I started feeling awkward. I couldn't really hear their voices, all I could hear were my thoughts and the idea of Ma smelling weed on me made me feel sick to my stomach. I looked over at the cable box and it was four thirty.

Ma got off work at five thirty, so I jumped to my feet and said, "Thanks, y'all, but I gotta go," and headed for the door.

Reggie looked me in the face as I made my way across the basement. Then he grabbed my shoulder and laughed. "Aww, this lil' nigga got his first lil' contact high. Shake it off, nigga, you good, son."

"Yeah, I'm good," I said as I rustled away.

"Well, come back tomorrow if you wanna put some money in your pocket, ya hear?"

I said okay and he gave me a strong dap, and as I started heading for the door he yelled, "And don't go telling your mama what you seen down here neither, she just starting to come around."

I said, "Okay," and let myself out.

From that day forward, once school let out at three, I power walked home, dropped off my stuff, hit the side alley, and grabbed the order and the cash. I got back from the munchies run around three fifteen and as long as I kept my mouth shut and stayed out of the way they'd let me hang out for a little bit. If the air wasn't too strong, I could cut out no later than four thirty, giving me a good hour for the contact to go away. When I got home I'd put my hoodie and coat on the back porch to air out from the smell in Reggie's basement. By the time it started getting warm out I almost felt like an honorary member of the crew, but they were all older than me and they spoke in a code they made up all on their own and I couldn't crack it. I laughed when they laughed but half the time I didn't know what they were talking about.

Even though I'm cool with them, they're just friendly to me.

My real homeboys are Chucky Taft and Beezy, and our moms are all friends.

Chucky's mother, Mrs. Vernice Taft, is like the mayor of Lothrop Ave. Her and Chucky were the first people who rang our doorbell to introduce themselves when we moved to Milton. As Ma tells it, the doorbell rang and when she answered the door there was a jug of sweet tea sitting beside the doormat and in our walkway was this white lady Mrs. Vernice picking up a plastic-wrapped foil tray of fried chicken and waffles with Chucky slung around her hip. Ma said they sat at our kitchen table and ate, while me and Chucky played with pots and pans on the floor.

Ma was convinced from day one that there wasn't any racism in Mrs. Vernice Taft, not to say she didn't see it in some of the other white people that lived on our block. The Tafts live five houses down from us, just before the hill starts to rise. Beezy lives on the tip-top of the hill, we used to only really see him in the summertime because he went to private school, but this year he transferred to Tucker Elementary and he wound up in Mrs. Power's class with me and Chucky.

Spring always used to be the loneliest season. Chucky's never around, he plays for the all-star travel baseball team. After school he's either doing homework or off doing baseball stuff with his father. With the warm weather, them Squad Six boys are outside, and I know better than to linger on the corner too long and risk being spotted by Vernice Taft, who'd tell Ma. But with Beezy around things were all good. Finally I had a homie my age to chill with. I started taking him with me on the store runs, but the way them Squad Six boys would come at Beezy snapping jokes was off the hook. I mean, sure my dude was fat but he was still my homeboy. We knew our peoples didn't bang with each other, but they all went about their business as if the others didn't exist, like they weren't hustling on different ends of the block.

One day them Squad Six boys weren't around after school, so I dribbled my basketball in the street, crossing up the sewer caps. When they came back to the block they were all fired up and D-roc kept telling me, "Dre, don't let me catch you rolling with that fuckin' nigga Smoke's little brother no more. We don't fuck with them. Period."

To stay loyal to the game, from that day forward me and Beezy were strictly school friends. It was weird having a best friend that only lived up the block yet we had to sneak around like criminals just to kick it. I was loyal for a little bit, but shit, Beezy was one of my best friends. Plus I couldn't really be in on all the real Squad Six dirt anyway, like why I wasn't supposed to be talking to Beezy in the first place.

"Andre. You only 'bout what? Ten or eleven? You got some shit going on for you, lil' nig. Just play your position, keep your eyes peeled, go to school, and be a good kid, son-dun. Shit, you see us out here all day, these house-broads calling the cops on niggas, haters trying to run up and shit. Just enjoy now, because once you punch that clock the work don't never stop, ya dig?"

This is the sermon Reggie used to give me every time I would try to get in on the good stuff, like riding out with the boys. Then came the day. Ma asked me why she hadn't seen Beezy around lately, and when I told her that I wasn't supposed to be chilling with him she told me, "Negro, this is the U-S of A. If you want to hang out with Miss Myra's boy from up the street, then you do that. I like Reggie but the rest of them punks ain't 'bout nothin'. Listen to Reggie. Not Claude, not Buggy, not Sticks, not Tony, and especially not that fool D-roc, or any of the rest of them fools."

With Ma's good ammo winding up my back, one day me and Beezy snuck away after school and went to the basketball courts at Kelly Park to play some one-on-one. As I was working Beezy's chunky butt out I heard some noise coming from behind us. It was the boom from the bass in D-roc's car. I can tell his speakers from anywhere. You can hear them before you see him. When I heard the bass my heart dropped. I wanted to run and hide in a trash can. I knew it was him and the Squad Six boys, that's how they roll. I also knew that when they got here they were not going to be feeling this little stunt. Really there wasn't shit to do but just whoop Beezy's ass in the game. Whoop him long and strong. That way at least I might get some props after the game. I had been working on my jump shot, like Reggie said to do.

As if things weren't already getting funky enough, about five minutes after my Squad Six boys got there and didn't even address me, I looked down off the court and I could see Smoke and company rolling toward the park too. Right as Smoke and his crew got to the court I had game point. Both crews were postin' on picnic tables on opposite sides of the court.

From the roar of both crews I could tell shit was about to hit the fan. Me and Beezy returned to sworn enemies. Beezy checked me the ball and I drove baseline on him. Up and under and the game was over. With both crews watchin' close, the tension in the air felt like Nana Tanks's homemade pickled pepper sauce. I thought my heart was going to pop out of my throat.

D-roc yelled out, "Man, we just the best, ain't it! *Squad Six!*

We got little niggas that'll body ya!" He jumped up and down with his fist pumping into the air like he was letting off shots. Now I don't really think he was speaking to anyone in particular, but Kendrick, Smoke's homeboy, seemed to take a special offense to D-roc poppin' off at the lip like that.

"Yeah 'ight, nigga, you better shut the fuck up before y'all niggas get exposed."

D-roc rumbled back, "'Ight bet. What you trying to do?" Reggie shot him a look. Then D-roc said, "Fuck it. I'll put five hundred on my little soldier right now, what!"

Reggie smirked. "Naw, fuck that. We'll put up a whole stack. These niggas is puppy treats. I got faith in my little nigga." He looked down at me. "Andre, get at these bum-ass niggas."

Then he looked back over at Smoke. "We go hard out here. I'll send my little nigga to merk you. Game's to fifteen."

I really didn't even want to play anymore, but then Beezy slammed the ball in my chest talking about "Check up, pussy."

That's all the invite I needed to oblige him in a good old-fashioned Squad Six beat down. I shoulda just socked his fat ass when that ball touched my chest. Instead, I gave his punk ass fifteen straight buckets. Beezy had nothing for me inside or outside. I ran circles around his jiggly fat ass. He should have known not to pull my gully card in front of my crew. When the ball dropped through the net on my fifteenth point, I caught it and slammed it down like a touchdown spike.

"And take that to the bank, fuckhead! Now go get our money, bitch!" And I chest-bumped him in the back as he walked away. Beezy ain't say nothing. Smoke had a whole lot to say, though. When Beezy got over to his side, Smoke mushed the stack in his face. The dollars drizzled everywhere.

"What a waste you are, you fat shit," Smoke said as Beezy brushed by him and started walking home. Smoke's eyes got small and his nostrils flared and he started scratching his head. "Hold da fuck up. I know you ain't 'bout to bounce without touching this little nigga up. I wish a nigga would chest-bump me in the back. Beezy, bring yo ass!"

Beezy turned around. I wanted to evaporate. Shit, I won, why I gotta fight? But from the devil in Beezy's face, I knew he was about to buck. I told Reggie to hold my stuff.

Reggie looked me in the eyes. "Yo, break his neck, ya heard me? Don't be afraid to hurt 'im 'cause he ain't afraid to hurt you. These boys ain't ready."

After Reggie told me that, I turned around and *boom!* Beezy tagged me in the face. "What up? I ain't the only one leaving here with a L today," he said.

At first I didn't think Beezy was going to fight me for real. I mean, we were boys no more than an hour ago. But I tasted the blood flowing from my nose and it was on. I grabbed the fat fuck by his shirt and chopped him right in the voice box.

"Yeah, kill all that noise, bitch," I said as he crumpled down to the floor holding that fat-ass double chin he called a neck. He fell and I hopped on top and started hooking off. It was like everything went fuzzy. I couldn't feel any of the licks he was laying on me. I just kept swinging until I heard Smoke say, "Ayo, that's enough, yo. Y'all got that."

D-roc, barked, "Nah, you the one that done wound up your little toy soldier, let them niggas fight."

But Reggie grabbed me. "Now that's how the fuck you hold it down, Andre! See, I told y'all bitch-made niggas, *you don't want no drama*! Now where the fuck is my *money*!"

Reggie put his hand out. Smoke took out a rubber band and slung it around a roll of cash and flicked it halfway across the court.

Reggie laughed, "Boy, I tell ya, these new age cats sure are disrespectful." He patted the top of my head. "You earned it, playboy, go grab that up."

As I jogged over to midcourt to grab the cash, I watched as Smoke walked Beezy away from the court like a principal who'd just broke up a fight, except he was choking him by his shirt collar like a dog.

Beezy turned around and looked at me. We made eye contact and it hit me. I really just fought him. When our eyes met we agreed, silently, that was stupid. I wanted to say I was sorry and probably would have if Reggie and D-roc weren't jumping up and down in my face, shouting at me 'bout how I looked like "Tyson on that nigga, son." I earned my stripes and I kept 'em. But it didn't feel right.

The whole ride home in D-roc's car with the bass boomin', all I could think about was how badly Beezy was getting it for letting me do him like that. All them Squad Six boys came to the conclusion that it wasn't Squad Six no more; it was more like Team Seven.

Ruby Battel

When that boy strolled in my house looking like a crash test dummy, trying to act like nothing happened, I was ready to go. "Dre, what in God's natural world happened to you? Look at you. You were fighting! Where was Reggie?"

He looked at me like I was talking to him for my health. He sat there like he didn't have crusted blood around his nostrils.

"Oh, so I get it. Code of the streets, huh? You're not going to tell Mommy what happened because you don't want to be a sissy, huh? I know how this game works, Andre. Don't forget I married your father. A cut above the rest, Dre! What don't you get about that? All this foolishness in these streets ain't for you. You're not like these corner boys going nowhere fast in these streets. I'll make sure of that. So who was it, huh?"

When that boy told me that Reggie and Smoke put my baby and little Beezy up to fighting, my blood started to boil.

When I asked him why he didn't just come home, I wanted to smack him, talking about how he "couldn't look like no punk." I told that little boy, if I hear he's out there fighting anymore I'm going to punk him and whoever else wants some. It's times like this that I really just wish I had a little help. Maybe if Eddy would be around more that boy wouldn't feel like he had to be so damn tough all the time. Lord knows, it's not easy raising two. It's just me. Even with the change Reggie drops off over here, it's hard to make ends meet.

No games. I took the situation into my own hands. The next morning when Andre left for school I called into work and told them I was going to be late. Hell, if them boys are too pig-headed to make peace, I will. See, I know Smoke, his mother and I are actually friends. I remember him when he was just a little stinka butt running around this block. Back when he wasn't nothing but little Stanley Taylor, Miss Myra's boy. Now he thinks he can terrorize my baby. Oh, I don't think so.

And I know Reggie loves Andre and won't disrespect me. Smoke, or should I say Stanley, he better not make me have to call his mother. He wasn't afraid of much, but when it comes to Myra, she got that boy in check.

I set out on a relaxing stroll around the neighborhood. Right when I got to the gate I could see Reggie and the rest of his squad hanging on the corner. I saw Reggie looking over. From the look on his face he could tell I was ready to begin acting up. I started in his direction and he left the corner and met me halfway. See, I appreciate the money Reggie gives me, but if he thinks I'm going to let him ruin my baby, he can take that money and wipe his ass with it. Before I could get a word out he gots to explaining, "Check it out, Miss Ruby. Before you come over here riffin' and shit, let me tell you. You should be proud! The boy has hands. I mean, hot damn, he served that boy up something proper."

I took a step back. "Reggie, what the hell do you think this is? You think I'm trying to raise the future Mr. Get Bad? That boy ain't but ten years old . . . I'm trying to raise up a good man!"

"And I'm trying to help you, Miss Ruby. You think I started that fight? Naw! Shit, if someone up rocked your jaw then what you gon' do?"

This Negro must have thought I was one of his little around-the-way hoes. He wasn't fixing to run that preschool game on me. I told that Negro, "Well, however it goes, I don't want my child being used as a pawn in your foolishness. Dre came in the house last night looking hurt. I've got enough weighing down my heart without worrying about y'all fools messing with him. Come hell or high water, there ain't nothing going to harm that boy. Especially these games y'all playing in these streets. Now I've got to live here, Reggie. It's on you to make this right. I ain't playing either. And you best tell your little gooney squad there will be no addition to y'all's little crew. So rethink it. Y'all stay with that Squad Six business y'all like to write on the walls everywhere, and Dre's going to be a kid."

He cut me off.

"I got you, Miss Ruby. You right. I'm grown. I'll make it right with Andre and Beezy. Just understand, you really stretching out my box on this one."

With that being said, I turned around and strutted away. And to my delight, I didn't even need to raise my blood pressure going up the other end of the block and dealing with

Smoke and his pure ignorance. As I started walking back toward my house, Miss Myra was heading my way.

"Ruby, I know you've heard about this. Little Brendan cried himself to sleep last night. Them boys didn't want to fight, girl."

"Girl, who you telling? I know them knuckleheads put them up to it. I just got done setting Reggie straight."

"Yeah, Stanley knows what's up. Ain't gon' be no more problems. He values the life he lives. Girl, these boys think they tough. I told that boy if I hear he's messing with his little brother anymore, bone marrow gon' fly. He knows."

4

Progress Report

Me and my older sister Nina were setting the table for dinner when I heard the tick of Pop beating on his snare drum rising from the basement. My smile met Nina's frozen face. The tick followed by the kick of his bass drum immediately broke me out with chill bumps. I didn't even know he was home. Pop liked to sneak in and out of the house through the basement door, that way we couldn't keep track of his comings and goings. Ma was on the back porch grilling some chicken. Nina's eyes got wide and then sunk into her face as she rolled them. "Guess we need to set one more, huh?" she complained and tossed me an extra place mat.

"I love it," she whined, "how he comes in here and tries to play it cool. Shit's not cool, Dre. When was the last time we even saw his sorry ass, huh?"

She paused. "Oh, yeah, you right, you can't remember, huh?"

I really didn't have much to say. She wasn't too far off. Ever since the night we saw him hit Ma and the police took him away, he's shown his long drawn-out face in the house less and less. It's just Pop's way, he's a rolling stone, always gone and no one knows where he's at or what he's doing other than drugs, his one true companion in life. Ma says she thinks he's out there hustling and working under the table so he won't have to pay child support, but I don't know.

Pop's timing couldn't have been worse. Of all the days to show up, he had to come home for the worst possible dinner of the fourth term. Progress report day. The barbeque chicken and grilled corn filled the house with an aroma that made me want to eat the air. But when I heard Pop in the basement, I started to feel the burn of the butterflies flapping in my belly. It was bad enough that I knew Ma would ask in her sweet little Negro-I-wish-you-would-lie-to-me voice, "Didn't progress reports come out today?" But to make things worse, Pop would get to throw in his two cents.

Ma's temper was not above coming upside my head and Pop's an erratic bungee-cord-type nigga, I never quite knew when he was gonna snap. Factoring all this together, I came to the conclusion that sitting the four of us at a table for dinner was like mixing all the ingredients for a Molotov cocktail. Shit was gonna jump off one way or another. The common denominator would be Pop. He was liable to get into it with Ma. They always seemed to be in each other's faces about God knows what. Then Nina and Pop couldn't get along for shit either. Nina said she hated the man. Me and Pop, we really didn't talk much about anything other than sports. It just seemed he took the ruckus everywhere with him like a devil with his pitchfork.

After we finished setting the table, I wanted to go outside and enjoy my last bits of okayness, maybe shoot some hoops, but with Pop and the progress reports I wasn't risking Ma having to look for me, with the possibility of a slap in the head at dinner turning into a leather belt beat down before we could even eat. Using our good sense, me and Nina took it to the living room to forecast how dinner was about to go. I told her I wasn't worried. Well, yeah I was. Just not as worried for me as I was for her. For me, science was a C, math and social studies were both Ds, and English was a D-plus. But with no Fs, I was living. No Fs equaled no knots on my head. I hoped.

Nina, she was buggin'. When my eyes rolled up and down her wrinkled progress report, I couldn't help laughing. Homegirl was rocking it with two Ds in math and science, a D-minus in English, and an F in gym class. I must admit I was impressed that she found a way not to pass gym class. Nina was going to spark the explosion at dinner, I could feel it. On the bright side I got to play the good child for a change. What a great sister, I thought for a quick sec. It was usually me getting in all the trouble. Nina was more like a quiet storm. She moved in silence with her dirt, but there was nothing slick about that progress report.

After I showed her mine, she hissed through her teeth and dropped it on the floor and sat down next to me. I clicked on the TV and we started watching *Rap City.* We could hear Pop downstairs trying to sing through his vibe-triggered Jamaican accent. The deep thud from the kicks of his bass drum rattled the house. The chimes from the vibrating plates and forks acted as the nerved-up countdown music to our soon-to-come Dinner of Doom. Depending on the riddims he was rocking at the time, I could get a good gauge on his mood. Pop liked the old-school classics. Old Bob Marley covers, Toots and the Maytals, Burning Spears.

When I heard Pop screech, "Old pirates, yes, they rob I," the first line of Bob Marley's "Redemption Song," rising through the floorboards I knew he must be in one of those thinking kind of moods. A bootleg Rastafarian in my opinion, there was always someone or something holding his broke ass down, or so he said. Me and Nina sat there on the cream pleather couches in our living room both frisking over the many very accessible hiding spots for our progress reports. Nina tried her hair but after pacing the room a couple times and seeing the tips of white poking out and hearing the paper crunching in her head, she realized that hiding her progress report in the mountain of braids on top of her head just wasn't going to work out and she settled for her sock. I hitched mine in the elastic band of my boxer shorts.

When Ma started to stir the Kool-Aid, I started to tighten up. Ma's very precise when she cooks dinner. Making the Kool-Aid was always the last thing she did before it was time to eat. She opened the basement door and yelled downstairs, "Eddy, come up and get some supper."

I took a deep breath and the countdown was on. As soon as Pop brought his dark lanky frame upstairs it was like pre-game warm-ups. When he sat down it was game time. Next call, Ma was going to let me and Nina know the food was ready.

Pop came upstairs with the suffocating aroma of ganja oozing out of him like a glowing force field. Ma sucked her teeth. She wasn't a big fan of the way Pop blew trees, but her disliking something never stopped him from doing his thing. As we all settled in, I glanced around the table.

"So, Pop, who you think's going to win the tag team title tonight, the Harlem Heat or the Steiner Brothers?" I blurted out with too much air in my mouth, trying not to sound too phony and overly excited.

Ma and Pop could smell me bullshittin' like crime-sniffer dogs smell crack. Pop ignored me, leaving his head hung, focusing on his food as he forked up more wild rice. Nina peeped my failed attempt for conversation.

Once Ma blessed the food Nina asked her daily dinner question.

"So, how'd y'all days turn out?"

"It went well, sweetie," Ma answered.

I tossed in my echo with Pop's "Fine."

Then it was back to the food. Dinner wasn't ever that dry. I felt left out, like everyone was in on something and I wasn't. Maybe I was the only person who had a good day. Hell, no Fs was a good enough day to me. We ate most of dinner in a very hot, uncomfortable silence. One-word answers and downward gazes. Nina, Ma, and Pop all avoided eye contact, trying to act like they weren't feeling the heat in the room.

As we ate, my eyes bounced face to face, trying to catch a vibe or anything that could help explain their silence. It wasn't finger-sucking, bone-biting, tip-your-cap-to-the-chef silence. It was different. It felt guilty. It made me feel like maybe Ma and Pop already knew about the progress report that was now getting sweaty tucked inside my waistband. But it couldn't be. Nina was in on the act too. She wasn't saying much. But maybe she knew what they knew and was trying to avoid the trouble that was brewing under all that silence. Whatever it was, I couldn't call it.

Things started to boil right as Pop started to chew the ends of his chicken bones and began to suck the marrow out. He kicked his skinny legs up in the air, resting his feet up on the edge of the table; bad choice. Pops's big old brown dingo boots busted up all the eggshells we ate dinner on. Ma was early wit' it.

"Eddy, take ya nasty doo-doo stomping boots off my kitchen table. It's evil enough you ain't putting no food on it, but now you want to help dirty it. Unbelievable!"

Pops raised his head slow. His forehead curled, exposing the community of worry marks living on his face. His bloodshot eyes squinted low, dipping deep into his face. His lips dropped and got thin as he bit down on his jaw, making the muscles on the side of his face pop out. But no words. He just rustled his feet off the table, shaking the whole meal. The ice in our Kool-Aid glasses clanged together and the serving spoons rung out. When I made eye contact with him the words came.

"Let me tell you something, Ruby. It's no secret or surprise you stay the way you do. Every time! Every time I come in here and try, we gotta go there. I'll tell ya what is true. Your encouragement truly helps this situation."

Yeah, Pop ain't have no real job that you could collect taxes from. Really, other than playing his reggae music, I don't know what he does. It seemed like he wasn't highly skilled at anything other than the art of working the hell out of my mother's nerves.

"Excuse me! So *you* gon' tell *me*? Me, simply pointing out the fact that your jobless behind ain't taking care of this family is what's holding you stuck in the unemployed bracket? Get real, Negro. Don't do me any favors. This house is just a convenient pit stop for you and you know it. Try. My. Ass! You just here 'cause you're in between"—she looked over at me—"things. And that's what's true. You can play the fool if you want to, but don't put it on me. How the hell you get up in here anyway? I know I been locking that basement door!"

She started viciously sawing her chicken breast. She let out a "Hmmppf" and turned her stare away from Pop and onto me. I darted my eyes away from hers.

"I ain't no criminal, Ruby. I walked in that basement door the same way I walk out of it," Pop shot back. Damage was done. Pop tossed down his napkin and stood up, took a couple steps into the hallway, then turned back around and sat right back down.

"That'll be da day I let a female run me from my table! Kids, how y'all doing?"

The heat was on. I looked over at Ma. Her eyes mirrored pure disgust as she glared across the kitchen. I glanced over at Nina. Her eyes told me she didn't know if it was our place to be talking either. Ma jerked back and pushed herself out from the table. She stood up and pounded down her glass of Kool-Aid.

"Eddy, in the room!" She fingered toward their bedroom.

At one point their bedroom was our dining room. When I turned about four, me and Nina sharing a room wasn't going to work out anymore. So Ma got Papa Tanks to put up a set of those paper-thin fake woodprint closet doors. The doors muffled the sounds but from basically anywhere in our apartment if you talked too loud everyone would be able to hear you.

I slid my glass across the table to Nina for a refill. Then Pop rolled his eyes and slowly got up. He let out a deep sigh and headed for the room like a kid that had to come in from the park for dinner before the game was over. When he got out of the kitchen Nina punched her fist into her palm. "OOOOoohhhhh, NIIGGAAAA. That's fixin' ta be some shit right there. The bastard. Some nerve!"

Then she pulled out her crunched progress report from her sock and started to wave it around above her head. "We still got these, though."

I smiled and dap'd her up and she came over and sat next to me. We sipped our Kool-Aid, both of us sitting on the edges of our seats with our heads cocked in the doorway, ears pointed toward their bedroom. It wasn't long before we heard things get cooking in there. Pop must have been working Ma's nerves again.

Them paper-thins kept in their voices for a quick second

until Ma roared, "Don't give me that bullshit! It's hard for a black man to find work? Not you. It's hard fa yo ass to keep a job! What happened at the post office, huh? Fired! Or how about the bank? Cloudy piss! Negro, you ain't 'bout shit. Giggin' all over Boston chasing the riddims, smoking weed and sniffin' to the vibes. You got a family, Eddy! How far you think that receptionist money I get working at the health center is gon' get us? Nina's in eighth grade and Andre's in sixth. Do you even talk to them? What are their favorite colors, foods? What are they afraid of?"

There was a short silence. "At a loss for words? Don't worry, nigga, I'll wait." She paused again and lowered her voice, but we could still hear her. "Yeah, I thought so. You don't know. Bet you know where to find a fix on Blue Hill Avenue. You make me sick."

"Get 'im, Ma," I whispered to Nina and we laughed.

"Serves him right. He thinks he can just come through that basement door whenever he wants. And it's supposed to be all good," Nina whispered back.

Then I heard the rustling of the leather from the million handbags Ma kept hanging over her 'bout-to-break doorknob. Nina stuffed her progress report back into her sock and flew back around the table and out of Pop's seat. Ma walked back into the kitchen and sat down. Her eyes were red, but she wasn't crying. She picked up her fork and took a couple of bites of food and tossed it down. She stared down at the table and started rubbing her temples. Nina took another piece of chicken and got lost in it. Ma looked up with a half smile.

"So everyone's day was good?"

Me and Nina just sat there and hung in a weird silence. I perked up. Now was go time. "My day was great!" I said and glanced behind me. "Hey, anyone know what time it is?

'Cause *Monday Night Nitro* comes on at nine." I looked back at the clock and it was seven forty-five. With my fumble on time, Ma sniffed out all the bullshit in my fake excitement. Her next string of questions was the true heat check.

"Didn't progress reports come out today? How'd you two make out? You two didn't get any, did you?"

I didn't know how to answer because Ma's tricky. She liked to ask them questions that were liable to get you smacked up three or four times. If we had grades of C-plus or higher in our classes in the Milton public school system, there was no need for one. But Ma, she knew us too well. She knew we both had progress reports, probably even knew the grades on them. When my face lit up with the guilty fear of oncoming danger, I was caught.

"Uh-huh!" She clapped and stomped her foot. "Out with them! Lemme get a look at the two of yous' quest to under-achieve! Y'all are too damn smart to be getting progress reports."

I reached into my boxers and pulled mine out. Nina grabbed hers from her sock. I looked over at Nina and slid mine to Ma first. When she scanned it, I could just picture her chasing me around the house. Hair all wild-looking, crazy with her hand cocked above her head yelling, "Don't you run from this whoopin', little boy," right before she caught me and palmed my face.

Ma's Costa Rican. Down there I guess they really like school, because she was a golden little goody two-shoes in her day. She ain't quite understand how we "new age kids" could do such things like getting an F in gym class. Ma was that girl in the library being quiet, looking smart and shit. When she met Pop, she was in college at BU. He used to hang out around Berklee and float his way around, campus-hopping with his bands. She stopped going to school freshman year when she got pregnant with Nina and they decided to get married.

When Ma got done looking at my progress report she shot me a look that made me feel like the smallest person in the world. She tossed it down on the table and grabbed Nina's. When she picked it up I couldn't help but laugh. When I giggled, Ma shot me another look.

"Somethin' funny, Dre? Last time I checked your progress report was sitting right in front of your sister's."

She put out my fire quick. Even no Fs wasn't gonna get me out of this one. Ma glided her eyes back across the table to Nina.

"Gym class, Nina? Be serious! Nina, gym class! Really! What you want me to snatch first, that weave out your head or should I just take your whole head off? Sure ain't using it bringing these grades in my house!"

I heard the rustle of handbags and knew things were about to get way more funky in a second. Ma and all her unnecessary racket disturbed Pop, who I'm sure was still cooling off from his run-in with her. I was actually surprised he was still here. Usually after them two screamed on each other, he'd be gone. Back out the basement door until whenever. But tonight just wasn't an average night. Pop blazed into the kitchen.

"Ruby, fuck you yelling about now? I'm tired of hearing this shit. It's always something. Fuck's the issue?"

Ma grabbed the progress reports off the table, got up, and slapped them into his chest, and started heading back toward their bedroom. As she walked away she snapped off, "Maybe if ya fatha'd ya kids you'd care too. Or do you even know what those are?"

With his card solidly pulled, he looked at the progress reports.

"*Nina!* What are these grades? Andre, fuck is the problem here? I didn't make no dumb picknies. Nina, are you fucking kiddin' me? What the hell's wrong with you?"

Then the temperature in the kitchen rose about ten more degrees. Nina's whole face changed up, her body froze. Her eyes turned to stones as she looked at him. She looked deep, like she was trying to see into his soul. I felt like I should have tiptoed out of the room. But I didn't. I sat there and watched as Nina boiled over and spewed venom across the kitchen table.

"What, Ed? You want to know why my grades are like this? Well, I want to know where the hell you've been these past four months. What were you doing while you weren't helping me or Andre with our schoolwork? Uh-huh, and you're right! You ain't made shit in here. You have no right to comment on anything in this house! Ma's right, I don't know you! I hate you and I wish you weren't my father!"

She began to cry, her voice was small and high-pitched.

"I hate you! You weren't here, you've never been here to help me and Andre with anything. So you don't come in here and question not nothin'! You're the worst father alive. Why don't you go back to Lynn and stay with your other bitch and your other kid. That lil' bastard ain't shit to me. I'd spit in his face if I saw him."

Then she punched down on the table and got up. Staggering, fighting for her balance, she whimpered, rubbed tears from her face, and said, "You're the worst," as she stormed out of the kitchen.

It felt like I had fire in my chest. My heart was beating so fast my stomach started to hurt. I was so confused. Lynn? Other kid? Now I really felt left out. I didn't know what the hell she was talking about. What I did know was that Nina lost her mind going off like that to Pop. As she staggered away from the kitchen, I looked at Pop. He stood up and balled his fists. His eyes were glassy and his nose crunched as he started rubbing his balled fist while staring at Nina. She was walking toward her room and talking shit under her breath. I looked down at my empty plate. I could feel him glaring at me.

He was shaking his head. "Oh, yeah?" he sounded off. "Ain't no child of mine gon' talk to me like that in my house!" he yelled in the hallway. Then he took off after her.

"Ayo, Nina!" I yelled to her, but it was too late. Two long strides into the hallway and *boom!* he tackled her in the doorway of her room.

"Get the hell off of me!" I heard her cry out before he pushed her down by the shoulders and smacked her in the face. Ma rushed out of their bedroom and jumped on his back and started punching him and pulling at his nappy little matted puff of hair.

"Eddy, you'll kill her! Get your hands off her. You musta done lost your mind!" Ma screamed as she wrestled at his back.

My legs got numb and my hands tingled as I watched all of this unfold.

"Andre, call the police! Call the police!" Ma yelled to me, but I froze.

"Dad, stop! Stop! Stop!" I yelled to him, but he didn't listen. I ran into the corner of the kitchen and sat down by the cabinets. From there, I could see exactly what was going on. I hugged my knees and knew there was nothing I could do. I wanted to get up and call, but I was too scared. "You're next" was the only thing that came into my head when I thought about calling the cops. Nothing made any sense. I tucked my head between my knees and started to cry. I just wanted things to be okay. It felt like time stopped and all I could hear was tussling and yelling. Then I felt a hand on my shoulder. I jumped up ready to run, but it was Ma.

"You alright, honey?" She rubbed the top of my head gently. "Everything's okay. Come here." She pulled me tight for a hug. With tears in her eyes she looked me in the face.

"We're gonna be fine, Dre, I promise. Everything's okay now. We're fine, baby," she repeated as she rocked me side to side.

I wanted to believe her, but I was rattled down to my bones. Nothing felt okay. Nothing felt fine, not to me. I panned the house, trying to see where Pop was at. He was stretched out on the one-seater in front of the TV. My chest lit up again when I caught a glance of him. I power walked into Nina's room. Ma went into their bedroom, mean-mugging Pop the whole way there.

I got into Nina's room and she was balled up in her tan winter blanket, lodged in her closet, rocking back and forth. She looked like she was in a cocoon. All I could see was the top of her braids shaking like a pom-pom, sticking out from the tan ball in the corner. Once I closed the door she tipped down the blanket to eye level. She was still crying. When she looked into my eyes, she took a big breath and began crying harder.

"I'm so sorry, Dre. You didn't need to be here for that. Shit's just not okay, don't think this shit's okay, ya hear? I just wish he'd leave us alone. He just needs to go 'head and die," she said through the stutters of her cry. She chinned her face out of the blanket. I squinted at her.

"Where'd he get you?" I asked.

She rolled out her lower lip and showed me a purplish-red bust.

"Look. I bit my lip when that bum-ass nigga tackled me. You just wait. He's gonna get his. Believe that."

I sat down next to her. I looked her in the face and could see the puffy handprints running up her cheek and down her neck. I wanted to cry too, but I didn't want to make things worse. She put her arm around me and we just sat there for a while as her cries slowly turned to sniffles. Then she spoke.

"So yeah, I guess I blew it. Ma didn't want you to know. You half know anyway. Daddy's been out there in Lynn staying by some other bitch's place. They even got a kid. The lil' shit-head's a boy. Not sure how old, though."

I didn't really know how to feel.

"How you mean? Like in real life, I got a brother . . . for real?"

She nodded. "What 'things' you think Ma was talking about at dinner?"

For a second I almost got excited. I always wanted a brother. But it hit me quick. There was nothing cool about having a brother like that. After Nina shook up my whole world, we returned to silence. It felt like the lights in the room had gotten brighter. I sat there and began to question everything. What a good actor he is, I thought. I felt stupid. I should've figured there was more to Pop than just reggae music and drugs. Nina tugged at my shoulder.

"Andre, it's nine o'clock. Isn't your show coming on?" she asked.

The wrestling match just didn't matter like it did an hour ago. I didn't want to move or do anything. I wanted to sit and think on things. Just take it in, really.

"Andre," I heard Ma call. The butterflies fluttered back into my stomach. I looked at Nina.

"It's okay. You can go. I'm fine." She nudged my shoulder. "Go 'head."

When I got up, my legs still felt weak. I opened the door

and I saw Ma in the living room talking to Pop. I caught the tail end of their convo.

"And you better calm ya black ass down, you're scaring Andre."

Then she turned around and saw me. She met me a few steps in front of the doorway and knelt down.

"Baby, your father's very sorry. He promised everything's gonna be fine. He just lost his temper. But he's sorry. Now go catch some of your show."

Her hair looked wild. Her face was hard. She smiled, but I could tell there was no happiness in her.

"I've got to go to work, okay? I picked up the night shifts overtime. Your father wants to watch the match with you. It's about to start. Hurry or you'll miss it."

She bumped me toward the living room. I put on the brakes. "Ma, can I come with you?"

She smiled at me—for real this time.

"Boy, you haven't shut up about that match all week. Go on. Sit with your father. He misses you." She poked me, trying to make me laugh. I broke and started laughing. "Now go 'head, your father promised he'd be cool. I pinky-swear."

When I saw her pinky out in front of me, I knew it was serious business. We locked pinkies and she gave me a hug and a kiss on the cheek. I stood there in the doorway until I heard the front door slam. I walked into the living room.

I knocked off the lights before I got to the couch. I couldn't even look him in the face. I didn't know what to say to him. Right as I sat down Booker T and Scott Steiner were circling around each other. Jumping on the balls of their feet, arms half bent, looking for the right time to pounce. I hardly could watch. I could feel Pop's eyes side-glancing me. My eyes stayed glued to the TV, avoiding eye contact at all costs. The

TV made the room look dark blue. When he wasn't looking at me I peeped over at him as the flashes of blue bounced on and off his skinny chest.

When the match went to commercial break he turned on the end of the Hornets-Bulls game. Michael Jordan had the game under control. I figured he'd watch it for a bit, then turn my match back on, but when the game ended and he started watching the postgame show, I got nervous. My hands started to sweat. After a couple minutes, I squeaked out, "Pop, can you put the match back on, please?" My heart was banging like a subwoofer.

He looked at me. My hands were now shaking and sweating. He moved his calloused fist from the armrest. I jumped. He grabbed the remote. I flinched again. He clicked back on the match.

"So who you got ya money on tonight, Dre?"

"I dunno."

We shared a long pause.

"So . . . how's basketball season going? How's your travel team doing?"

"It was cool. It ended two months ago. I'm playing in the outdoor league now, it's springtime."

We went silent again and the match jumped back onto the screen from commercial break. Booker T and Scott Steiner had their hands locked, standing up, knees bent, playing a big game of mercy. They both swayed and pushed, trying to gain some leverage. I couldn't even enjoy it. I was too busy watching the live wire sitting across the room from me. I just looked as the shadows ran all over him. Wondering, why? And how? We made eye contact for a second, but I bolted my gaze straight to the floor. Then he looked me off. And I looked back at him. Then we did it again.

"Am I fucking bothering you, Dre?"

I got a jolt of lightning in my stomach.

"Nah, I'm just tired, Pop. I think I'm gonna head off to bed," I said and then got up and headed for my room.

It was cooler in my room, I thought as I plopped down on my bed. I rested my head on my pillow and closed my eyes. My head smashed with questions. How could he hit Nina like that? Now we done took some third-world beat downs in this house, but he looked like he really wanted to kill her. His eyes were so red, he looked possessed. He's the one who once told me, "Only a coward puts hands to a woman," and now look at him. With this business about some other lady and having a brother, I didn't know what to make of anything he'd ever told me.

I lay on my bed with my desk lamp on. Waiting. Waiting for him to leave. His job was done here. It was time for some peace. Until the next time he came slithering back in through that basement door. I heard him fumbling to hold the phone and the beep of him mashing down the numbers. Then he started talking, loud and loose.

"Just coolin' it at the house with the kids." He chuckled. "We just here chilling, ya know, easy vibin'. Who's all over there? Is EJ awake? Yep. Alright. I'll see you a lil' bit." And he clicked.

A few minutes later I heard footsteps heading down the stairs to the basement. Then a deep thud. I kicked my feet into my slippers, ran into the bathroom, and hopped into the tub. From the window I could see out into the side alley of our house leading to the next street over. Sure enough, there was Pop leaving out the basement door.

I ran into the kitchen, flicked on the basement light, and walked down the stairs. I looked over in the corner where he kept all his records and drum equipment. His drum set was still there. I walked over to the basement door and watched Pop out the peephole, walking, a dark skinny figure, bleaching into the night. He hit the bend in the alley heading toward Blue Hills Parkway.

I threw the bolt on the basement door.

I was the only reason it stayed unlocked anyway.

5

The Big One-Two

Pop pulled up in his rusty old blue Bronco. I couldn't believe my eyes. I hadn't seen him in about four months. I wanted to be so mad at him. He'd missed my whole rec league season and my all-star game too. We won the championship this year and I got the team MVP award. Man, he'd missed everything. Only because today was my birthday, I was giving him a get-out-of-jail-free card. I hadn't believed Nina when she said she'd overheard Ma telling Aunty Diamond and her boyfriend Lex that Pop was going to take me out for my birthday. When he stepped out of the car he looked kinda scary. He was so skinny, his hair looked ready to dread, and he smelled like cigarettes and liquor, but I still couldn't help being excited to see him. The first thing I said to him was, "Why don't you eat some food, man?"

He answered in his strongest patois, "Wat a gwanlick-lepickny. Happyburtday. Looks likes it's a'me n' ayu today."

I really didn't even know if it was cool for me to go out with him. I stood there real confused.

"I don't know, Pop. I gotta ask Ma if I can."

"It's cool, man," he said.

But I knew better than to believe him.

Right when I got to the porch, Ma came outside beaming. She had my Red Sox cap and my Celtics jersey in her hands. She knelt down and whispered in my ear, "This is your sur-

prise, Dre. I know you miss your daddy. Y'all have fun today."
She gave me a kiss on the cheek. Then she stood up and looked
at Pop. He was still standing at the fence. He never came past
the fence anymore.

"Eddy, y'all have a good day. I don't want *no* monkey business, ya hear?"

He didn't answer her. They just looked at each other like
strangers.

"Thanks, Ma," I said, and grabbed my stuff and ran to the
car before she could change her mind.

When we turned the corner of Verndale onto Blue Hills
Parkway, I couldn't believe he was there sitting next to me
and we were going to spend the whole day together. I'd only
seen him a few times since that night when he freaked out
and hit Nina. For a while we just rode, not really saying anything. He had missed so much I didn't really know where to
start. I wanted to tell him about how I got into my first fight,
or about my first game of spin the bottle or my rec league
season. I wanted to tell him I was onto him, that I knew why
his cigarettes smelled different. I had so much to say I just
stayed silent and looked out the window. I love Boston in the
daytime. It's so peaceful. No one's really out but the bums,
hustlers, and fiends.

"What's wrong wit' you, pickny? You alright? A surprise
coming for you today, man."

"Really?"

"Yup. We gunna have a good day, star, trust."

I wanted to be surprised, so I didn't ask where we were
going. I just enjoyed the ride. It seemed like we were going on
a tour of Boston. We passed Blue Hill Avenue and the Com-
mons. We passed through downtown and Harvard Square.
But when we got on the Tobin Bridge, I got really scared.

"Pop, where are we going?" I asked him. He just laughed and kept driving. "Pop, where are we going?" I asked him again.

"Relax, man, ya know? Today I figured you were ready."

When we got on the Tobin Bridge, I saw a sign for Lynn, and I knew nothing good was going to come of this trip. All I could think to myself was, "Lynn, Lynn, the City of Sin, ya never come out the same as ya came in." I knew my Pop's mistress lived in Lynn with my half brother. I had to stop this now. "Pop, I don't want to meet him."

He knew. He knew Ma didn't want me around his mistress and her kid.

Jamaican Pop came out again. Always trying to be smooth. "Relax, EJ is tense up ta meet you already. Mon, just cool it and tek it easy, mon. Dem already waiting for us."

I wanted to jump out of the car, but there was nothing I could do. He was driving and I was sitting there already regretting this trip.

"Pop, you know Ma doesn't want me with them."

"Now, Dre, who in da world said we haf ta tell ya mudda 'bout dis. When your friends at school do things, do you tell your teachers? I am your friend, right? So why would we have to tell her?"

He had a point, but I still couldn't shake the fiery flashes I was getting in my stomach. I let down my window to get some fresh air because I felt like I was gonna hurl. It was terrible. My belly was so tight it hurt to speak, so I didn't. I closed my eyes and tried to imagine how many cables held up the Zakim Bridge but all I could think to myself was how mad Ma was going to be when she found out. So I looked out the window and let the ride pass. Every time we stopped, I wanted to jump out of the car and run. I could still hear Ma's voice forbidding me to meet my "halfie." When we got off the exit, I really started to tense up. I wanted to cry. I didn't understand why he wanted me to disobey her like this.

"Yo, Rasta, I always hear say you want a brudda and ting, well it's time y'all link up and vibe, mon. Don't worry yaself. It's okay."

When we pulled up to Dunkin' Donuts, I saw them. A woman and a young boy. Pop turned off the car and popped open the glove box, brushed his hair back, and rested his cigarette on the window.

"That's EJ and his mother. I love her, ya know."

When he said that, I wanted to kill him. How could he love anyone but Ma? I wanted to ask him how he could have two families, but I was too scared. When I made eye contact with EJ, he smiled. I looked away. I didn't want to see him.

Pop got out and walked over to them. Ma was so much prettier than this trick. She was fat with a dusty old weave in her head. When he hugged her, I felt a piece of myself die. His face lit up. He looked so happy. Then he grabbed little EJ and picked him up and swung him around. I felt like I shouldn't have been peeping on this family. I wanted to mind my own business. But I couldn't help looking. When they all started walking toward the car, I didn't know what to do. I didn't even know where I was. There was nowhere to go. So I just sat there and put my seat all the way back so they couldn't see me.

Pop snatched open the door and said, "Boy, you don't know how to speak?" So I sat up.

"Hey, honey-dip, happy birthday," she said. "How does it feel to be the big one-two?"

When she smiled I could smell the coffee on her breath. It didn't make any sense how he could like her. She was so nasty. Her face was filled with little black freckles and she looked like she was about to burst right out of her green sweat suit. She was so big I could hardly see EJ standing behind her. She tapped my knee twice and said, "Y'all have fun now. EJ, don't go spend up all the paper route money." When she walked away, I wished EJ would have followed her.

EJ sat in the back behind Pop. I stayed in the front. When we left the parking lot, Pop threw on some old Bob Marley and said, "EJ, this is Andre and, Andre, this is EJ."

EJ threw me a handshake. I balled my fist and threw him a pound. Only herbs get pounds. If he didn't know, he knew now: I don't like you. He needed to know meeting wasn't my idea.

"Ha ha, EJ. Da nerve of dis guy. Him wasn't sure if he was gonna mek da trip, but he wised up and came around."

I hunched down in my seat because I didn't want anyone to see me with him. I knew this was all so messed up. I felt as though it was my fault. I should have just run inside when I saw Pop pull up. I looked at EJ out of the corner of my eye. He looked nothing like me.

EJ caught me. "Hey, man, what's up? What are you into, big bro? I've wanted to meet you."

I wish I didn't really know what was going on, but I did. I wanted to scream, "Yo mama's a home-wreckin' hooch." Instead, I just looked at him and didn't answer. All I wanted to know was when this was going to be over. He was why shit was so bad at home. If I erased him, we could be a family again. I hated him and his mother. I knew she was the lady that Pop had been staying with. I turned up the music. Bob always put a cool vibe in the air. I stared out the window as EJ and Pop talked. I wasn't even listening.

Our first stop was the liquor store. Before Pop got out of the car he reached deep in his pocket and pulled out a crinkled old picture of two baby boys and tossed it on my lap.

"You don't remember, do you? This isn't the first time you two have met."

Then he slammed the door, and I felt the temperature rise. I closed my eyes as if I was sleeping. I didn't want to talk to EJ. But when I peeked at him, he was just sitting there cheesing with his big ol' Kool-Aid smile.

"So, Dre, I've heard so much about you, man. Will you teach me to play b-ball like you? I hear you play for the junior regional team."

It hit me then that this little guy just didn't get it. I didn't want anything to do with him. How could he not understand? He was the only one happy in this car. I felt bad, but I had to do it. "Yo, pump the brakes, son. I can't even do all that. How old are you anyway, man?"

He said he was eleven, which hurt me even more. Pops had been cheating on Ma since I was one.

When Pop got back in the car, he threw his forty-ounce between his legs and ruffled down the brown bag just enough so he could drink it, and we breezed off. When I looked over at him, he was sniffling with a misty look in his eyes. I couldn't believe it, this asshole was really sitting there crying.

"I've been waiting years to finally have y'all two link up," he said.

Then he took a sip of his forty. That was the first time I had ever seen him cry. I wanted to cry right along with him. When he saw me staring at him, he quickly wiped his eyes and said, "So what you two picknies want to do today?"

EJ immediately said, "Daddy, can we get Big Bro a present for his birthday?"

My blood ran cold. Nina was the only other person I had ever heard call him Daddy. I wanted to correct him. And I wasn't his "Big Bro" neither. But instead I suggested we go to the mall. I figured I love presents and, shit, the little guy owes me for my troubles.

At the mall was the first time I got to take a real good look at him. There was just no way this kid was my brother. We looked nothing alike. We were exact opposites in every way. He was a geek. He had braces with black, green, and yellow Jamaican-colored rubber bands on them. He was a scraggly lil' guy. He wore glasses, and all he seemed to be into was anime and *Star Trek*. At the mall, EJ started running around like he'd never been outside before. I was waiting for Pop to say something, but he just let him do his thing. If that was me, he would have snatched me bald. The poor little guy was so happy to see me. And all I felt like doing was kicking his little annoying ass.

First we went to Cinnabon because EJ was bitching about his little sweet tooth. I wanted to choke him. It was my birthday, and we were sitting there catering to this little bastard. I tried to play it cool, but I knew in my heart everything about this day was just wrong. It didn't feel real. I felt like I was above everything watching the day unfold.

After EJ got his sugar fix, we went to Sam Goody to get some CDs. EJ bought me the *Wu-Tang Forever* CD, the one my mother said I couldn't have because of that stupid parental advisory sticker. Pop got me the Memphis Bleek CD *Coming of Age*. Both CDs I knew damn good and well I wasn't supposed to have. After that, we walked around a bit. I was hoping EJ would run off some of his energy so I wouldn't have to sock him in his lil' peanut head before the day was out.

EJ asked so many questions I started to wonder if he was working for the law or something. I felt bad, but when EJ gave me a wedgie, I yoked him up and told him to calm the fuck down. He was laughing, but Pop could see I wasn't kidding and broke it up.

After that, Pop decided that it was time to roll out, so we left the mall and headed back toward Boston. Maybe fifteen minutes into the ride, EJ started whining that he had to pee. So we pulled over at a Walgreens and let him out. Pop and I stayed in the car. We both watched him walk into the store. Pop said to me, "He's a good lil' pickny. He just needs some coaching. I was hoping that you would take him under your wing."

Okay, so now I was officially upset. I thought to myself, This guy is on crack. I was so mad, so mad I just spoke my mind. "Listen, 'ight. Let me tell you something, Pop. This ain't fixing to be no every week thing. After today don't bring him 'round me no more. Test me if you think I'm playing. I'll beat his lil' ass and then what? I don't fucking like him, okay?" Now I knew I was out of order for speaking to him like that, but I didn't even care.

He eyed me.

I was so scared I couldn't even raise my eyes from the floor. Pop was a loose cannon. I was waiting for him to snap and beat the hell out of me at any moment. I looked out the window and saw EJ walking back toward the car picking pieces of Laffy Taffy out of his braces. When the door creaked open and slammed, I let the seat back down again.

By this point it was about afternoon and I'd had enough fuckery for one day. I grabbed my belly and started rocking back and forth. "Pop, I think I need a washout. I think my insides are rotting. I feel like I'm getting the Hershey squirts. You gotta take me home." The only person in the car who believed me was EJ.

"Aww, Big Bro, I'm sorry, man. You're not feeling well?"

I wanted to ask EJ if I had an echo, but I let it rock.

"Yeah, son, I ain't feeling so hot. It's time to take it back to the hood, but I'll get up wit' you."

Knowing how I felt about him, Pop didn't really say much. He just looked heated at me, but I didn't care. He should have known he was dead wrong putting me through all this anyway. I was happy I was going home, but the fuckery wasn't over. EJ was still in the car.

I let the window down to get some air and rubbed my belly and started tapping my knee and biting my nails. About a half block away from my house, the car stopped.

"Alright, pickny, get out and don't shit yourself before you reach home."

EJ just thought "Daddy" was so funny. I threw him a pound and bounced. I didn't even say bye to Pop.

"You sure you okay? It was nice meeting you. Catch ya on the flip side," EJ said, hanging halfway out the window like a monkey as the two of them pulled off.

I didn't go home. I walked back two blocks to the Tucker, my old elementary school, and sat on the top of the monkey bars. How could I go home? I knew Nina and Ma were going to want to know what I did all day. I couldn't bullshit this one. Ma, she sees right through me. And I knew if I told Nina she was going to tell Ma.

For a while I just sat there, reading the credits of my new CDs. I felt like everything today was my fault. I just knew Ma was going to be so mad at me for going out there and fraternizing with the enemy. I decided that this day was a secret I would take to the grave. Once the streetlights came on, I started walking home.

When I turned the corner onto Lothrop, I saw everyone was outside. Ma, Nina, Nana and Papa Tanks, Aunty Diamond and her boyfriend. When they saw me, they started popping party poppers and singing "Happy Birthday" and throwing confetti. I just wanted to cry when I saw them, but I mustered up a half smile and walked up to the porch.

6

Objects in Motion

It didn't take long to be identified as one of the troublemakers in the seventh grade. In just one week I went from being a harmless wanderer to being a roaming troublemaker. My teachers in the sixth grade labeled me a hallway-wanderer and they stuck me in the "resource room" down in the basement where they hide the special education department. The school told Ma that I needed extra attention, but I think they just ain't want me wandering the hallways like I do. I don't really need the extra help, but the teacher, Ms. Lenny, damn near be doing my homework for me. I still feel like the punishment didn't fit the crime, but I shouldn't complain.

See, there's a big difference between being a wanderer and a troublemaker. Both stigmas raise teachers' eyebrows and neck hairs, but when you're a wanderer they're still nice to you, they just want you to get to where you need to be. But when you're a troublemaker you glow red in the eyes of the teachers, they straight up don't want you around. Once you're slapped with the troublemaker reputation, you're as good as being a criminal in the streets and teachers police you like hallway cops looking for a reason to accuse you of something. Whether it's a simple misunderstanding or not, if a teacher decides you're guilty of something, you hardly get a chance to defend yourself, because "talking back" is rude once you've been accused.

Nina laid down the troublemaker blueprint for me—her reputation hovered over me like a storm cloud. I think some of the teachers were a little bit afraid of her and they were glad she'd gone to high school. When I was in sixth grade and Nina was in eighth, teachers would see me in the hallways and ask, "Are you Nina Battel's little brother?"

I'd answer yes, and they'd break a fake smile and say, "Hmm, that's nice," and quickly walk away.

Nina was a terror when she was a student at Pierce Middle School, and it feels like the teachers half expected me to be a certain way. A bad reputation's a hard thing to outrun.

Nina warned me that my science teach Mr. Stow was a real-life asshole. She had a wild run-in with him just a couple days after our progress reports came out last year, when Pop showed up at the house and started arguing with Ma and tripping about our grades. Nina was in don't-fuck-with-me mode after all that happened, and I think Mr. Stow picked a real bad time to mess with her. He wasn't even teaching the class she was in, her English teacher was sick and Mr. Stow was only substituting. Nina's teacher left a worksheet for them to do and Nina said she wasn't in the mood for busywork, so she folded her arms out in front of her and rested her head down on her desk.

Nina said Mr. Stow wouldn't leave her alone about looking like she was sleeping and after the third time he called her name and she ignored him, he clapped his book shut, hopped out of his seat, and stormed over to her desk and screamed, "Wake up! No one else in this room is allowed to sleep in class. Do you think you're above the rules?"

Nina said she looked up at him and stood up on her feet. She didn't like how he rolled up on her like he was about to do something. As Nina tells it, she told him, "Wasn't nobody asleep! Why you don't get out my face with yo hot-ass breath? You know what? Write me a pass to the nurse's office 'cause your fuckin' face is making me sick."

She was sent to the principal's office immediately, and she gladly took her three-day suspension. Ma screamed on her pretty bad about it and put her on punishment: no phone or TV, no friends over the house or going out on the weekends. Ma put Nina on lockdown and she acted like she didn't care the entire time, which seemed to piss off Ma even more. I thought what she said to Mr. Stow was pretty funny and I was impressed with how she handled the whole situation, but in my case I wasn't even looking for no trouble.

Science has always been my best subject. I figured I'd just lie low and let the time pass, and kind of stay out of his way. But from the second I walked into Mr. Stow's room on the first day of class, I felt him put the hawk-eyes on me. I took out a notebook and a pencil and I leaned back in my chair as he walked around the room desk to desk handing out the syllabus. When he got to my desk he paused holding the syllabus like he didn't want to give it to me, blinking all fast behind his thick rectangular glasses. I looked up at him and he sort of snorted as he pushed his glasses up over the bridge of his nose.

"Four on the floor, Andre Battel," he said as his bushy eyebrows arced toward his receding hairline. I was surprised he already knew my name, but then quickly remembered what Nina had told me. He waited until I put all four legs of my chair on the ground and then he dropped the syllabus on my desk.

The first unit was on Newton's three laws of motion. Our homework assignment was to read the handout he'd given us explaining the whole concept and to come to class prepared to ask any questions. I read the handout and the concept seemed simple enough to me. Stuff doesn't move unless something makes it move. Once something's moving it'll keep moving until something stronger stops it. It refreshed my memory, we learned that crap at the end of last school year. It seemed like the lab we did where we poured vinegar into a beaker with baking soda inside and it bubbled and fizzed over.

The second day of class, I had no questions, so I sat in the back of the room gazing out the window, bored out of my mind. Even though it's been two years now, I still daydream about having recess, being able to run off a little steam in the middle of the day. It was the only thing I looked forward to about school and I don't know why they took it away.

It's so hard to sit through class with nothing to look forward to. My problem accepting school with no recess is what made my sixth-grade teachers start calling me a wanderer. I'd find any excuse to slip out of class and I'd walk around the hallways making faces at my friends in their classes, looking for someone to help me find recess, but all I ever found was myself in the principal's office. My guidance counselor, Ms. Judge, was the one who called Ma and told her the teachers noticed that I was having trouble sitting through class. She recommended Ma take me to the doctor and get me tested for attention deficit disorder and that I start going to the "resource room." Ma reluctantly agreed to me going to the "resource room" for more specialized attention, but when Ms. Judge kept urging Ma to get me tested for that attention disorder, Ma got really angry.

I was in the living room when Ms. Judge called and I heard Ma tell her that I was an energetic growing boy and that I didn't have no attention disorder, I just needed to listen better and behave. She also told Ms. Judge that her problem was that instead of working with the kids, she was trying to medicate all their personality away and that it was the last thing she was going to do to me. Ma ended the call and told me that they just don't know how to deal with kids who are strong-minded.

The kids at school call the "resource room" the "romper room" and they say only Skippys and Speds have to go there. God did not skip over me when he was giving out brains and I never really imagined myself being a special ed kid. At first I hated it, I sat out of window range so no one would see me in there with all the slow kids. I didn't really need extra help all the time, and I hate the way Ms. Lenny talks to me like I'm dumb, always hinting me toward the right answer. There was a bunch of times I tried to tell her that I was okay and didn't need her help nor did I belong in there with the slow kids, but it was like screaming underwater—it did no good. Soon enough I just gave in and got used to having Ms. Lenny breathing over my shoulder and spoon-feeding me the answers. I'm not stupid, class is just boring as hell but most of the time I got all my homework done before I went home. I hardly ever bring any homework home anymore, leaving me plenty of time to play basketball after school.

The resource room was my next class after science and Mr. Stow's deep voice felt like a sleeping pill, making time crawl. All I wanted to hear was the bell ring. It was warm outside and the window was open and a bluish-green dragonfly flew into the room. I watched it dart around for a while, it stole the entire class's attention while Mr. Stow was writing on the board. When he turned around and realized everyone was watching the dragonfly, he rolled up a piece of newspaper and swatted at it until it flew back outside.

Everyone refocused on him and I looked around the room.

It felt like church, everyone was involved in something I didn't completely understand. I mean, I understand church is about God, the pastor, and the congregation, and school is about class, teachers, and students, but what makes people pay attention and listen to teachers and pastors the way that they do? Looking around the room at everyone taking notes and paying attention, I just couldn't figure it out.

I got tired of thinking, the heat in the room made me start feeling sleepy, so I raised my hand and asked Mr. Stow if I could use the bathroom. He gave me a hall pass and I left. I figured maybe if I stretched my legs a little bit it would take the edge off. I was only gone for about ten minutes, which was good considering how long I would've been gone for last year. He didn't even have to send someone to come looking for me.

When I walked back into the classroom all my classmates were staring at me and giggling. I sat down at my desk and looked up at the blackboard and my name was written in big capital letters under the word "Detention" in the top right-hand corner of the board. All my classmates were sneaking glances at me and I felt my hands start shaking. My stomach dropped and I started feeling my heart beating in my throat. I couldn't catch my breath, it sort of felt like I was breathing into a small paper bag. I raised my hand.

Mr. Stow paused his sentence about inertia and called on me.

"Excuse me, sir! What'd you give me detention for? I wasn't even in the room. How'd I get detention when I wasn't in the room?"

I couldn't hide the anger in my voice. I crossed my arms and glared at him. He snapped the piece of chalk in his hand and his face soured as his blue eyes narrowed on me. He said, "Mr. Battel, you were gone much longer than it takes to use the washroom. Now please stop interrupting. We can discuss this after class if you'd like, but for now—Newton's first law of motion."

He turned his back on me and wrote Newton's first law of motion on the board:

> *An object at rest remains at rest unless acted upon by a force. An object in motion remains in motion, and at a constant velocity, unless acted upon by a force.*

Mr. Stow turned back toward the class and wiped two big yellow streaks of chalk dust on the pockets of his black corduroys.

"Let's see if I can give a more practical example of the law of inertia. Say, for example, a student decides to go off wandering the hallways because he or she is bored. So boredom is what set the student wandering. Unless I, the teacher, stop this wandering, it may never stop." He was looking straight at me but swung his arms wide while asking the class, "Now, does that make sense?"

No one answered him, the bell rang, and everyone started packing up their stuff. He walked over to the door, saying bye to everyone as they walked out of the room. As I walked toward him I put my head down and brushed past him.

"See you at two o'clock, Mr. Battel," he called to me as I walked up the hallway heading toward the resource room.

When school let out I walked straight to Kelly Park to play some basketball. I didn't show up for Mr. Stow's detention because I hadn't done anything wrong. What gave him the right to keep me after school for being at the bathroom too long? What if I'd had the bubble guts or something? I didn't, but what if I did? After school, before the streetlights come on and Ma gets home from work, my time is mine. I don't need Mr. Stow busting my balls. I get enough headaches just being at home. Between Ma, Nina, Nana Tanks, and Aunty Diamond, there's enough eye rolling, finger snapping, and teeth hissing to last me a long while. Especially now that Aunty Diamond and Ma been beefing. Aunty Diamond started it really, she's crazy. She thinks the entire world has beef with her, but I think it's the other way around.

When Aunty Diamond divorced Uncle Elroy, she got all weird. She started wearing all black and stopped hanging out with us and talking to Ma, and even though she lived upstairs in their apartment, she started being mean to Nana and Papa Tanks. She'd explode on them for the pettiest things, like one of them warming up her leftovers the day after she ordered food. She stayed in her room and didn't really come out unless she was going or coming from work, getting something to eat from the kitchen, or using the bathroom. She wouldn't even come out of her room to eat with us on Thanksgiving. She'd come out maybe for Christmas but that was only if one of her two boyfriends was around. There was her skinny, pale-as-pasta boyfriend Lex, he's Haitian and deejays on the weekends but he ain't got no real job. He's usually hanging around the house waiting for Aunty Diamond to get off work. That's only until she gets sick of him always mooching off her, which seems to be every couple of weeks, and she throws him out and calls her married boyfriend Brent. He's not around as much, but sometimes I can never quite tell who I might see upstairs in Nana and Papa Tanks's apartment.

This summer, after years of acting like all of us didn't exist, Aunty Diamond emerged from her bedroom like an animal fresh out of hibernation. One night we were sitting down to eat dinner when Aunty Diamond knocked at our back door.

She had a bright smile, a paper plate and plastic spoon in her hand. She looked ready to sit down and eat dinner with us. Ma stood in the doorway. Aunty Diamond sniffed over her shoulder, "Smells good, Ruby. Whatcha making?"

Ma didn't budge from the door.

"Nice to see you, Diamond. Wish I'd known you were being social again, and maybe I'da made enough food for a guest." Ma closed the door, she didn't slam it but it didn't seem as if their conversation was over. The next morning I woke up really early. I sat eating a bowl of cereal while Ma was in the shower, Aunty Diamond snuck downstairs and shushed her finger to her lips and crept into Ma's room. She came out with an armful of Ma's work dresses. Again she shushed her finger to her lips, laughing like we were playing some kind of game. She skipped back upstairs. Ma got out of the shower and noticed immediately. She went upstairs in her bathrobe and I couldn't hear what they were saying but I heard yelling. As I was finishing my bowl of cereal Ma busted through the back door with all of her dresses in her arms. Aunty Diamond was behind her and Ma slammed the pile of dresses on the ground and blocked Aunty Diamond from coming into our apartment.

"Ruby, just let me wear the dress," Aunty Diamond demanded.

"Diamond, you can't just up and decide we're sharing clothes, especially when before yesterday it's like you didn't even know my phone number. Why didn't you ask me first? That's your problem. You just do whatever you want to people. But I'm done letting you walk all over me."

Aunty Diamond folded her arms, looked at Ma. "So quick to burn a bridge, Ruby. Don't forget, one day you might need something."

Ma slammed the door in her face and Aunty Diamond yelled, "Bridge burnt, Ruby!" and walked back upstairs laughing this evil high-pitched witch-sounding laugh. Ever since Aunty Diamond started coming back out of her room it's like she feels like Ma owes her something. Whenever Ma gets anything, Aunty Diamond wants it, no matter what it is, money, a new hairstyle, a dress, a new set of friends. It just seemed like Aunty Diamond was plain jealous of Ma and everything she did. She's always trying to compete with Ma but the one thing Ma has that Aunty Diamond will never have is kids. In this department Aunty Diamond can't compete, and she'd complain to me and Nina and get mad at us, claiming we always forgot about her, leaving her out of the things we did as a family. I try to avoid her when she's around the house, she's forever crying and complaining when there really isn't much for her to be bitching about. She's always swearing to the high heavens that the world doesn't care about her. The weirdest thing about Aunty Diamond is that we're so broke all the time, it's crazy to even think we got anything for her to be jealous of. She has her own car, pays no rent living upstairs, has a full-time job, and supports Lex the full-time mooch. She has the most money out of anybody in the house and she seems the most miserable too.

Besides that, ever since Pop took me out to Lynn and forced me to meet EJ and his fat-ass mother, it's the only thing I can think about. I never told Ma or Nina about what happened that day or where he took me. I didn't tell so I could protect Pop either, I didn't want Ma to feel bad about trying to do something nice for me. I can still hear his voice ringing in my head, fooling me into thinking that the whole thing was okay, "Now, Dre, who in da world said we haf ta tell ya mudda 'bout dis. When your friends at school do things, do you tell your teachers? I am your friend, right? So why would we have to tell her?"

I knew there was something flawed about his reasoning and the more I thought on it, the flaw was that me and him ain't friends, he just wanted to cover his ass. Ma's been suspicious of me since that day, no doubt. She asked me why I came walking around the corner and why Pop didn't drop me off in front of the house. I panicked and told her that I'd asked Pop to drop me off at Kelly Park because there was good run up at the courts. I told her I'd played for a bit and came home. She asked why I wasn't sweating and I didn't answer her. I could tell she didn't believe me, but she didn't press the issue any further. I didn't know how to tell her what'd happened. I was mad at Pop, mad at myself, and I didn't want Ma to feel bad about setting the whole thing up. Plus, there was no telling what would happen if Ma found out. Now when I'm home I try to stay in my room listening to music or upstairs in the den watching cable. If I'm not doing either one of those things I try to be asleep. Ma always asks me what's wrong and I always tell her nothing, but the weight of the secret from my birthday has been weighing me down, thoughts and images from that day are always playing in my head, bouncing around and itching at my brain like a mosquito bite. I want it all to go away but it seems ain't nothing that can be done to change the truth.

I don't know what I thought was going to become of the detention, and I knew better than to tell Ma about it, so I did like Nina, acted liked I didn't care and let it ride. I needed to be at Kelly Park, at the basketball court. It's the place where my standing doesn't change as long as I work on my game. It's where I have control over how people judge me. The basketball court is the only place where everything that makes me uncool doesn't matter. I can turn it all over on its head. It doesn't matter that my sneakers aren't name brand or that my father's a deadbeat, or that Ma doesn't drive a nice car. At the basketball court it's simple, all that matters is putting the ball through the hole, whether or not you're good at it. There's a big gap between talking and talented and everyone's truth is revealed at the basketball court.

The best part about basketball is all I need is me, the ball, and the rim. Even if there's nobody running full court I'll shoot by myself until my arms are tired or the calluses on my fingers start to crack. Ma always tells me my life's "off balance" because of how much time I spend playing ball, but at the basketball court I can be what I can't be everywhere else: good.

Ma asked me how the first day of school was, I told her "fine," ate my dinner, and went to my room.

The next day of school, I walked into science class and my name was still written on the board. This time it had a big yellow check next to it. Again, I raised my hand and asked why.

Mr. Stow clasped his hands and rocked on his heels as he said, "I missed you yesterday after school, Mr. Battel. So much so that now I'll be seeing you after school for the next two days."

Then he told me again to stop being rude and interrupting his class.

I heard a few girls in the front of the room gasp, and the new kid Roy Shepard, who was sitting behind me, started laughing and kicking my chair.

I'd stepped on Roy's sneaker in the cafeteria on the first day of school and he tried to make a scene. He dropped to his knee all drastic and started spit-shining his Jordans. He looked at me and pointed at my sneakers whining,

"Dammmn, man, don't be stepping on my J's with your cheap-ass, Boe-Boe-ass sneakers."

I wanted to smack him in the mouth but no one really paid any attention to our exchange so I let it slide. But now whenever I see Roy he calls me "Boe-Boe."

Roy kicked my chair again as Mr. Stow asked everyone to take out our textbooks. As I turned in my chair to get my book out of my bag, Roy gave me the middle finger and I could feel my face heating up. He kicked the back of my chair again and I edged my desk forward, out of kicking range. I could tell if we kept going at this pace, we were going to fight.

I felt my heart sink as I looked at the clock and saw that there was forty minutes of class left. I tried drawing circles, scribbling big bull's-eyes, ignoring Roy, watching the passing clouds, and thinking to myself. First off, I ain't coming to no two days of detention because I took too long going to the bathroom. Even if I did walk around for a bit before I got there. I mean, who the hell does this guy think he is?

What I wanted to know was, who polices the teachers, who sets their rules? Because Mr. Stow's pretty damn rude too. I mean, what's the motivation to stop "being rude" once your name's on the board and you've been singled out? Isn't that an outside force acting on an object at rest? I didn't even get a warning, I didn't start any trouble with him until he started with me. Isn't it rude to call me out, trying to embarrass me in front of the whole class? It's bad enough already that since middle school started I don't hardly get to see Beezy and Chucky no more and every day Roy Shepard has something new to say about what I've got on, calling my sneakers "Boe-Boes," saying I dress like a white boy just because I've got on a pair of cargo khakis.

The tag was sticking out from the collar of my T-shirt and Roy read it aloud, "B.U.M. Equipment, isn't that the brand they sell at the discount store Bradlees?"

I could hear Roy hissing at me and slowly scooting his desk forward so he could try to kick my chair again. My legs started shaking. I sat clicking the top button on my pen, trying to calm down. I stabbed my pen into the notebook and started raking tears down the page.

"It's all about power and friction," Mr. Stow rambled on about the second law of motion.

Roy kicked the back of my chair again and I leaned to the side like I was trying to tie my sneaker and spat a big wad of phlegm onto his sneaker. He kicked out and yelled, "Ayo!"

Mr. Stow looked at him and said, "Roy, what's wrong? If you'd like to add to the discussion, please raise your hand."

Roy didn't answer him and my breathing steadied and I started thinking about the idea of power. Where does power come from? And how do people get it? And why do they have it? What gives people the right to have power over other people when we all start off as little helpless babies born to our parents? Why does being a teacher give them the power to give out detentions and why do cops get to arrest people when they're just people too when they're not working. Who gives churches and schools the power to operate? Churches are inspired by God and schools are funded by the government, but it seems like the two things don't mix, so they can't get their power from the same place, so then where does all the power come from? Some things I just can't figure out.

After I got tired of racking my brain about power, Roy started kicking my chair again.

I raised my hand and asked to use the bathroom.

Mr. Stow sighed and said, "No, Andre, you can't." He looked me off and resumed talking about Newton's second law of motion, he had it written on the board:

> *The change of momentum of a body is proportional to the impulse impressed on the body and happens along the straight line on which that impulse is impressed.*

I was bored and pissed off and, sure, maybe I wanted to take a little walk, but I did also have to use the bathroom. I tuned out Mr. Stow and sat in my chair shocked, Roy Shepard lightly chanting in my ear:

> Boe-Boes, they make your feet feel fine,
> Boe-Boes, they cost a dollar ninety-nine.

I tried to tune him out too. What was it about being a teacher that gives this jerk the power to take away my right to go pee? It's crazy and unreasonable to deny anyone the right to use the bathroom. It seemed like a joke. I could feel the side of my head pulsing and heard Roy chanting that damn Boe-Boe song, and all I want to know is why everyone thinks they got the power to fuck with me. My legs started shaking again. I knew I told Ma that this year would be different, but it feels like I'm losing control.

Ever since Ma joined New Day Pentecostal and stopped letting us go trick-or-treating, she's always going on about how if you stand for nothing, then you'll fall for anything. She was talking about Jesus, but I was thinking more along the lines of my pride. Without recess, or Chucky and Beezy, I was right back at the bottom of the social totem pole, and Roy Shepard was on top. His father's a doctor and drives a Range Rover.

He lives in a nice house and he's already damn near got a full goatee. Roy crushed me in the coolness department, but the more he whisper-chanted the Boe-Boe jingle in my ear the closer I came to the conclusion that it was time for me to take a stand.

Roy will learn to stop fucking with me.

I hated the way things switched up once middle school began. I liked going to Tucker Elementary better, everyone knew my name there, and not because I was a troublemaker either. Everyone knew my name because I had had enough playground fights that they knew I wasn't afraid to fight and was actually pretty good at it. It's not my favorite thing, but it goes hand in hand with being the best athlete in our grade, and everyone knew that too. Every day at recess me, Chucky, and Beezy dominated the playground. I wasn't ever afraid with them around, but none of that really mattered now.

I had to make a new name for myself.

Roy Shepard stopped kicking my chair and started throwing pieces of paper at the back of my head. It was only Wednesday of the first week of school and I didn't want to start off the year fighting, but Roy was grinding on my nerves. Another piece of paper hit the back of my head and Roy said, "I bet yo mama cuts your hair in the kitchen. Huh?"

It was true but I ignored him and raised my hand again. I made eye contact with Mr. Stow, and he brushed me off and called on someone else. Another piece of paper hit me in the back of the head and I turned around. Roy grabbed his pen like he was writing notes and looked up at the blackboard like he wasn't doing anything. I could feel my shoulders getting tense and right then I decided, Before I tear this classroom up, I'm out of here.

I stood up, put my book and notebook in my backpack,

zipped it closed, smacked everything off of Roy's desk, and walked across the room. The whole classroom paused, then broke out into a chorus of "Oooooohs" and laughter as I turned the doorknob and walked out into the dimly lit hallway. Mr. Stow ran to the doorway and yelled, "Get back here right now! Where do you think you're going?"

"To take a leak," I called back.

I heard more laughter and Roy's voice yelling, "Look at Andre go, in those ugly-ass Boe-Boes."

I kept walking and I thought Mr. Stow would just let me go, but I heard his voice getting closer to me as I walked and when I turned around his skinny body was striding right at me. I ran a couple steps and stopped. I turned around and stomped my foot and screamed, "What!"

He caught up to me, winded and pink-faced.

"You need . . ." He wheezed clutching at his chest. "You need to . . ." He coughed and took a big gulp of air. "You need to return to class."

He slouched down, resting his hands on his knees, panting.

"Look, Mr. Stow, I told you I needed to use the bathroom. I don't know why you been sweating me anyway. I know them three motion laws you talking 'bout. The third one's for every action you get a reaction. You did what you did, and so did I."

He started laughing sarcastically. "Young man, I'll see you for a full week of detention, starting today."

I turned around to start walking toward the bathroom when I saw his hand coming toward my shoulder and I jerked away dodging his grasp. I jumped toward him, balling my fist, ready to swing.

"You better don't touch me, old man. Touch me and I got the right to defend myself. I ain't wrong."

He put his hands in his pockets, shaking his head. "After

the bathroom, take yourself to the principal's office. And I will be seeing you for detention."

He looked back over his shoulder and clapped his hands and roared, "Hey! Everyone back in your seats. Now!" Everyone disappeared from the doorway. I shrugged my shoulders and said, "Whatever," and kept walking toward the bathroom. I didn't know what I was doing exactly, but all I knew was how to carry it like Nina, just act like I didn't care and let it ride. I wandered around the halls for a bit after I used the bathroom until the bell rang and I just went to my next class. When the school day ended I was going to skip Mr. Stow's detention again, but he met me at my locker.

"I believe you're going to be clapping the chalk out of my blackboard erasers today after school, isn't that right? Come on, we'll get the erasers."

He started walking toward his classroom and I didn't argue, I just followed him. I put my stuff down, he gave me a stack of erasers, and I went outside to clap them on the side of the building. As I clapped the erasers chalk dust flew up into the air like smoke and it made me sneeze. I clapped out the second eraser and went into one of those rapid sneezing frenzies. Right as I decided I just wasn't going to clean any more erasers, I heard Roy's voice singing that damn Boe-Boe song as he walked toward me all alone.

> Boe-Boes, they make your feet feel fine,
> Boe-Boes, they cost a dollar ninety-nine.

His words stung like alcohol in the eye. I looked around and there was not a teacher in sight. So I took a deep breath and I charged him. I started launching the erasers at him and the chalk dust puffed up everywhere. He was crying for me to stop, coughing in a cloud of chalk dust before I even made it over to him. He tossed his arms over his face and hunched to the side, pleading for me to "chill," but there was no more chilling, I'd already tried to chill. I punched Roy in the ribs and he moaned and grabbed his side. He left his face wide open and I gave him three quick jabs to the face. Roy pushed me back and took a wild swing at me and I tackled him, gripped his throat, and squeezed as tight as I could. I looked down into Roy's face, he's light-skinned, he was turning red, all the veins in his forehead wiggled like they were about to burst.

"Please, Andre, stop!" I could see the blood smeared on his teeth as he struggled for air. I held his head in my hands and started knocking it off the dirt on the ground until I felt a set of arms lock around my body, yanking me backward and I tried to wiggle away.

"That is enough! Break it up. Stop it right now, Andre." I kicked free of the arms and stumbled to my feet.

I looked and it was Mr. Stow and Principal Brutus.

Principal Brutus walked toward me, eyes bulging out of his head. He snatched me by the arm with so much force I knew better than to try and fight his momentum. He led me to his office, where he yelled at me about being one of the troublemakers that are now on his radar and how we make his job much harder. I sat blank-faced until he was done and gave me my first ever three-day suspension notice. I took the notice and walked out into the hallway reading it when I saw Mr. Stow locking up his classroom. He turned out the lights and shut the door. As he was turning the key in the lock he turned his head and looked at me, snickering, "For every action there's a reaction, eh, Mr. Battel?"

I ignored him and walked outside.

7

Praise

Ma asked me to ride with her down to Mass Avenue near Hynes Convention Center. Pop and the crew were rocking out, having a jam session at the Berklee College of Music. He and his band of clown-ass Rastas think they big-time, rehearsing at Berklee. Anyone with green dollars could rent out studio time there, they ain't special. Ma rushed up in my room looking like she'd just won the lottery or something. She claimed Pop had bought us a bag of groceries, but I wasn't really trying to roll out for this one. She promised she'd make her famous barbeque chicken for dinner and when she said that, it was game over and she was gone. I heard our front door slam and the rusty chokes and coughs of Ma firing up the Catalina. Disarmed before I could come up with an excuse. She was always good at making deals with me before I could respond.

Pop wasn't never around anymore. These days he was more of a wrecking ball than a rolling stone. The only way to get in touch with him was through his pager, on the shaky chance the bill was paid. That was only half the battle. He wasn't the best at returning phone calls. Drugs, music, and under-the-table paychecks—that's how he stayed fed and made sure he didn't have to feed us. Me, Ma, Nina, we're no more than third wheels in his life and he made that no secret anymore.

This little trip was seriously fucking up my flow. Basketball season was coming and I needed to be at Kelly Park grinding out on the blacktop, getting my hustle on. At Kelly Park I get busy running fools' pockets, playing one-on-one. Ain't no need to chase this bum-nigga around is what I wanted to tell her. As I walked up to the car I could already see Ma's head bopping to the beat. When I opened the door, "God is great! And greatly to be praised! *God is great! And greatly to be praised!* Sing unto the Lord a new song!" jumped out at me. Ma was bouncing her shoulders and clapping her hands, smiling bright. She was having a little praise party but the gospel music was playing too damn loud for me. I sucked my teeth and plopped into my seat.

Ma looked at me, turned the music down, and yelled, "Negro, please! Fix your face and stop hissing your teeth. Praise God for supper tonight. Act like I ain't had a long day too. I'm praising. A little praise ought to take that sourpuss off your face. Cheer up, son, we're going to pick up dinner, ya know. Or would you prefer a bowl of sleep for dinner? It's not like we have to watch him play. Now act right. This won't take long." She tossed her head back and let out that hyena cackle of a laugh and started nudging my shoulder with the beat. I brushed her hand off me. She laughed louder and we took off.

The only thing I loved about riding down to Mass Ave. was watching the red CITGO triangles flash over the skyline, throbbing out Boston's heartbeat for the city. Ever since I was a little kid I've always watched that sign: one big red triangle dissolving into three and pulsing away from each other, almost like there's a giant windmill separating them as they fade. White lines pin-stripe down the whole sign as the triangles flood back in, making them one again. When I was a kid, I'd watch that sign, excited, hoping that maybe it would change or do something different. But now I just watch it. It's the only thing to look at other than the bustling bullshit in the hood.

Nothing special today, all different types of sketchy hangin' on the corners: crusty-mouthed yellow-chip-toothed crack-heads, or a bum swirling a bucket of dumpster water with a squeegee begging to rinse off your windows, or a wacko with a sign on his lap that says nothing close to what his eyes tell you he gon' do with that money. At least the street perform-ers work for their change. Pop was just another bullshitter like the rest of the broken niggas on Mass Ave. I can't even remember the last time he came by. The nigga was good to play us out tonight, really. After I got tired of watching them triangles, I deaded off the gospel and clicked on the radio and drifted off to sleep. I woke up as we pulled up in front of a store across the street from Berklee. The sun was fading away, the city beginning to look like a violet. Purplish shadows were beginning to take their places between the buildings and alleyways tinged with daylight. But I figured all wasn't lost of my evening.

I hopped out quick and paged Pop 3663, our code for food, from the pay phone on the corner in front of Spike's Junkyard Dogz. Then we waited. And waited. And waited some more. We just sat there as the streetlights began to blink on. The cars zipping past us swayed the Catalina side to side. Wasn't much else to do but sit and listen to the Catalina's ancient shell squeal as she rocked. Sitting and waiting in that stuffy-ass death trap of a car made me feel like twice the fool. I wound down my window, letting the dirty Boston city air smack against my face. I kept hearing balls bouncing in my head, feeling the burn of my time lost at the park. The smell coming from Spike's made my belly start talking to me.

Ma's head was resting on her clenched fist as her eyes scoured the swells of trendy no-name musicians letting out of their jam sessions. Her nail polish was chipped and her dry-ass Gerber-baby ponytail was crying for a relaxer. Dark wrinkle-puffed half circles draped down under her eyes. She began biting her nails and tapping her foot on the brake pedal. When the rockers signed off on the radio and David Allan Boucher signed on for *Bedtime Magic,* the mellow sleepy music that 106.7 plays at night, I knew. *Bedtime Magic* starts at nine and the streetlights don't come on until eight.

After the fourth commercial break I sat up. I let my window down the whole way and looked out into the herds of black instrument bags, dreadlocks, weird piercings, and tattoos. My heart heated and cooled every couple of seconds. It felt like a game. Like we traded off tapping the side panel with excitement, saying, "I think I see him," every time a dark-skinned wiry musician with a Zildjian drum bag strapped to his back passed us by. After a cool twenty minutes I could feel my temples beginning to pulse and I started to tabulate the cost of all this bullshit. Twenty good-old American dollars. A whole night at the park lost over what?

I coulda hustled that within my first three games at the park. We weren't waiting on steaks or even chicken, regardless of what Ma said. Pop's punk ass only ever came through with a package of cold cuts, cheese, bread, chips, maybe a box of cookies and some Kool-Aid packets. I wanted to put my fist through the windshield when I saw the tears tightroping the rims of her eyelids. And she was talking 'bout praise? For what? Fuck we got to be happy for? We been hungry the whole way down to Mass Ave. and Pop grimed us, again. He never brought anything but bad vibes, as far as I'm concerned anyway. Ma's eyes were becoming more frantic.

I glanced back out the window. The car hiccupped on, and without a word we were off sailing down Mass Ave. Her sniffles aggravated me. I flipped down my mirror from the overhead and felt like giving myself the finger. I turned and watched the embarrassment pour down her cheeks. She slid her head away from me, gazing at the road sideways. Once a shame, twice a fool, and after that it's on you. I decided right there and then that this scraping-by shit wasn't for me no more. I can do this better and I will. Scared money don't make money and what better time to start getting some money than now? I mashed off the radio. We rode in silence. Played out once again, same old tired-ass song. With the way we set ourselves up for this shit, the pleasure was all ours, right?

Around Egleston Square we pulled up to a red light and there was Mr. Trixy, the street performer, giving the stop sign a red-light special. I smirked. Ma looked at me and put her hand on my shoulder.

"You alright, sugar? I'm real sorry about tonight. Just know I didn't plan for things to work out like this."

I nodded and jerked my shoulder away from her. I dropped my head to the side, resting it on the seat-belt buckle and letting the blowing wind drown away her little sermon. She slapped me in the chest and I popped up.

"Show a little respect. Look at me when I'm talking to you!"

"Ma, I know what you mean and I hear you, but all this out here is real tired. Real sorry! I'm tired of this shit." She didn't hesitate. She clean broad-hand-palmed me across the back of the head, catching a little more neck than hair.

"You watch your mouth, little boy. You ain't grown yet and you will show me some respect."

I wanted to hit her back. Instead I looked her in the eyes.

"What the hell you hitting me for, Ma? Tonight was stupid

and you know it. Twenty bucks, Ma! That's what my whole night was about, twenty bucks. And now what? We still riding home on empty. I know this ain't all on you. Never said it was, but it don't hurt no less. I already got the rap sheet on Pop, and so should you by now. You ain't gotta tell me nothing. I got eyes."

She had no response for me. The light turned green and we pulled away. She clicked the radio back on. I could feel the palm print bubbling up out of my neck. How can't you feel like a sucker when you volunteer to play the fool? What the hell was she acting so damn hurt and surprised about? This wasn't anything new.

I pressed my neck up against the cold glass window to cool down the palm burn. From the corner of my eye I could see them sad-ass tears dropping off her chin like a melting icicle. She was looking at me and I could feel it. But with a hot-ass handprint bubbling out my neck, if she thought I had words for her, she could go phone a friend. She can stay bright-eyed like a puppy looking to this bum-ass nigga for a handout. And that's exactly what she can do—keep her hand out and wait for him to spit in it. Pop couldn't even come home at night, and she thought he was gonna get some grub for the kids. I bet he tossed in some bucks for his corny-ass crew to be up in Berklee, fronting like they were somebodies. He probably don't even remember which set of his kids he's neglecting.

"Dre." I kept my head resting on the side panel, neck snug to the window. She sucked her teeth.

"Andre Battel, don't be so hard. You're only fourteen years old. You ain't even begun to taste what the world has for you. You gonna get to where you're going in life, I swear it to you." I really wasn't listening but she kept on talking anyway. "We might not always have what we want, but we always get what we need. God's never let us go, even when it isn't looking so pretty. Right?" I didn't say a word. "We always get by. Don't take this entire burden with you into the world. It'll break your back. This is just a hurdle. You've got bigger battles to fight. Don't wear yourself down so soon. The Bible promises the few days we have will be filled with trouble. But we're good, baby boy, we're alive. We're good."

I sure was about to see what the world had for me. I wanted to argue back and smash out. Tell her to get a grip and be real, realize we broke as hell and don't no one give a fuck. That taking the high road shit ain't doin' nothing for my empty belly, and as far as I could see God didn't have anything on my dinner table for me tonight neither. I squeegeed my neck off the window, dropped my seat back down, and let the palm print sizzle as I looked up, watching Blue Hill Avenue blaze on by.

"In due season, son, in due season. Remember, this too shall pass. Nothing lasts forever, especially not living like this. God will never leave you nor forsake you. And His promises will come to pass. Blessings have to come."

It felt like she was pleading with me to believe in Santa Claus. I had a couple things to say but I didn't. If she'd hit me again, it woulda been nothing but a scrap-up in that car. I just played it cool. Nothing lasts forever—I knew that. *Bedtime Magic* filled in our silence as we rode. There was nothing left to say, no more old wisdoms and proverbs were true. Only so many times you can do a DNA test before the cold hard facts are in, and life's proven herself to be a coldhearted bitch time and time again.

We pulled up to our house and Nina was standing on the porch with a bright smile, rubbing her belly up and down. I stepped out of the car empty-handed and she knew. Her eyebrows shocked back and her mouth dropped open. We locked eyes and her face went limp. I shook my head at her. Before I could get up our walkway and onto the porch she was on it. She looked at me, snapped her neck back, and grabbed my shoulder.

"Word! Niggas ain't got no dinner, though. Ain't that some bullshit."

I said, "Well, praise God," brushed by her, took down my bowl of sleep, and knocked it the fuck out.

8

Chocolate Chip

All the little birds flittered through our block, cocoa-buttered up in their poom-poom shorts, ankles strapped tight with sparkling plastic jelly sandals. The suntan ladies of Lothrop Avenue were lying out on the sidewalks in their bikinis, soaking up mineral oil, tanning-mirror dents in their chests. They had the block feeling like a sauna. I was ready. That summer all I did was play ball and hustle. It was time for the V-card to go and when I kicked that note back across the floor to her in math class, I knew: I could have her. See, there's a code in the corridors, so fuck what you heard and call me shallow if you want to, but listen! In the hallways of our high school, Tunnetta and me didn't make no sense.

She's smart and quiet. She be up in the student council and doing smart shit like getting honor roll. No one paid her any mind. The kids in student council were like shadows in the halls. They were around us but mostly behind and under our feet. She didn't even have a perm in her hair. She couldn't compete with the wifeable girls in school like Sade Fulton. Sade runs the step squad. They call themselves the Hot Girls.

They liked to parade around in their NBA jersey-dresses and Adidas shell-toes, sweating them BRC—Bed Rock Crew— niggas. The BRC cats were the muscles in the halls while the Hot Girls wrote the law. Together they made sure that everything in the hallways made sense. And if things didn't make sense, believe and trust they'd be the first to let you know—only the Hot Girls' announcement might be sketched across the lockers closest to your homeroom in red and orange permanent marker for everyone to laugh and see.

Or one of them BRC boys might run up and try to beat you to sleep. It would probably be Big Maal, but their whole crew's a handful of spark plugs. At school now, I'm just an athlete. We know our roles and play our positions. Like, we know better than to go after a girl like Monika Allen. She go out with Tito. He's the most money-gettin'est nigga out the BRC. A nose candy peddler, he don't even sell weed no more. Everyone in our high school had a position and most played 'em, but Tunnetta "Chocolate Chip" Johnson plain didn't give a fuck.

She moved here around the way from some dirt-road town in Alabama. It showed in her whole swag with them fuzzy cheese-puff plaits she kept twisted up in her head. She wore these clunky headphones like them boys that ride the short bus. She didn't really talk to anyone. Well, at least anyone that ran in my world. On paper, Tunnetta don't make too much sense, one of them girls with a few cute features and one or two sexy parts but it all don't sum up to equal sexy.

If you stared at Tunnetta long enough, you'd probably get a headache and be confused. Juicy, plump lips and a flat stomach. Wide hips with a pancake-flat booty. She had that tall mushy frame. Her hips pendulumed slow and seductive like a grandfather clock. She stepped strong like pistons pumping an engine and she was knock-kneed so it looked like she was smuggling newborns that were trying to jump out of her hips. Not quite an hourglass, she was like two sweet potatoes stacked on top of each other sideways. Her appeal was different, more something you'd want to get inside of.

Reggie and them Team Seven boys on my block saw it too. They'd all howl every time she'd piston down our block with them headphones on, zoning out how she do. We go to the same church. Her and her father sit all the way across the congregation at service. She has a little cottage cheese bubble-wrapping the back of her legs and a few skin-tone stretch marks snaking up her inner thighs, but she could wear the hell out of a Sunday dress. She never dressed nice around the way, and that made me curious about her. Reggie and them Team Seven boys always told me I was crazy not to pipe her. Before she bloomed, got gassed up, and started thinking that she was somebody and deserved shit, is what they'd tell me.

Two things couldn't nobody take away from her were those honey-brown hazelish eyes and the big ol' ripe mangos she had slang-a-dangin' from her chest. We never spoke until early in August when I caught the shock in her eyes as I focused in on her with a request at her father's bodega. Me and Beezy had just come from chilling at Kelly Park. He was hungry and I needed some Zig-Zags. Beezy grabbed the door handle and froze.

"Fuck!" His arms tantrumed out to his sides as he limboed back toward me, bouncing at the knees.

"Go, nigga!" I nudged him in the back.

"Look inside." He elbowed me in the chest. "All we need on a Sunday."

I got a nauseous tingle in my stomach. Sade Fulton was in there with her pops. He's my Regional All-Star team coach. Forever rocking them black undertaker sunshades and cussing somebody out on his cell phone. The type of cat that turned a phone call about practice into a forty-five-minute hot-seat roast session. Wanting to know my dreams. Where I saw myself in the next ten years. My plan to combat the white man's glass-ceiling system. He drove a sexy chromed-out black-on-black 745 Beemer. A nice sound system but he didn't play music in his car when I rode with him to our games. He told me what he had to say was more important than anything the crackerjacked radio box could tell us knuckleheaded kids. He drove by us every day after school, never stopping to politick. He'd just thump on by, slow-freezing every nigga in their pose. Rumor is he used to be a dopeboy, but I don't know. Shit, my plan was to stoner-glide the Sunday breeze. All I did know was he'd spoiled Sade into a rotten bitch.

He was standing at the counter filling out a money order slip, the mean-mug on Sade's face stanker than a bowl of chitlins. Mr. Fulton had on a black Adidas jogging suit with a Sunday *Boston Globe* tucked under his arm. Sade was behind him holding a lip gloss. Mr. Fulton answered his cell phone and we seized the moment and broke. Sade acted like she ain't seen us hiding in the back near the watercooler and fresh fruit. She stood there stone-faced, sucking on the lip gloss that she hadn't purchased yet, slow and steady like it was a popsicle or cigarette or something else. Gawking and thinking about her lips, she glanced over. We met eyes.

"Ummf!" She folded her arms and rolled her eyes, craning her body away from my direction.

She's too much. The baddest dark-skinned girl in school but a crazy birdbrain too. A bad bitch that knows she's a bad bitch—the worst and most dangerous kind. She always had the freshest Jordans on, wrists dripping with gold bamboo bangles, ears swinging low with door-knockers. She's been crumbs in my bed ever since we went out for three weeks last school year. We never broke up; we fizzled out. She been evil-glaring me ever since. She likes to start shit for the sake of starting shit.

Mr. Fulton got off the phone and glanced around the store. I hunched into myself and acted like I was reading the back of a box of Theraflu. He paid and walked out the door. Sade moved up in line to pay. She looked through Tunnetta, gave her one of them blank stares almost the way people do to ATMs. She dropped her lip gloss on the counter like she was rolling a hand of dice. It rolled on the floor behind the counter. Tunnetta squatted quick and bobbed back up.

We waited for Sade to leave the store, then got in line. When it was my turn Tunnetta hopped out of her seat and took three steps into the middle of the counter, just where her pops stands so he can see all the mirrors. She thought I was going to steal something, so I caught her in the eyes and leaned in toward her. Her face went sour and twitched. She stepped back and dropped her stare to the floor. I looked out the door and Sade was grilling me as she pulled away in the 745. I turned back to Tunnetta. She stood weird and meek, her body half turned away from me, hands clasped together at her waist.

"Ay, sweetheart?" I squinted down at the name tag Velcroed to her cannons. "Tun-netta," I drawled. She glanced up at me. I smiled.

"Can I help you?"

"Think I can get a pack of Zig-Zags, lil' mama?" I licked my bottom lip and smiled harder.

She was fidgety, like a child waiting in line to pee at the carnival. We caught eyes again but she didn't look away this time. She arched into herself like her shoulders wanted to high-five. Them honey-browns got wide, pinballing side to side like I was stressing her out. She stood there blinking, looking dumb.

I thought she was going to call the manager—her pops—but she didn't.

"On the low," I shushed my index finger to my lips.

A grin melted into her face and she spun around. I slid two Kit Kat bars in my back pocket. She turned back around with a bag of Swedish fish and my pack of Zig-Zags underneath.

"Seventy-five cents, please."

I dropped the change on the counter. She sucked her teeth.

"Just came in from church. Shouldn't even be doing this for you."

"Bad girl." I winked at her and she broke another smile.

"Smoking weed on a Sunday, uh-uh." She shook her head. "Ain't you on the basketball team at school too?"

I smiled back. "Don't they say not to judge folk up in that church house?" I tossed her the deuces and walked out. That was the extent of our interaction that summer.

"Andre Battel! If you want to talk to Jamal then you do it outside of my classroom. Otherwise you need to shut up."

The room rang out with an echo of "Oooooooos," then fell pin-drop silent. Shut up? Mrs. Rosetti told me to shut up? We weren't the only people in the room having a side conversation. She glared at me, then turned around to write more notes on the blackboard. All eyes were on me and my face was getting hot.

"You gon' take that, my nigga?" Big Maal leaned over and whispered in my ear.

That's when I picked up the ruler and threw it at her. I missed to the left of her and she pushed the intercom on the wall.

"Main office? Yes! Andre Battel is being sent to the office for being rude and obnoxious. He is becoming belligerent in my classroom."

"Well, that was a lot of name-calling, lady." I got up and started walking out. "Bitch!" I said under my breath.

She heard me and that sealed my three-day suspension. I also had to switch out of her class. I wound up in Mr. Stigs's class.

My first day back post-suspension, my name tag was sitting on a desk in the front of the room, of course next to the resident big brain. Teachers always loved to yin-yang the front of the classroom this way. I was late so I just sat down. A few minutes later a paper folded into a tight triangle slid under my desk. I looked at her and she looked at me and then the note. I acted like I had to tie my shoes and picked it up.

"Remember me from the store, smoker boy?" the note read.

She glanced me up and down and it turned me on. Tunnetta finally brought her Sunday church game to school. No more clunky glasses. She'd run a hot comb through her frizzy hair and ditched the plaits. She had a hazy look in her eyes. I could hear them Team Seven boys barking in my head, thirsty and beginning to bloom.

"Sure do!" I wrote back and she giggled.

She tucked the note in her pocket, then got up, earthquaking her hips as she walked over to the pencil sharpener. Her stance looked stronger, like she'd been hitting the gym or turning down meals. Her skin was even starting to clear up. Well, as clear as chocolate chip skin could clear.

Tunnetta's skin was tough. Her acne was for-real-for-real jacked up. Her cinnamon-brown skin made it look worse too. Her cheeks would look like there were fire ants clawing out constellations on top of sand mounds. One morning at breakfast, before school started, Big Maal stood up right as Tunnetta walked into the cafeteria, red-faced from the cold. He ripped open his chocolate chip muffin and held it in the air like he was Rafiki from the *Lion King* holding Simba toward the sun.

"The side of Tunnetta's face, ladies and gentlemen!" He spun himself around in a dramatic circle and curtseyed.

I never called her that but the nickname stuck, and bad skin, big tits, and pretty eyes was all Tunnetta "Chocolate Chip" Johnson was known for around school. She wasn't really a good look for me, but I was curious.

"So tell me, what's it like to be high, smoker boy?" the note the next day said.

I told her I could show her better than I could say and she blushed. She was just as curious about me as I was about her. Later that week I got around to bringing up sex. She told me she was a virgin. I lied and told her I wasn't. She believed me and I think it turned her on. She started asking me questions about what it was like. How long did it go for? Where did you do it? Does your mother know? Why weren't you scared? Brand of condom? She said they made it sound like the most dangerous thing in the world at church, and I told her about how great it was. She asked me my favorite position and I told her all of 'em. I told her how tired I'd get in my lower back if I did it really good. I even told her that sometimes I'd lose my voice and be hoarse after. She ate it up.

We switched notes every day in class and she'd laugh at me when I'd fail my tests. She told me all her good business up front and I told her what I wanted her to know. To be real, only the Bad Girls were fucking in the ninth grade, and even that was kept on the low-low. Either that or you had to have one of those committed-for-life relationships and the sex actually meant something. All them BRC cats got to smash down the Bad Girls. And us, we athlete boys, we were stuck with the mind-gaming, hard-stepping Hot Girls. Getting laid meant convincing a broad we wasn't doing something wrong, or at least that we weren't going to tell and make her a whore in the halls. Or scribble her number on the walls in the bathroom or the railing of the bridge under the words "Call for a good time."

Once we tickled the topic of sex, I wanted to scratch her. The next day I wrote my phone number on a piece of paper. It took me three whole weeks to strap on a pair of nuts and actually give it to her. She called me that night. Nina answered the phone and walked in my room wide-eyed like a day-ghost. She handed me the cordless, then backed away from me slowly like I had a gun pointed at her. "Let me find out," she giggled under her breath and slammed my door.

We talked until about two in the morning and it wasn't about anything in particular. There's only so much to say about the sex neither one of us was having. It didn't matter, though; the conversation always flowed. Sometimes my mother would pick up the phone in her room right in the middle of our conversation and tell Tunnetta I had to go. She never made fun of me for it. We started talking on the phone every night but never in the halls. We stayed strictly math class friends. Math was her only normal class anyway. All the big-brain-smart-guy classes were in another part of the school, away from kids like us.

On some weekend nights we'd stay up late and watch all the uncensored videos on *BET: Uncut*. A top-notch bullshitter, she'd always act like the big booties twerking in the videos repulsed her. But it's not like she turned the channel. She'd get quiet then, randomly ask me shit like, So is this what guys like? Or, Is this how the other girls at school get down? Massaging her brain, I'd always tell her yes. I'd spoon-feed her anything to move her mind toward where mine was. Our notes started getting longer and realer. She started telling me about her deep thoughts.

Her mother died last year, before they moved up here. A leaking gas pipe caused a flash fire in the middle of the night. Her mother didn't make it out and it haunts her daily. Her daddy took to bourbon and bringing home prostitutes. She said he only paid attention to her when he got to brag on her big-brainedness at church during coffee hour. She told me the only thing he cared for was his bodega and the money that came in through its doors. I told her about my lame-ass father and how I do a little more with weed than smoke it. She didn't hang out with anyone at school, but she'd hang with me. I thought there was something really cool about that. She was like my little secret. And I was hers.

When school lets out, the drama of the hallways turns real. You'll get your issue if you got one. This is how it worked. Basically you had to be some type of somebody. We latchkey kids all walked together in a huddle, but don't get it twisted, we were not together. The pack was like a prison yard, everyone had their territory. People step out they zone and it turns into a jungle.

Me and Beezy got to walk up front of the pack behind Big Maal and Tito, a few big-booty Bad Girls peppered between us and the Hot Girls. Sade Fulton made me a somebody when Keyona Lawson, the next in trust of the Hot Girls, approached me after basketball practice one day last year and delivered a note.

You wanna be my man? Check Yes or No.
—Sade "so-easy-to-love" Fulton

She drew two hearts next to her name. Keyona handed me a black marker and sucked her teeth. I looked at the hearts.

"Check something, nigga!"

She started snapping her gum like I was the one who ran up on her. I checked the "Yes" box.

"Sooky-Sooky Chile," she yelled, then scrunched the note into her bra, winked at me, and ran off.

I was officially POS—Property Of Sade. We were scandalous news in the hallways. The buzz from me dating a grade up set the thermostat for all the girls. Once Sade liked me, all the girls did. She was a mind-fuck, though. Whenever I was close enough to talk to her one-on-one she'd act like she ain't see me, then seductive-glare and eye-fuck me from afar, putting on a show for the halls. If it wasn't for her pops I woulda cussed her out. Sade still writes me these long-ass notes every now and again like we were in love and had been through some shit. She slips them in my locker. I ignore them. Most of the time I don't know what the hell she's even talking about. She writes these corny-ass R&B lyrics in the margins of the page. Her and Big Maal's crazy ass were like a match made in heaven. All 'cause I played up on the varsity basketball team and she was the captain of the step squad she decided to like me. We didn't even speak to each other, but I was still off-limits in the halls. But anyway, anything could be the spark that set a forest fire on the walk home, however big or small.

Tunnetta was usually a little late coming out of school. Something about being smart also meant staying hella late after school. I'd walk home with my peoples, then stop off by Kelly Park to hoop and hustle. That's what I'd do until she'd walk by. She'd never stop and say anything. Wouldn't sugar me with one of them caramel glares or nothing. And that's why I liked her. She played her position right for me. She'd stroll by the court and I'd see her. She would keep it moving. I'd eventually breeze off from the court and catch up. Me being seen with her was a no-no.

One day after the basketball season was over Tunnetta got into a fight with her pop. He was drunk and beat the piss out of her, with a belt too, all because she got a B on one of her English papers. All during math class she was stressing it. I just put it out there and asked, "Ever met Mary Jane? Bet she'd make you feel better about it."

She wrote back, "I haven't but maybe I should." I didn't think she was serious, though. But sure enough, that day after school we met up inside my grandfather's toolshed.

Now, I really ought not smoke so much of the weed I'm supposed to be selling, but as long as I keep killin' on the ball court, my main man Smoke will break me off. He breaks bread with me, an ounce or two here and there to hustle and smoke, nothing major. He never sweats me 'bout no re-up money. I get it to him when I can and leave my extra around the house, where I know Ma will find it. Sometimes I put it in the mailbox and I know she thinks it's either Pop or Reggie putting it there. Sometimes she trips for days off that shit. Hollerin' and stomping her feet. Talking 'bout the Lord and His sweet mercy miracles. Ma would lose it if she knew drug money was sponsoring her dinner and church plate tithes.

I feel bad, but shit, the lights ain't got shut off lately so fuck it. At the court playing one-on-one is the real hustle. And old-timers come by Kelly Park all the time. They can easily drop a prideful hundred on a lunch break trying to prove they still got it. Usually that's the money I use to pay back Smoke for a re-up. Anyway, me and Tunnetta walked inside my grand-father's toolshed and I took my stash out from under his grease-cutting sink and rolled us up a joint. The whole time I rolled, Tunnetta's leg bounced as she watched me, her eyes bright and focused.

"Can you teach me how to do that?" she asked.

"What you know 'bout green?" I laughed.

"I can learn. Be nice!" She slapped my arm.

"Ever ate a Fruit Roll-Up?" I sparked the joint. "Just think about stuffing some weed inside. Then up, up, and away."

I hit it a few times, then passed it to her. She held it like a dirty thong she'd found mixed in with her laundry or some-thing. She squinted and sniffed. She sucked.

"Now hold the smoke in your mouth and inhale again and hold it."

She sucked again. Held her breath in like a yawn. Her head fell back and she put her hand to her chest, sighing a thick stream of milky smoke. She hugged her sides and started humming. She hit the joint like a champ and I was half jeal-ous, half impressed.

> Birds flying high, you know how I feel.
> Sun in the sky, you know how I feel.

She moaned, rocking side to side, waving the joint like an orchestra conductor. She kept singing that one verse like she was in a trance. I didn't want to interrupt her. She took another toke, coughed, and then burped. Her face got pepper red and drooped into her cupped palms. My head was tingled-fried and I was starting to feel spacey. She sniffled and I thought she was laughing. I snapped my fingers loud and she looked up. Tears in her eyes, her lips pouted out as her jaw bounced.

"I just miss my mother is all. It's lonely in the house without her," she gasped.

She closed her eyes and it felt like she was leaning toward me. I didn't know what to do so I touched her face. Her skin felt like fuzzy Braille. I kissed her and we fumbled over each other. We stood and I cradled her back, pulling her closer to me. I slid my hand down the back of her jeans and she let me. Even though it was wide wit' no weight on it, it sure was soft. We bumped up against the shed door and it blew open. We both jumped back and almost fell, the daylight squinting our eyes. Flustered, she said she better go. We never talked about the kiss, but the next day in class I asked her what song she was singing.

" 'Feeling Good' by Nina Simone. It was Mama's favorite song," her note read.

Tunnetta liked weed and we started smoking together after school a lot, like two or three days a week. She told her father she was tutoring, and I mean, that was our initial idea. We'd get high and sometimes she'd sing. She never cried again, though. Sometimes we'd kiss. Sometimes I'd even get halfway between second and third base and freeze up. I don't know why, but I would.

Mostly we just chilled and talked. I don't know what we were but I did know that friend shit was officially over. It started feeling like we ought to be more, but I was plain embarrassed of her too.

Beezy was the first one that caught us. It was a half day of school. Her father didn't know this, and we'd planned to kick it until school usually got out. We were walking and Beezy was right outside in his front yard all sweat-greased up, look-ing like a water buffalo ass-deep in the shrubs. I told Tunnetta to wait at the edge of his walkway. She posted. When he saw me he went up and sat on his porch. He looked at me, then down at Tunnetta.

"Let me find out you chippin' it," he said.

"She's my math tutor. Relax." I kept stone-faced.

"Your stupid ass for damn sure ain't taking no math lesson on no Friday afternoon."

Caught. "Come out of my business, son," was all I could say. He shook his head. Beezy's funny as hell and my best friend, but two things I know about him: one, the nigga got a loud mouth and, two, he likes to show off. I didn't like the way he kept looking down at Tunnetta.

"Man, I'll catch up with you," I said and dap'd him.

"Going to study, huh?"

"What! You wanna come?"

I started walking. Beezy's nosy ass couldn't let it lay, though. He leaned over his porch railing and started eyeing us. Tunnetta was bugging the fuck out too. She asked me if she could use his bathroom like my crib wasn't only down the street.

"Come on up, Chocolate Chip." Beezy yelled from the porch and held his screen door open. I don't even know how he heard her. Tunnetta smiled at me and took one of them strong stomps.

The *106 & Park* countdown was on BET. I tossed my backpack on the floor, kicked my Timberlands off, and stretched out on the three-seater. Beezy sat at his computer. He's forever zombied-out at the computer screen. Tunnetta rustled her way out of the bathroom and into the doorway. She stood there waiting for someone to say something to her. I nodded my head at her and put my palm flat up to my chest a little bit under my chin and twisted so Beezy couldn't see. I walked two fingers across my palm. Her face went soft and she nodded.

"'Ight. Bye, Andre. Thanks, Beezy."

Beezy looked up from the computer and muted the television.

"What about studying?" He looked at me and chuckled. "If y'all ain't gon' study you ought to stay and watch 'Freestyle Friday,' Chocolate Chip." She looked up cheesing all bright, batting her eyes back and forth, smearing honey between me and Beezy.

"Okay! My dad thinks I'm tutoring anyway."

She sat down on the other couch across from me. Beezy played Teddy Pendergrass's "Love TKO." He was sampling the hook for a beat he'd been working on. It was like he'd plugged the red peg into a Lite-Brite. She reached between her legs and popped the CD out of her Discman and sat next to him at the computer. I couldn't hear what he was saying to her, but I looked over and she was cracking up, slapping her leg and clapping her hands. I'd never seen her laugh like that. She never laughed at my jokes that way. I saw his forearm on her knee and got a flash of fire in my chest. He was showing her a scar but I felt like he needed to keep his hands to himself. I unmuted the TV and let them rock out.

Tunnetta had a CD full of baby-makers, some old-school rhythm and spice shit, Al Green and Marvin Gaye cuts. They seemed to have so much in common. The freestyle battle came on *106 & Park*. This nigga Beezy was so busy flapping his gums to Tunnetta about how he and his older brother Smoke be doing this and doing that that he missed the first contender, Poster Boy's whole verse. This he realized right as it cut to commercial break. He tossed a pillow at my face.

"You couldn'ta told a nigga the joint was on?"

Tunnetta thought that was hilarious too. I was pissed off

beyond words. The show cut back and the second contender, Young 'Tastic, was terrible. Poster Boy won the battle.

"Glad I got to see the whole battle, *nigga*!"

Beezy gave me the stank-eye and smiled. I wanted to kick him in the teeth. He felt my heat and said he needed to go and shower. He clicked off the light in the room and walked out. Ginuwine's "So Anxious" was the old-school joint of the day on the countdown. I turned the volume all the way up. Tunnetta was wearing her glasses for the first time in a long while, and the video was reflecting off her lenses.

"Come here," I said.

She sat on the far end of the couch, one cushion between us, her staring at the wall, me staring at her. Her eyes looking buttery and sweet. I scooted over toward her and leaned my head back into her lap. She started tracing my ears and I closed my eyes.

"They're so little and cute," she whispered.

She laid her left arm across my chest. I raised my hand and wiggled my finger in between hers. She started swaying to the video and I opened my eyes. She drizzled them caramel eyes down on me and we kissed. Her hands were clammy too. Her fingers started to wander and soon she was rubbing her fingers over my chest. My heart was beating so hard my whole body was shaking, I tried to think. Think of anything. I opened my eyes and sat up.

I turned and kissed her and she kissed me back harder. I pulled away, then looked at her, then over in the corner to the attic door. I hugged her and I began rubbing my hand on her back under her shirt.

"Wanna go upstairs?" I suggested.

She bit down on her lip and nodded yes.

Inside Smoke's "Poom-Poom Room" we sat at the foot of the bed.

"Why don't we get comfy?" I asked. We both slid back and I snaked the comforter over us. She turned and grabbed me by the chin, looking me in the face.

"Andre, I want to ask you something. Do you like me?"

"Yeah," I mustered out, slightly winded.

"Look, I know this isn't going to work out, but you at least have to still be nice to me."

Buzzkilled. I didn't answer her. She grabbed my belt buckle and bobbed down, disappearing under the blanket. I tugged her hair and lifted the covers.

"You sure?" I asked her and she ignored me.

My knees bucked and my stomach tangled in knots as I felt her mouth's warm repetition. I leaned back groaning and grabbed the back of her head. I looked over on the nightstand and grabbed the gold-wrapped Magnum sitting there. She came up for air and I waved it in her face. She took my shirt off and I struggled with the buttons on hers. She laughed and got undressed by herself. I got the condom on and straddled her, poking around until I popped her piñata and felt a tight rush. Her back arched up and I looked down into her face. It looked like she was in the middle of a painful shit. I stopped.

"Am I hurting you?"

She grabbed my hips and told me to keep going. I pumped a few times more, but she clearly was not enjoying it. I saw the crimson contrast against the condom and almost gagged. We both hopped off the bed naked, mad-dashing for our clothes. The room smelled like a long day's walk, and it was time to roll. I realized the shower water was off and the TV was muted and that Beezy had probably heard everything.

"Maybe I ought to walk you home," I said and we started moving toward the door. We got down into the TV room and Beezy's bitch ass whistled as we walked out. I didn't say anything to him.

"Bye, Beezy," she said and we bounced.

We rounded the corner of Lothrop onto the parkway. We got a block away from her father's bodega and I forgot it was a half day at school. Everyone was still out: Hot Girls, Bad Girls, BRC, and my Team Seven crew. I didn't say anything. We just kept walking toward them. They were all posting outside the store, huddled up in a circle. Sade Fulton and Monika Allen were in the middle of arguing about something. Sade saw us and put Monika on pause. She pointed and led the pack toward us. We met paths and I stopped. Tunnetta had no clue what was going on.

"Excuse us," Tunnetta said and stepped to the side.

I looked at her and thought, Us?

"And look at this ol' saggy-ass chocolate-chip-faced cellulite-body-ass-bitch," Sade said.

Tunnetta pulled my sleeve. "Come on, Andre." It was a good move.

Sade grabbed Tunnetta's hair. "Bitch, you gon' act like you know something!"

"Let me go!" Tunnetta struggled.

They fell and Sade was on top. She started hooking off rapid-fire. I watched, sandwiched between Big Maal and Reggie, cringing with every hit. I stepped and put my arm out about to break it up, but Big Maal put an elbow in my chest.

"What's it to you? Let 'em," he said.

"Reggie, you don't think this shit's foul?" I asked. Tunnetta's mouth was bleeding and I could see the beginning of a dotted eye.

"Stop acting like a lil' bitch," he replied.

Tunnetta wrestled away from Sade and staggered into her father's store. I started walking in after her, but Reggie put his arm around me and said, "Creeping is one thing, but ain't no Captain Save-a-Hoes in our clique. Let it go."

The next day she didn't look at me. I didn't talk to her or Beezy that entire week. One week turned into two and then three, and I heard she's fucking Beezy now. I really miss her, but in the hallways I guess that makes sense.

9

Running Rebel

The bed shakes and I wake up facedown in a soggy pillow. I turn onto my back and glance over at Janet, she's naked. She slaps the bed and stands up. Eyes like two green olives, she's glaring at me.

"Now you're awake. You nasty motherfucker!"

A baby is crying. Whose baby? Not sure, guessing it's hers. Janet's a regular jungle-fever hooch on the reggae circuit, she's at all our shows. I cough and push up on my elbows, I feel the piss ooze out of the mattress and know it's been another one of them nights and I know I must do better. She looks at me again. I am sorry, but saying it won't help so I don't and roll over on my side. Pipe in hand she pulls open the curtains and the foggy sting of whiteness from the snow floods the room. She bangs the pipe on the sill and blows in it. Loads it with a hit, flames the lighter, and inhales. I listen to it crackle as my head begins to accordion in and out. Every time I blink the room kaleidoscopes in front of me, shuffling our lust trail from last night leading up to the bed: empty red tops, Colt 45s, dirty clothes, fabric roses, and our underwear.

She walks into my view facing the window, and all I can see is her lower half. The bottom tips of her greasy blond hair, her dimply pimpled raspberry ass and the topless fairy riding a half-moon tramp-stamped on her lower back. She turns around and grabs the golden tuft of hair on her crotch.

"Motherfucker! Don't look at me like I don't love my god-damn husband. I love my goddamn husband!"

She bounces at the knees, pelvis thrusting to emphasize her words. She squats while yelling it again and flails her arms out, dashing over a bottle of orange pills across her nightstand. The pipe falls out of her mouth and shatters. Pills everywhere. She crumbles onto all fours.

"Save them!" She looks up at me.

The baby's cry is now louder and gurgled. My mouth is beginning to film over and it feels as though a boiled egg is forcing its way up my throat. I jump and run out of the room naked, sticky, and cold. I make it to the kitchen sink and this is where I let it go. Throwing up makes me feel no better as I lean dry-heaving against the counter and looking at the floor. It sounds like that damn baby is screaming on a megaphone in my ear now, and I look up under my armpit. It's in the living room snugged to the couch's armrest, a roll of newspaper propped up under its chin, an empty bottle on its side.

I turn around and it's a white-black mulatto baby, head shrouded in curls. I walk over to it and it's a boy. His chest puffs up and he slows the cry down to a groan. His eyes twinkle at me and his little arms stretch up in my direction. His bib looks like it's made of yolk. He's thrown up too. Poor little bastard. The place smells like a burnt diaper. This seems more like a job for a mother, and so I turn back for the room.

Janet's in bed spread-eagle, her arms crossed at her chest, head slumped back, geekin' out, biting at the air, making nasally moans. I sit down next to her. All them curls and crying this morning got me to thinking about Ruby, Nina, and Andre—my family—and when it was I was last home. These thoughts always lead to worries and worries lead to ganja smoke, so I grab my jeans and put on my boxers. I pick up an old Boston *Metro*, fold it in half, and take out the last of my 'erb and start breaking up on it. The crumbling is over and now I'm beginning to spin my spliff.

As I start tucking it together Janet shakes herself awake and starts looking at me as she kneads her nails into her thighs. Her eyebrows crouch together and she leans forward and smacks the joint out of my hand. Looking at the last of my 'erb sift into the carpet has the accordion in my head feeling motorized and the baby sounding possessed.

I reach and pick up one of the orange pills she forgot to grab off the floor and eat it. Then I look at her. She tosses her hands at her sides as we both look down at the carpet.

"Bring home E-Bone Battel. And you piss the bed and don't even fuck me right." She grabs at her crotch, gyrating again. "Thought Dom said you were one of those Mandingos."

I hear a ding in my brain and the accordion stops. My body begins to feel like a hot-air balloon and the fire's taking me up. In moments like these I've learned women want this, they're crying out and begging for it, so you'd better let your hands go.

I reach and snatch her hair and it feathers out in front of me. Feels like I'm baling hay as she squeals. I stand up and pull her with me. Things get hazy and somehow she bites my chest and scratches at me. I swing and release her. There's a thud and that's her head on the wall. She's down and crying too. I minute-man around the room getting road-run-ready but get stalled looking for my other boot. In the midst of looking around she says she's calling the police. I ignore her and fish my other boot out from behind the bedpost. As I kick my foot into the boot I look over and she grabs a box cutter out of her purse. I start for the door and she hops up and stands in the doorway, box cutter in hand.

"What?" I jump at her. "Cut me if you gon' cut me then." I wind up like I'm 'bout to smack her and she flinches back. I knock the box cutter out of her hand and bodycheck her to the floor. Her and the baby together sound like an engine running, and that's exactly what I do. I bounce out the door of her bedroom.

"You ain't shit," she yells as I bolt from the apartment. "I'm telling Woodley about this!"

"Tell 'em, bitch, worry 'bout your fucking kid," I stutter as I run.

It's snowing, I have a hoodie but no coat, and I'm in East Boston. Janet stopped chasing me at the door of her apartment, but I'm still running 'cause that's all I ever seem to do. Run, run with my rebels, Dom Dixon and the Running Rebels. That's my band, for now. Dom's our lead singer, Ziggy's on the keys, I'm on the drums, and Denzly's on the bass. We gig up and down the East Coast but mostly stay in New England.

I don't know why I always seem to go, but I just do. I run, 'cause in moments like this, when my heart beats like a nail clipper puncturing my eardrums, I think of Ruby the most. I wonder if I'll ever get back to her and pray I do. She never believes in what it is I'm doing while I gig, but I'm trying to make things better the only way I know how—the music.

I stop running when I see a cabbie on the corner and I hop in winded. My lungs feel dipped in rubbing alcohol and that pill's got the driver's head looking like a big tater tot. He keeps talking to me. I'm not sure what he's saying but I keep nodding yes because my head is starting to feel too heavy for my neck. Now, I'm pretty sure I didn't say so, but South Station is where the cabbie has brought me. Well, I yacked a little bit on the backseat and he put me out free of charge. I get out of the cab and all the gel-heads in business suits sniff up their noses at me like they're any fucking better.

I pull the drawstrings on my hoodie, hop the turnstile, and get on the next Red Line train to Ashmont. I doze off and wake up as the doors ding open, and I can't tell if I was sweating or drooling but my hands are wet. The conductor's voice announces that we've arrived at Broadway. A familiar hand is stroking my knee. I look and don't move it because it's Beatrice, one of our band's favorite groupies. I've had her before, many times. She's a paper-thin biddy, always had a thing for drummers and the way we swing our sticks. Her teeth may look like broken piano keys but she knows how to use her mouth.

At the JFK stop a rotund woman gets on our cart wearing all white. She looks like a sea lion wrapped in a snowman suit, only her top hat is white and covered in glittery fake baby's breath. She waddles in licking her lips, humming "Amazing Grace," and snugs into her seat clutching her purse and Bible. Beatrice tries to lean in and kiss me as the train takes off, but I feel the scratches and the bite on my chest and push her away.

"Good to see you too." She raises an eyebrow and slaps my arm.

"Rough night. Got a Tylenol? 'Erb? 'Trice, I need something."

She bites her lips and then starts rummaging in her purse. She sandwiches a blue pill between what look like two credit cards and crushes them together against her knee with a lighter. She sprinkles a bit between her thumb and pointer finger and raises it to my nose.

"Here," she says. I sniff. "That'll put ya down, sugar." She strokes my face.

The train takes off and I begin to feel like a conveyor belt is spinning in my ears and it's tickling the back of my tongue.

My eyes feel like cold orange slices, but the rest of my head is piping hot. I'm sweating and Beatrice is sucking my ear now. I don't stop her. The big woman's angry and charging toward us. I can't move. I want to yell but instead it's she who's yelling.

"It's the people like you two who are why our children are so lost. You and you. You're prostitutes. Turning tricks for the devil. No shame for yourselves in public."

Beatrice stands up and waves a finger in the lady's face. "Fuck you, Miss Lady, you ain't seen me doing nothing. I work for myself."

Beatrice jumps at her and the woman swings her purse, and it seems they've exploded into a bouquet of doves and roses. And then I wonder if the woman that sat next to me was Beatrice at all, but I know that the big older woman's not wrong and I wish I could say what happens next but I don't remember. Many sounds muddle together with the conveyor belt and I begin to nod. I wake up at Ashmont to the butt of the conductor's flashlight in my chest.

"End of the line, Daddy-O. Get off the train."

I take the trolley to Mattapan and walk over the bridge to Milton. What I remember next is falling down somewhere in the snow and more crying. Stern voices and warmth. Gentle hands carefully undressing me. More warm sensations and delicate arms embracing me and guiding me to my sleep, and the word: "Daddy."

Ruby mushes me in the chest. She's dangling the keys to the station wagon in my face. She's in her bathrobe, silk scarf wrapped tight.

"I called Mr. Watson and told him Andre won't be needing a ride to the tournament today. You will be taking him to his games this morning!" I clear my throat and wipe the sleep out of my eye. "What!" she says. "Act like you got something better to do."

"Relax, I'll take him." I cough.

"Yeah, you will. You're lucky your daughter is the one who found your sorry behind slumped against that basement door last night." She sucks her teeth and walks over to the dresser. I smell the grease burning off the curling iron heating up next to her makeup tray and it's turning my stomach. Her dress is hanging from the door. She drops her robe and she's developed a little back fat, but, damn, she still looks good.

It's always this way between us. We deserve each other. She'll never leave me and I'll never let her ass go. We ain't right, but she's my bottom bitch and we're something and that's all anyone ever needs—something.

A car outside beeps its horn twice and Ruby turns electric, patting over her face in the mirror, putting on her panty hose. She's wearing a black lace bra and panty set and she's got one of her gold necklaces on too.

"Where you going?" I ask her.

"Out."

"Where out?"

She sucks her teeth and shrugs her shoulders.

"Eddy, don't ask me no damn questions. It's a women's group at church. Roland's taking me. The real question is where the hell you been the last four months—that's the real question."

"Out," I answer her.

"Eddy, you're insulting. You know that? I hope you run them streets smoking that stuff until your head pops off or someone pops you."

She got her shit together and turned super Christian all of

a sudden a couple years back. Roland's supposedly one of her Christian brothers. He's a fucking whitewashed Uncle-Tom-ass nigga if you ask me. He lives next door with his soon-to-be wife and stepdaughter. He likes to slick-eye me from afar and look down his camel nose at me. One of them dark, pretty, slim-waist niggas that makes white folks feel comfortable. Graduated college, uses SAT words, got big teeth.

I don't like him meddling in my garden when I'm away, but Ruby allows it. Andre thinks the motherfucker's cool. And I don't like the way he likes to hug up and grin in Nina's face neither. I been away a bit, but I know what I know. Andre's standing in the doorway with his gym bag.

"Andre, where's the game?"

"East Boston High School."

He doesn't even make eye contact with me and walks out. He's always been her kid. First fucking word was "Mama." Ruby trained it into him just to spite me. What the hell was I supposed to do with a kid that calls his daddy "Mama" every-where we go? Wherever the time goes, it's gone, 'cause he's about my height, it seems, and the kid's got a chest that looks like two couch cushions. And his neck's about the size of my thigh. I may not have been here in months but I can't recall the last time I've seen him. Even when I do come around he's always gone away playing for some team somewhere.

I kick on my boots and head out the door to warm up the car. I stop in the hallway to loop my belt and look up into the kitchen. Nina's box braids are dangling around a bowl of cereal. I walk in there. She looks up and cuts her eyes at me. I put my hand on her shoulder and she flinches away and stands up.

"Leave me alone." She turns her back to me. She's crying.

"What's wrong, baby?"

She turns back around and pushes me in the chest and I grab her arms and pull her close to me. She rests her head on my chest, I wince and look down at her.

"Look at you, Daddy—why you always doing this to yourself?"

"I'm sorry, baby," I whisper in her ear. "Thanks for getting me last night, okay?" I rock her side to side. "You're the only one I got in my corner, you know." I stop rocking her because I'm getting dizzy and falling down wouldn't help anything. I really hate it when she does this shit, but she's got plenty to be upset with me about. I know. I pull back and brush two of her box braids behind her ear.

"I gotta take Andre to his game."

She sniffles and looks down.

"Yo, we gon' be late, Pop." Andre's voice tumbles into the kitchen all gritty, like I'm one of his homeboys on the corner, and my hands begin to tingle. I don't turn around. I kiss Nina on the forehead.

"Get your stuff, baby. I'll take you to lunch." I stroke her cheek.

It just came out and Nina takes off down the hallway and I got not a penny to my name. I turn around and want to sock Andre's jaw. I chuckle at him and walk over to the hallway closet and put on one of his jackets and an old knit hat. I zip the coat and turn to him. He smells fresh out of a ganja field and I step back and he steps back and looks at the floor. He's higher than bat pussy and what am I supposed to say to him? I just brush by him and walk outside before I do something to him. Kid's got a lot of stripes to chalk in the streets before he thinks he can get one over on an old dog like me.

Outside I see Papa Tanks's little legs sticking out from beneath his gold Volvo.

"Afternoon, Pop!" I say. He inches out from beneath the Volvo and lifts his goggles to look at me. He takes out his handkerchief, blows his nose, then flips the goggles back on and disappears back under the car. He's never liked me.

I look up the walkway and Roland is idling outside the fence. I want to spit on him when he leans his head out the window stretching his arm toward me as I pass by.

"To what do I owe the pleasure, Eddy Battel? Put it here, brother."

I keep walking and don't respond. I get in the station wagon and fire it up. It backfires twice, then starts and the gas light flashes on. I hop out of the car, jogging to catch Ruby before she comes out of the house. Roland smiles at me as I jog by.

"Ho! Thought I was going to have to give ya a jump, man."

I stop because he's the right nigga to say the wrong thing.

"Fuck you, crackerjack." I smack the roof of his car. "Test me if you want. I fail every time."

We make eye contact and he starts winding up his window. This is when the tough guy disappears and the bitch comes out. Roland suddenly becomes winded and develops convenient amnesia. The foolish-chatter stops and his head recoils into his little neck and all of a sudden he's got the helium voice.

"Whoa! Eddy, come on! Relax, man, brother. Chill!" he squeaks out through the crack in the window. I keep walking and meet Ruby in the doorway of the house. Her makeup's fresh, curls tight, and she smells sweet. I put my hand on her hip and she stiff-arms my chest and steps back.

"Eddy, move!"

"The car needs gas." I grin.

"You are so trifling." She rolls her eyes and digs a twenty-dollar bill from her purse. "Now move!" I step to the side and she booty-bumps past me, then stops and turns around and hands me another ten. "And make sure the kids eat." I watch her walk to the car. Roland is eyeballing all of this and he smiles again with them fucking teeth. Ruby gets in the car and unbuttons her jacket and pulls off her scarf and freezes. He's tattling, he couldn't wait. He turns back around with his bitch ass and waves again, and now Ruby's mean-mugging me. He rolls down the window.

"Good day, pal. Be blessed."

They burn rubber and pull away in his red Acura Legend. The sky is still ash gray, and I watch their black silhouettes in the rear window as they pull off. Ruby's arm raises and she rests her hand up on the side of Roland's headrest.

Like I said, we deserve each other.

Andre power walks by me with his hood on and I watch him bop to the car, clutching his gym bag. He slams the passenger door behind him. My head hurts, I still ain't got right on the day and I don't care how bad he thinks he is—I ain't in the mood for no shit. I hear the front door slam and I look up as Nina's locking it. She starts walking toward me. She's wearing makeup too. Her jeans are spandex-tight and her shirt's about a half inch too short, showing off a chrome belly button ring that I was not aware she had. She too brushes by me and gets in the car and I follow behind her. I put on a cassette tape from one of my shows a few weeks back in Providence, and we pull off.

As soon as we get over the bridge into Mattapan Square we hit a red light. Andre sucks his teeth like he's offended. He snatches open his gym bag and takes out his headphones. He rezips the gym bag and stuffs it between his legs. He turns his music all the way up and resettles into the seat. As he rustles around I can smell the weed all over him. Feels like I should say something but I don't 'cause there's nothing to say.

He pulls the drawstrings on his hood, hiding his face, and slouches deeper in his seat. I look at him.

"Just leave him alone. He's always crabby before his games." I look up at Nina in the rearview mirror.

"Well, maybe he—" She raises a finger in the air and stops me.

"Well, maybe you ought to know." She cuts her eyes at me. "There's a lot you don't know about!" I can feel her mounting her daddy-do-wrong soapbox, so I turn up the music.

"You can't hide behind that music forever!" She crosses her arms and braces back into the seat, pouting and looking out the window. I don't answer her and keep looking ahead as I drive. Andre takes off his hood and headphones.

"Easy!" He turns around and looks at Nina. Then turns back around and slaps the dashboard. "Look at the time! Damn, man, we 'bout almost late. Coach hate it when niggas is late!" He lets out a growlish groan. "I should've just rode with that man."

"Yeah, you'll have your chances," I shot back.

"Well, don't do me no favors then, nigga." He looks at me.

And here he goes again with that corner-boy tough-voice. I jerk the wheel as we swerve across three lanes onto the rumble strips of the breakdown lane and I stomp the brakes.

"I won't!" I clap my hands together. "You think you hard? You got something to prove? I'm right here, make a move!" I peer over into his face and we lock eyes. He doesn't look scared, but being scared ain't got nothing to do with getting your ass beat.

Nina's arm slices through our glares.

"Come on, y'all, can we please just make it to the game?"

Andre looks away. I keep my glare locked on him for a few

more seconds just to make sure we're clear. I take my foot off the brake pedal, turn up my music, and we ease off.

We pull into the parking lot of East Boston High and I already don't want to be in this part of the city. A fat little white man with rosy red drinking cheeks is pacing out front of the gym smoking a cigarette, his hair gelled up all hedgehog-like. He's got on a yellow-and-black swishy suit, the same color as Andre's gym bag. Andre looks at the man, lets out an aggravated sigh, and rolls down his window.

"Coach, I'm coming, I'm coming—my bad," he yells to the man and starts grabbing for his gym bag. "Let me out. Let me out, Pop."

The man looks down at his watch. "Battel! Fifteen minutes to tip-off and you're draggin' ass. Get in there!"

Andre snatches his sneakers from his gym bag, tosses the bag in the backseat, and runs up the steps to the gym. "I should bench your ass," Coach Hedgehog says as he blows smoke and Andre runs past him inside.

I take my foot off the brake and the car rolls a bit as I hear the squeak of Nina's open door and hit the brake pedal again.

"Excuse me! Forget I was in the car?" She sucks her teeth.

"I didn't mean—" The door slams and she starts walking toward the gym.

I park the car and a black family in a white minivan parks next to me. The side door opens and a young boy and girl run out to the back bumper and stop. The parents get out and the mother takes her time unclipping the hinges of their other little girl's car seat. I wait for them all to exit, then start walking up to the gym behind them. The older two run ahead playing as the parents hang back, walking the little girl between them, each parent holding one hand as her arms stretch up and she waddles along. I remember back to when I thought having kids was all it took to keep us all together.

As I get closer to the gym I see the brightness of the lights and hear a buzzer going off. It ratchets up my headache and I stop to rub my temples. I watch the family walk up the stairs to the gym. Nina's holding the door for them. She waves for me to hurry up.

We walk in together and there's an admissions and concession table set up in the little lobby. It sounds like a million basketballs are bouncing and it's not helping my headache. I can see Andre and his team in the layup lines. A stout white woman with a floral turtleneck is sitting behind the table.

"Would you two like to buy a weekend family admission pass for twenty dollars?" she asks.

I almost laugh in her face and look at Nina, who looks offended. She fixes her eyes on the woman, who is stressing her jaws with a smile.

"We're assistant coaches. You sure coaches pay to enter these things?" Nina grabs her back pocket like she's going for a wallet and the woman hunches into her double chin looking embarrassed and crosses her hands over the bulge of her stomach.

"Of course, of course." The woman chuckles and motions her arms toward the door.

We walk past the table into the gym. Nina winks at me and I smile. The game hasn't started yet and Nina heads off to grab us seats while I head for the bathroom.

The dirt under my nails looks metallic as I wash my hands. I see myself in the mirror. My eyes have dark raccoon circles and I have a few little cuts on my chin. The back of my head feels tender from falling down last night. I lift my shirt. Janet got a few scratches off on my stomach too, but the bite didn't break the skin. I run some cold water and wet my face. My jaw hurts from grinding my teeth. I dry my face and walk back out to the concession table and use a couple of Ruby-dollars to get a coffee. I'll give myself till halftime before I grab some smoke and a beer so I can start feeling more normal about things.

Nina is sitting with a bright-skinned black couple, clearly parents of one of Andre's teammates, both wearing the same black-and-yellow team travel gear, looking as square as can be. The husband has a *Boston Herald* stretched across his lap and the wife is knitting something. Nina knows these people. They're all laughing as I walk up the bleachers. The man stands up and flaps his arms open like he wants to hug me. He has a wet-looking S-curl in his hair with matching patches of gray on the sides.

"You must be Andre's father. Charles Watson, I'm Aldrich's dad. It's a pleasure. Andre was just over to the house last night for the team pasta party. Some kid you got there. You must be proud."

"I'm Eddy." I stretch my hand out and look down at his big shiny watch. He gorilla-grips my hand and snatches me close for a half embrace. I almost spill my coffee and force a smile.

"This is my wife, Trina." She drops the yarn balls in her lap and tilts her glasses down to see me, raising a limp hand in my direction. She smiles, showing no teeth, and gently touches two fingertips lightly on both sides of my hand and we make a shake motion, being careful not to actually touch hands. We make eye contact and her eyes open shock-wide and narrow and I look her off and say nothing and settle into my seat.

I watch as both teams' starting fives walk onto the court,

milling around slapping high fives and saying, "Good luck," waiting for the ref to toss the jump ball. Andre's a starter and I don't know the last time I saw him play. Maybe when he was in grade school. The ball tips off and bounces to Andre, and immediately he attacks the hoop and gets fouled. He makes the layup and pounds his chest, yelling, "And one!" Everyone starts cheering and my head pounds harder.

Charles leans into me, bouncing his eyebrows.

"God, I love watching that kid play," he says.

"So, Charles, what number's Aldrich?" I ask as Andre shoots his free throws.

"He's number seven."

"Where's he at?"

"The bench." He points.

I nod okay, and say no more. It looks like this is the game to see. The gym has five ball courts of games going on but everyone seems to be packed in around this one. As the half unfolds, Charles sits telling me more than I ever knew about my son. First off, this league is called AAU. This is one of the best AAU teams in Massachusetts and all these kids are supposedly "pipelined"—as Charles put it—to play ball in college. On the weekends, more often than not Andre rides with the Watsons to tournaments.

Charles's got Andre caddying golf at his fucking country club and they take him along with them on their Martha's Vineyard vacations. I don't really know how to feel about all this. But it's more than I can do for him, so again I say nothing.

Charles says he's been teaching Andre to play the guitar. He's thinking about giving him one for his birthday. This sends an electric jolt up my spine. I turn and look him in the face.

"Oh, yeah? What kind of music you teaching him to play?"

"Just some rhythm and blues, a little Muddy Waters." He tosses his hands up. "Oh, you don't mind, Ed-O? Andre said you're a drummer. I'd hate to step on a musician's toe. I only play for fun."

I don't answer. The more Charles keeps talking the less I want to hear what his light-skinned country-club ass has to say. From the sounds of things, Andre's better off without a nigga like me around.

I look out at Andre on the court and his eyes are still red, with the slant of sideways sunflower seeds. He might smoke a little reefer, but he's nothing like me and maybe that's good. I tune Charles out as he starts blabbering about the life insurance company that he runs and playing squash at the YMCA on the weekends. Now what kind of black man plays squash? I focus in on the game.

Andre's out there tearing shit up, bullying kids, cursing out the refs, talking shit to the other team's coach. Aldrich finally gets in and throws Andre an alley-oop right as the time expires, and Andre dunks it on a scrawny little Spanish kid as the buzzer sounds. Then he turns around and chest-bumps the kid, screaming "Penga!" in the little yellow boy's face.

The gym erupts, everyone's standing, the kids lining the courts are jumping up and down falling all over each other. A lanky ref runs up in his tight black pants and windmills his arms in Andre's face and blows his whistle, spiking his hands together into a T to call a technical foul on Andre. Andre looks at the ref and starts laughing as Coach Hedgehog runs onto the court and ushers him back over to the bench, sitting the whole team down.

Coach Hedgehog's pulling at his collar, his face is tomato

red, and all the kids on the sidelines are reenacting the dunk and laughing. Nina is more embarrassed than amused, but Charles is right, I am proud.

That's my boy out there and who'da knew, he's got Battel blood in them veins after all. Charles can take him wherever he wants, but I made him and he's my son. Andre looks across the gym and we make eye contact and I smile and give him the thumbs-up. But then I realize he's looking at Nina, who's fanning her arms up and down, puffing out her cheeks, telling him to breathe. She nudges me.

"So, where we going to lunch?" she asks.

"You don't want to see the second half?" I ask.

"Get with it, Daddy, these things go all day. The Killer Bees got four games this afternoon. We'll see him play."

Charles gets up and walks over to the team bench after Coach Hedgehog finishes yelling at them. He has a Gatorade in his hand for Aldrich. I follow behind him empty-handed because I guess this is what fathers are supposed to do. I don't know what to say, so I just sit down next to Andre on the bench. I look across the gym and see three white girls holding signs that say "Battel's Babes." Again I feel strangely proud.

"You doing your thing, man." I look at him.

He's huffing and puffing, looking down at the floor. Some kind of energy on the guy. Seems I'm the only one with the nuts to be within ten feet of him.

"You need anything?" I ask.

He doesn't answer me.

"You thirsty?" I ask again, and again he doesn't answer.

I want to punch him in the side of the head. Fuck's he so mad about anyway? Look around, he's got a cheering section and every dad in the gym stiff-dicked wishing he was their kid. The whole place is watching his every move. Such a fucking ungrateful little bastard. He's got it a whole lot better than me when I was his age. I get up and walk back over to Nina and we head out the door.

We pull out of the parking lot and again I can feel Nina looking at me. "What are you in the mood for?" I ask her but then see a Dunkin' Donuts and pull into the drive-through. The sour look on her face says she was expecting more, but shit, I still need to get right today. We both get coffees and breakfast sandwiches. We cruise around for a bit looking for a place to park so we can eat, Nina's eyes burning on me from the passenger seat.

"Daddy, can I ask you something?" She doesn't wait for me to respond. "What's your life like? I just wanna know. Really, what is it you do out there when you're gone?"

I stare at the road ahead. I hate it when she does this shit and for some reason her voice feels like acid melting my insides and I don't know what to say. The answer isn't good enough. It's too simple: I'm a fuck-up. What am I supposed to tell her? I turn tricks for the devil? Niggas like me just don't learn. I been caught up in this tumble cycle and can't seem to stop.

"You don't have to answer me today but I *do* deserve that much . . ." she continues.

Back in the day I would've popped those overgrown words back down her throat, but she's not wrong to want to know. I turn the tape deck back on.

"Aw, baby, come on. Why don't we talk about the good times, ya know?"

"What good times, Daddy?" She's yelling now. "They're all dead and cold. Why don't you care, Daddy?" Her eyes are glassing over with tears and my heart's racing.

"Baby, I'm sorry." It's about the only thing I can offer.

"Yeah, you are sorry. You sure are sorry, Daddy! You sure are."

Now I've apologized and bought the girl a meal and she sits here insulting me. I am her father and she is my daughter and she needs to know her place in the world. I grip the wheel and look at her.

"Since everyone seems to be so curious this morning, why don't I ask you some questions, Nina? When'd you start wearing your jeans paint-on tight and smearing makeup all over your face like a blinking raggedy nightwalker, huh? When did you get your belly button pierced like a little hoochie mama?"

"So that's what you care about?" She lifts the flap of her shirt over her belly button and rips the ring out. "It's a magnet!" She throws it at me and spills her coffee down her lap and throws her breakfast sandwich against the windshield. She's sobbing. The magnet hits my neck and I swerve a bit looking over at her as we pull past a gray Crown Victoria stopped in the entryway of a mobile mart.

It pulls out after us and I don't know what the hell we did wrong but he's turned on the red and blues. I reach into my back pocket and realize my wallet must be back at the house and wonder if I have any warrants.

The officer walks up to the window and it's Officer McDevitt, one of them South Boston Irish good ol' boys. We know each other from more encounters than I care to speak of. He looks down at me, braces back smiling, thumbs in his belt loops. He squints his eyes looking at Nina and the mess she's made.

"Everything okay in there?"

"McDevitt, whatchu want?"

"You know the drill. License and registration."

That's when I pause. "I don't have my license on me but I know my license number."

He shrugs his shoulders and his eyebrows raise. "Without a license how am I to know who you are? Out of the car!"

"For what? I didn't do you nothing. Why you even pull me over?"

"Red rejection registration sticker. I smell marijuana. Out. Of. The. Car! Battel!"

"Bullshit you do. Ain't nothing in this car."

"Oh, mind if I look around a little bit?"

This is when I hear the sniffer-dog barking and know I'm tripping. How could I not realize he had the fucking dog with him? But shit, it's Ruby's car and I felt a tinge of confidence.

"Not a problem." I look over at Nina. "This won't take long, baby." She folds her arms and looks away from me. I step out of the car and stand beside McDevitt's cruiser with my hands crossed behind my back "for safety reasons," with another backup officer standing next to me.

A woman cop arrives as more backup and walks Nina to her cruiser and they stand there waiting for McDevitt to start the search. He takes the German shepherd out of the cruiser and walks it up to the station wagon. He walks the dog around the car as he opens all the doors, and then lets it off the leash. It goes berserk and springs into the backseat. The dog jumps back out of the car, chomping down on Andre's gym bag, trying to rip it in half. McDevitt looks at me and grins, then speaks into his radio as more backup officers arrive.

"Good boy, good boy. Who's a good boy?" McDevitt pets the dog and takes the bag from him and returns it to the car. He unzips the back pocket and, sure enough, the motherfucker pulls out what I figure to be four ounces of weed.

"Click, click." McDevitt looks at the officer next to me.

"You fucking planted that shit! No way you're getting me on that."

The officer steps behind me and I feel the bite of the handcuffs chomping down on my wrists. At this point pleas are for a later time and the officer pushes my head forward and takes a step.

"No no no no no no no ... Officer, please!" The officer pushes me toward the cruiser and I jump up and buck back at him. McDevitt rushes in, slide-tackling my legs out and I start kicking at him. More backup crowds around and they are pig-piling on top of me. I feel a gust of wind and they're carrying me now, chanting, "Stop fighting!" I watch the female officer restraining Nina.

"Jesus Lord!" Nina screams. She's giving the officer a run for her money too. They slide me into the cruiser and the door slams. My skull is bleeding somewhere, I can taste it in my sweat. I sit up and look out the window at Nina as I pull away, and in some weird way this seems like one of the better things that has happened to me lately. I'm a piece of shit, it ain't hard to tell. Maybe it's time for this prostitute to pay his pimp.

10

Slipping

I'd riffled through every bag of nuts, bolts, washers, and screws twice looking for my stash and found nothing. Maybe I shouldn't have smoked that joint on the way home. My wristwatch beeped. I only had ten minutes until Drop Everything and Read time was over and my midday absence would be noted by my fourth-period science teacher, who would alert the office, whose secretary Mrs. Agnes would pass the message along to Ma and the assistant principal. Fuck, I muttered to myself rapid-fire as I rummaged my hands through the darkness inside Papa Tanks's toolshed. Detention, suspension, or an ass whooping? Trouble's a-coming, I know, but it don't matter none 'cause I ain't going nowhere without my trees—considering my last lapse in accounting for them, and how it resulted in Pop being accounted for 'round-clock by guard, iron lock, and key.

A cold breeze whistled the shed doors open and I thought I heard some rustling behind me. I turned around but didn't see anything moving and in my high haze I dismissed it. The doors wheezed shut. Usually I could nose out my weed simply by rustling the bags. Frustrated, I began to throw and kick through the clutter of bags on the floor until I heard a few more distinct thuds behind me and I froze. With the shed doors closed, beams of lights broke through the cracks in the wood. Everything else was tar black. I turned around and took a few steps, reaching out in front of me. Feeling nothing, I resumed my search and attributed the sounds to a mixture of the blowing leaves crunching outside and my own stomping around—until Papa Tanks clicked on his flashlight, spotlighting my face, breaking his stealth. He lunged at me and snatched me by the base of my neck, kneading his tamarind-thick fingers into the collar of my polo shirt.

"Andre, you crazy 'r wha?"

He thundered his hand across the back of my head. Neon fireworks exploded into my vision and I jolted forward. Papa Tanks spun me around gripping my chest, balling my shirt around his hand, and slowly pulling me closer to him. The veins in his forearm pulsed out his rage. He peered down at me and his eye smoldered. He held me still as I wavered away from him like a little turtle suspended in the air by its shell. Papa Tanks tightened his grip to a choke and continued to tighten it until I rasped out, "Pa-Paw, I can't breathe," and tried to squirm away. He took it as an act of aggression.

Papa Tanks drove a hand into my sternum, knocking the wind out of me, and I doubled over. He grabbed me up with both hands and pulled me in close and squatted back gathering his momentum and charged me back into the wall like a lineman. Yoked up on my tippy-toes, I felt my legs give out and I clutched at his forearm for balance. His eyes popped wide, the wrinkles around his temples looked like clenched fists. He reached behind me and rustled free a tire iron and held it above his head. My eyes snapped shut, cheeks quivering with anticipation. After a short pause I peeked at him and he bashed the tire iron into the wall next to my head, splintering the wood onto my cheek. My arms flailed out and Papa Tanks pushed me to the ground.

"Mussy-be dis. De reason yu mashing up de whole place!"

He spiked a crinkled brown paper bag off my chest. The aroma wafted out and I felt a fucked-up sense of relief.

"Mari-Juana! Andre! Why? You nah t'ink I see what you a'do. Me grun-sun running roun' actin'a Al Capone, like we nah have bread in'ayawd? In truth, we all mus' tek up our life wit' God. Jus' 'memba, an honest man's sardine taste betta den any devil-steak."

Shaking his head, he turned and walked away.

"Pa-Paw," I called after him.

He ignored me and kept walking. He was a boss back home in Costa Rica. He didn't repeat himself. The flashlight clicked off and he slammed the doors and the room returned to black and he was gone, leaving me clutching my product, lying on my back panting and bewildered. I sat up and glanced into an old mirror leaning against the shed wall but couldn't see myself through the dust caked all over it. The wind flapped the doors again and I flinched.

"Fuck!" I grumbled. I punched the floorboards, stood up, and stuffed the weed in my pocket. I let out a long sigh. I slowly ran my hands down my face. Time to pull it together. Shit's all fucked up—it always is—but for a change I sort of wished someone would save me from myself. All I wanted was a summer day when everything tapered off and I could run ball at Kelly Park all day and nothing really seemed to matter.

As I walked out of the shed, the rain stopped and the sky shattered itself into a sunny day. Me and Papa Tanks both know I know better, but the fact remains: morals can't override hunger. Besides, I can't stop hustling anyway. Not since Pop blew back into town, fucking my flow in true Pop fashion.

As I started walking up over the hill back toward school the silver spoiler on Smoke's Honda Civic emerged from a blind spot over the hill like a shark in shallow water. I wished I could go up inside their house and chill with Beezy, but Beezy's at school. Plus, since Tunnetta, shit ain't been the same. She Beezy's girl now, even though I still touch her from time to time. When I reached the top of the hill I saw the ends of Smoke's cornrows dangling out from the back of his Red Sox cap in the rear window. My heart sped up and I stopped and turned down a side alley leading to the avenue. Smoke wasn't being very friendly these days.

Once the high school basketball season was over and AAU ball got under way, I realized I could extend my clientele—until Pop left my basketball game trying to convince Nina he wasn't a piece of shit. He got himself bagged. If he had his license on him or simply kept his ass at the gym, nothing would have happened.

That shit's on Pop more than it's on me. It don't matter where he is when he is gone. Jail or the streets, he wouldn't be home anyway. He'd probably be in Lynn with his other family. The bigger problem is that Pop lost sixteen hundred dollars worth of product. The money was a matter I had to take up with Smoke. It was his product, really. Charge it to the game. I started small, but once the clientele's hunger grew so did the weight I dealt with. This is also the point when the games were over and things began to unravel.

Smoke wasn't hearing the whole Poppa-got-bagged story. One month. I had one month to get Smoke his money. Or else! And that deadline has come and passed and now I'm working for Reggie. Of course, he fronted me the weight. Trying to pay back two debts at the same time, I'm basically working for free.

As I walked up the parkway looking at the mounds of wet

fallen leaves, my wristwatch beeped again. Fourth period was well under way. I had fourteen gram bags to move and wasn't going back to school. I still felt a bit hazy from the joint, plus Ma probably already got that call from the school office. I walked by the Tucker, my old elementary school, the shriek of kids playing at recess in the air, and I leaned up against the chain-link fence, watching them play.

A group of little ones stood around a rainbow-patterned parachute and raised it above their heads in unison. The parachute belled up into the air as they all ran inside and sat on the edges of the balloon, hiding as it toppled down on them, a wilted mushroom. In the front of the playground on a patch of concrete a group stood squat-legged around a silver spray-painted baseball diamond playing kickball, waiting for the next pitch. The smell of pizza floated across the playground, making my stomach gurgle.

The fence rattled and I heard the approaching buzz from the custom exhaust on Smoke's gunmetal-gray Honda Civic hatchback, and it straightened my stance like a zipper up a dress. I turned around and the car darted by and didn't stop. Not irregular these days, considering, but as they sped past I saw Nina in the passenger seat ducking down, clearly trying not to be seen. I recognized her silk head wrap. High or not, I know Nina when I see her. She was supposed to be at the same place I wasn't: school.

At the stop sign Nina's head popped up completely. I paused at the sight. I'd ignored the rumors in the hallways about them two dating, 'cause I'd never seen them together, but there was no denying it now. I kept walking and I didn't really know how to feel about them two. Shit sure is changing. I'm big enough to fist-fight Smoke now, which has been crossing my mind more and more lately. But Smoke now carries a gun. He and Nina blow through the stop sign, bang a right, and vroom-vroom up the avenue.

The avenue was still and quiet as I walked away from Tucker toward Mattapan. The bell from the Methodist church announced that it was noon and a green SUV honked its horn at me from the other side of the avenue, breaking my trance. I looked over and it was Aldrich Watson, the last nigga I wanted to see, and he had his sidekick Eric Saucionni riding shotgun too.

The Watson family lives on the other side of town, where the money's at. Aldrich is one of them uppity Fresh Prince of Bel-Air minstrel-show-type niggas, always touting a so-called genuine version of blackness that he so desperately wanted to connect to. He's a nice enough kid and we play on the same AAU team, but we're two different breeds. The Watson family ushered me into their upper-crust black world and Aldrich marveled at my everyday blackness and the roughness around my edges, jockin' my every move. Only reason I let him come around sometimes is 'cause I feel indebted to his folks for all they're doing for me. Mr. Watson likes me, he always says I remind him of himself when he was younger. He usually rides us to our games, and when Pop got arrested Mr. Watson offered to employ him upon his release.

"Yo, Dre, you got any work on you?" Aldrich called to me.

I just looked at them and didn't say anything until Eric called out too and I thought, Fuck it, and approached the Land Cruiser. I pulled the chrome handle to the back side passenger door and it was locked. Eric popped his head out the window.

"Got any work?" he asked, looking confused.

"Yes, dickhead. Not 'bout to give it to you right here in this school zone, though. Aldrich, ride me 'round the block."

Eric Saucionni irked the shit out of me. He was a wigger if I ever met one. We go to school together. Big Maal and them BRC cats let him hang around. "Somebody gotta talk to the cops and somebody gotta buy the weed," Big Maal would laugh.

The doors clicked open and I got in.

"What y'all looking for?"

Eric placed sixty dollars on the median and I retrieved it.

Eric turned to me. "How far can that get us? We gotta get back to Cambridge. Aldrich's on a free period so we took a ride. It's bring-a-friend-to-school day."

Just this year Aldrich transferred to a private school to play ball and it seemed like it was the only thing Eric ever talked about. Eric always had the dopest gear and rocked it wrong. It irked me that Eric would prance around the hallways at school bragging about going to all the hip-hop concerts hosted by Jam'n 94.5. It irked me that Eric was like Aldrich's mouthpiece. And Eric irked me most of all because, other than me and Beezy, no one else seemed to notice.

We pulled 'round the rotary out front of Kelly Park and stopped. I tossed three gram bags on the median.

"That far," I said as I looked at Eric, grabbing the door handle.

Aldrich perked up. "Yo! You ain't try'na smoke my nigga. It's been a minute. Feel like we lost touch and shit." Aldrich tossed me a Dutch Master. "Here." He handed me back a bag. "You roll one. I'll roll one."

I nodded and started unwrapping the cigar's outer leaf.

"Where you wanna burn at?" I asked Aldrich.

"Right here. Cops never come to Kelly Park, especially during the day," Eric answered. Me and Aldrich made eye contact in the rearview mirror and continued to roll in silence. I finished and lit my blunt and soon after Aldrich lit his.

"So where you been, my nig? I been blowing you up, yo!" Aldrich looked at me, looking genuinely hurt, as though us not speaking over the weekend was a legitimate gripe. "You missed the tournament too."

I ignored Aldrich and continued to smoke. I looked out the window and watched the basketball courts. Reggie was shooting around by himself under the far basket near the picnic tables.

The higher I got the more I felt the need to get out of the car. Especially when Aldrich started blasting Jam'n 94.5. Nothing worse than a radio gangsta. The session wasn't over but I caught Aldrich's eyes in the rearview mirror, gave a salute, and slapped Eric in the back of his head and opened the door.

"Hey!" Eric glared at me.

Aldrich tossed a hand across Eric's chest and shook his head no. At least someone could smell the danger.

"I get out of school in 'bout two hours," Aldrich said. "Why don't you come by the house. It's Friday. Let's hit a party."

I looked at Aldrich and said, "Yeah yeah yeah," and turned my back to them. My legs felt heavy, like I was wading through a sludgy grayness. I watched Reggie draining threes as I approached.

"Yerp," I called to Reggie.

Reggie yerped back, took a few more shots, and held the ball, watching me walking toward him.

"Lil' nigga, you ain't got school?"

I giggled into my hands and looked down as I walked and didn't answer.

"Ain't I just ask you a question, lil' nig?"

I shrugged my shoulders. "Shit got all fucked up today."

I was so blunted I couldn't even look him in the face.

"You smoking up my shit?" He grabbed my shoulder. "Same thing that'll make you laugh'll make you cry. Tell me what the fuck you are doing out here at twelve twenty-five on a Friday afternoon stinking of product."

We walked and sat down on a picnic table.

"'Ight, so I wasn't skipping school. I was just stepping out to grab a re-up and—"

"Wow." Reggie interrupted. "You a liability. You know that? I don't need your moms coming 'round giving me the third degree 'cause you out here playing a grown man's game." He put a blunt to his lips and lit it. "You're hustling backward. You know that? Why you don't stick to ball? Something you're good at."

I'd heard the little sermon a million times.

"Why you ain't stick to ball?" I blurted out, maybe a little too fast. "Reggie, you was the nicest."

Reggie's nostrils flared. "Nigga, I balled till I falled. You already know. But me, I'm built for these streets. I ain't no puppet for the blue-eyed devil, just to be his fall man. I got my team. I'm the Team Seven MVP. I ain't built for no campus. Niggas like you know how to talk to white folk and shit. It's too late for a cat like me. I picked my lane. Why you don't be like that nigga Aldrich? Get the fuck out of here. Before you get caught the fuck up, fucking around."

I reached for his blunt. "I could hit that?"

Reggie pulled it closer to him and turned his shoulder to me. "Fuck outta here, nigga, look at you. You ain't high enough, huh? Maybe that's why your stupid ass got caught up in the first place."

Reggie looked me in the face and I glanced away.

"Not even," I fired back and took out a joint of my own and sparked it.

"Oh, you big now, huh?" Reggie laughed. "All I know is you better don't play with my money, fuck around and get in over your head. Miss Ruby won't be able to save you on that one. I ain't Smoke, nigga."

Reggie gripped the back of my neck, squeezing my pressure points, until I shook myself out of his grip.

"Dawg, I'ma have it. Don't worry about it." I rose to my feet.

Reggie spiked the ball at me, I spun away but it grazed my side and rolled off into the grass behind the courts. I stood there looking at Reggie sort of stunned, and took a drag from my joint.

"Oh, I'ma worry about it, nigga! Fucking up the money causes big problems, Andre. Keep thinking nothing can happen to you until something does. You better be ready, how you act like you are." He looked at me in the eyes and blew a thin stream of smoke. He started shaking his head. "What you tryin'a be out here anyway? A hustler or a ball player? Instead of trying to be what you ain't, why don't you be good to the things that are good to you, and protect that. Everything ain't for everybody, Andre."

I turned around and walked off to get the ball and dribbled back over to the picnic tables and sat down next to him.

"But I'm saying, Reggie, what happened, though? Why didn't you take it further with basketball?"

"Look, I ain't 'bout to sit here and get into all the particulars with you. A lot of shit happened. Life happens, Andre, that's what I been trying to tell you. I got responsibilities you wouldn't even begin to understand." He snatched the ball out of my hands. "What? You think you're gonna go to the NBA or something? I got real. I grew out of that chasing-hoop-dreams shit. I was four times the hooper and hustler you are when I was your age. Back then I was moving too fast, all the attention went to my head, and a couple of the mistakes I made back then set me back. A few of 'em still follow me around now. I lost a lot of time sitting in a box, and it took me a while to get back on my feet. And I swear on my mama's soul, I ain't never going back to jail, especially not for gettin' caught up with a lil' reckless nigga like you."

Reggie took a long drag and looked up at the cloudy sky. He blew a couple of smoke rings. I don't know what Reggie did time for, and I knew better than to ask. We both sat smoking and listening to the crackle of the blowing leaves until the rumble of Smoke's Honda Civic approached. This time him and Nina didn't even see us as they sped by.

"And what the fuck's up with that?" Reggie blew a stream of smoke in my face as we both watched Nina's profile slide by.

"I dunno but I'ma fix that too. Dawg, I'm on top of my shit." Without dap'n Reggie, I started walking away.

"You ain't on top of shit," Reggie called to me. "Where your daddy at? And how'd he get there? You, nigga, that's how!"

He'd hit a nerve. I stopped and looked back at Reggie taking a drag off his blunt. I balled my fist. Reggie looked at me and laughed out a cloud of smoke.

"Keep walking, little nigga, 'fore I smack a high note outcha. Remember who the fuck you dealing with. You already know how I get down."

My better judgment told me to keep walking and I did. With every step I took it felt as though I was sinking and getting smaller. The day spoiled again and returned to rain and my joint went out and I tossed it in a sewer. What the hell was I doing walking up the street smoking weed anyway? The rain chilled me as I walked. I couldn't think of anywhere to go but home so I did.

When I walked into the apartment I heard the shower water running. Nina's sneakers were outside the bathroom door.

The water turned off.

"Hello?" Nina called out.

"Nina?"

"Andre?"

"What the hell you doing home? Riding 'round town in Smoke's car and shit?"

"Nigga, please, whatever—hold on." A gust of steam engulfed me as Nina swung open the door in her bathrobe. "So what, you my daddy now? Why you ain't at school?"

"Nina, what the hell is wrong with you? You know that nigga Smoke gotta gang of hoes. What you doing riding 'round wit' him for? You better not be fucking him neither!"

I stepped into the steamy bathroom and got in Nina's face. Nina pushed me back against the wall.

"And what if I am? At least he's nice to me." She cut her eyes at me and stomped past.

"So you're his new toy, huh?" I shook my head. "It's sad to see you like this, Nina. Real disappointing."

Nina stopped and turned around.

"Oh, fuck you. See me like what, Andre? What? You're better than me now? You ain't no better, nigga. I seen how you did that pasty-face bitch Tunnetta." Nina folded her arms, shaking her head at me.

I took a few big strides up the hallway and again we were inches from each other.

"You got something to say, Nina?"

"Ain't nobody scared of you. You need to get the fuck up out my face. Huffing and puffing wit' your hardly hustling ass.

Gettin' Daddy locked up." She sighed and rubbed her chin. She looked at me. "Disappointing."

It was a low blow. She knew it would hit a nerve and I got the overwhelming urge to put my hand through something. I chuckled with her a few times, then I jerked back and smacked Nina across the face, knocking her into her bedroom door. She jumped at me with a flurry of punches and kicks.

"You ain't no better than Daddy—you just like him, matter fact!" Holding her face, Nina ran to the phone. "I'm calling Mommy too. You gon' hit me, nigga. Fuck you, Andre!"

I stood watching Nina dial the phone and said nothing. I began to feel the scratches Nina landed on my cheeks, grabbed my backpack, and walked out of the house, heading toward the Watsons' side of town. I stepped off the porch into the grayness. As I walked, the rain mixed in with my tears. I was slipping and of this much I was aware.

11

Born Again

Subwoofers circled Bishop Jackson where he stood at the podium with his head bowed, stroking the bottom of his goatee, winded from having just finished bringing forth his sermon. Clergymen sat in pulpit chairs on both wings of the podium, regally robed in purples, reds, greens, and gold. The choir hummed along, entrenched in pews rising up the walls toward a spread of stained-glass windows. Every eye glued onto Bishop Jackson as he looked out at the crowd and wiped the glaze of sweat from his face. He set the rag down and picked up his Bible. The air went still for a moment as he clapped it shut. Glaring around, sizing up the crowd, he stretched his arms up toward the wooden pews. High heels clacked, boots thudded, and the choir stood.

Ma stomped her feet and swam her arms side to side.

"Use me, Lord, use me!" she screamed.

"Glory, sister! *Glory!*" shouted a baritone voice from somewhere in the back.

The band readied their instruments and the drummer ran a finger across the chimes and started a slow patter on his snare drum. The sobs and praises from those deeply communing with the Lord subsided. A calm began to fall over the congregation.

Ma had begun sobbing around midservice after Deacon Harris stood from his seat in the middle of the stage, looking like he had a hot poker sticking up his spine, eyes rolling back in his head, speaking in tongues.

Bishop Jackson moved toward Deacon Harris and poured anointing oil on a rag and slapped it on Deacon Harris's forehead.

"Speak, Lord!" Bishop Jackson yelled.

His touch crumbled Deacon Harris like a wave splashing a sand castle. Bishop Jackson knelt down and gripped Deacon Harris's forehead as though his head were a heart and his hand were a stethoscope.

Bishop Jackson closed his eyes and began prophesying.

"We're living in the last days, sayeth the Lord of hosts. We need stronger vessels to weather these perilous times." Deacon Harris was still down, half convulsing. Bishop Jackson was kneeling, palming oil onto Deacon Harris's forehead.

"Do not fear or shun the wicked ones in your life, for I am God and boundless redemption lives through me. Do you believe in redemption? Greater is he who knows my name, sayeth the Lord of hosts. Will you be a vessel carrying the lost back to light? Be a vessel! Stand with me today and watch me restore all that the devil has *stolen* from *you*! sayeth the Lord of hosts." Bishop Jackson stood, wiped his hands, and walked back to the podium.

Deacon Harris's eyes began to steady and he came back into himself. The ushers hefted him up off the floor and back into his seat. Deacon Harris's wife stroked his back and held his hand. As Ma watched the scene unfold, she broke down and started bawling. Me and Nina watched her mortified as the sermon switched gears into Bishop Jackson's famous pitch about redemption through the blood of Jesus—the one that gets Ma every time.

Ma slid onto her knees in the pew and sobbed into the lap

of her cream-colored Sunday dress. It was like she needed the Lord to plug her in and recharge her battery. The organ pipes bellowed from above the balcony and the overhead lights dimmed to a glittery darkness, reducing Bishop Jackson to a silhouette carved out by the fluorescent glow from the crucifix in the middle of the podium. The bassist strummed into the drum patter and thrummed under the beat.

"Every head bowed, every eye closed. I'm going to pray the benediction," Bishop Jackson intoned.

I hated it when the lights dimmed inside the sanctuary in New Day Pentecostal. The wails and screams of church elders twitching with the Holy Ghost, barking in tongues—it kinda scared me. It felt like there was some kind of magic in the air, the Holy Spirit flowing around the congregation like vapor, filling folk with the Spirit at random, playing a big game of duck-duck-goose. As I sat in the darkness I always feared the Holy Ghost would envelop me one Sunday like an ill-fitting suit and transform me into a holy roller like the rest. The stained-glass depiction of Christ splayed across a crucifix, bleeding out in his crown of thorns, made everything the color of rotten apples. Sitting in that stiff darkness made me feel like I was in a dungeon, trapped with my thoughts.

I could never catch Tunnetta looking at me from her seat across the congregation next to her father. But when those lights dimmed I knew she was looking, I could feel it, at least I hoped she was 'cause *I* was looking, trying to see her. In the darkness, all the wails and groans reminded me of the same ruckus I'd heard throbbing through the floorboards from my grandparents' room a few weeks back.

Since I've been fucking up and digging myself deeper and deeper into a hole, at night I haven't been sleeping. I just lie in bed looking up into the nothingness as worries carousel around my chest. Regrets race through my mind as I lie in bed playing back where I went wrong or how I let things get so messed up with Tunnetta, and I wonder what Smoke will do to me when he gets tired of waiting for me to give him his money.

It was three in the morning, and I was awake thinking on things as usual when I heard the hollow panging of Nana Tanks waddling to the bathroom using her walker. Ever since her botched knee surgery her legs haven't quite worked the same. I tracked her slow footsteps to the bathroom, the pause, the flush of the toilet, and her slow trudge back. Her steps stopped near what I imagined to be her nightstand. I heard a loud scream and one strong clang from the walker and then it sounded like the fridge upstairs turned over on its side. Nana Tanks yowled like a banshee. My ears popped and I sat up. She wailed into the floor and then went silent and my heart-beat felt like a bee stinging me in the chest.

The entire house woke up and snapped into crisis mode. All preexisting house beefs were put on truce until further notice and everything turned electric. I could hear all the commotion of everyone moving around and it felt like I was hiding under a jungle gym.

"Mother, talk to me! Talk to me!" I heard a few more light thuds and I imagined my mother shaking Nana Tanks. "Call an ambulance!" Ma cried.

I wanted to move but I was too locked in my fear to go and see the chaos rumbling through the floor into my room. I stayed put, listening to the sounds muffled by the pillow I'd clamped over my ears. The boom of the paramedics storm-ing into the house is what got me up out of bed. The red and orange lights pulsed through my shades as I put on a pair of sweatpants.

.I opened my door just in time to see the apartment door open and Nana being taken out of the house on a half-bent gurney. Her cheeks pouted down like a bulldog and she had an oxygen mask suctioned to her face. She was tucked in white blankets up to her neck, head slack to the side. Two EMTs were wheeling her out, and when they pushed her through the ambulance doors, I thought she was dead.

The memory now played in my head on repeat, wild and vivid, like the congregants of New Day Pentecostal, stomping feet, clapping hands, screaming in praise and pain. Some people were passing out while others were doing sanctified shuffles up and down the aisles in conga lines.

"Can we all please join hands?" said Bishop Jackson.

This was the part of church I hated most. I'd always sit next to Nina and her hands would sweat. They reminded me of raw chicken flesh. I'd tell her they smelled like cheese and when she extended her hand I'd reach out and hold her wrist. She'd shake her wrist free and punch me in the knee. Or she'd lick a finger and run it along my ashy ankles, pulling at the cuffs of my too-tight high-water church pants. It was like a routine between us.

Today, though, Nina and I watched our mother fizzle down into what looked like a certifiable lunatic. We held hands and locked arms, huddling into each other. I looked her in the face and she appeared so sad, so innocent. I didn't think I'd ever forgive myself for hitting her like I did.

The saxophonist blew into the rhythm, speeding up the tempo.

"It's never too late to reclaim all that the devil has stolen from you! Today! If you'll surrender your life, repent, and accept Jesus Christ as your Lord and Savior, your future will be secured. If you haven't already, will you accept the Lord today? If that's you saying to yourself, 'It's time to make a change,' please come down to the pulpit, I'd like you to join me in prayer. Come on down. Are you ready to be a vessel? Are you ready for the rest of your life today?"

Bishop Jackson stepped down from the podium.

The organ elevated from a shrill moan to a high-pitched trill, drowning out the band's rhythm. Nina and I held each other in disbelief, listening to our mother melting on the floor, but I doubted Ma was embarrassed. "Ain't no shame in the Lord" was her motto. She had plenty to cry about but, truth be told, I didn't know what exactly triggered this.

"Let it out, sister. Let it go, girl." A pint-sized elderly woman with wax-smooth olive skin rubbed her back and held her hand.

"Will you join me in prayer? Are you ready to start the rest of your life now?" Bishop Jackson's voice repeatedly crooned through the speakers.

The lady nudged Ma. "Go on, sister, reclaim your life."

Ma lifted her head and cleared her throat. The lady handed her a napkin and Ma wiped her face and stepped out from the pews, holding the wooden rail. I just about wanted to die as I watched Ma all unraveled staggering down to the pulpit among the other newfound souls.

See, the thing is, Ma's been a believer four years strong, a faithful servant, pious and devout. She moves like a lily pad on windy waters for the Lord. She takes on all assignments.

Bishop Jackson and his fellow clergymen splashed oil on all the converts' foreheads and ushered them into a small side room to distribute some literature. As the line of converts entered into the back, Ma walked back to her seat, all shined up with oil like she just came out of a bag of fried chicken. She had regained her composure. She stopped in front of the pew and looked at me and Nina like we had just as much a role to play in her stress as anybody, then she smiled at us and took her seat. Nina and I knew this was a very bad sign. Before Ma accepts any of the Lord's assignments, she always answers an altar call and gets herself born again.

Pop's imminent release from jail was a tension in the house too. Ma and Mr. Watson had a long-standing friendship, so he plucked a few strings in his rich nigga network and set up a work-release-type deal for Pop. Somehow he got Pop's charges balled up into a year of probation. He was scheduled to be released in a few weeks and the topic of where he was going to reside had yet to be resolved. Mr. Watson assured Ma that she'd receive her child support or he'd garnish Pop's checks. I knew Ma considered her friendship with Mr. Watson a blessing, but I wasn't feeling it. Mr. Watson's goodwill didn't always seem to do good in my opinion.

"My family, my family," Ma said as she sat hugging herself, rocking side to side, watching Bishop Jackson as he finished out service, having everyone recite the Lord's Prayer. When the part about debtors came up, she glared over at me. Service let out and Ma stayed in her seat, smiling up at the ceiling and shaking her head. Nina and I bumped our way out of the pew and waited in the aisle for Ma to snap out of it. When she did, she strong-stomped out of the sanctuary, blowing past us out into the parking lot, click-clicking along. Nina and I trailed her, trying to keep up.

"Ma, where's the fire? . . . What's the rush?" Nina called.

"We need to get to the hospital to see your grandmother and then get home so we can clean up the house. You know your father comes home soon and he likes a clean house." Ma turned back and smiled at us with that glow, and Nina stopped in her tracks and balled her fists. Her eyes crammed shut as she took a step back.

"Why you don't make that nigga go live in a crack-way house?" Nina shook her head at Ma. "You just gon' keep on letting him in, Ma? Come on." She rolled her eyes. Ma kept walking.

We reached the car and Ma opened her door and got in. Nina and I sat together in the backseat, a unified front. Nina's eyes seared on Ma from the rearview mirror. Ma started the car, turned around, and slid her sunglasses down so we could see her eyes.

"Be a vessel? Give your life to the Lord!" She looked at us blankly and sucked her teeth. "Y'all two just need to be born again, y'all been acting like demons in the street. Now I'm taking back what is rightfully mine. I am a child of God and I want my husband back. I want my marriage back. I want my family back!"

She did a little praise dance in her seat and put the car in gear.

"O ye of little faith, why are you so afraid? Your father's coming back home to live with us and we're going to be a family again. I am taking back all that the devil has stolen from me."

She'd never looked crazier to us. She snapped her fingers above her head and pushed her shades back on, turning up the gospel music. We pulled out, passing the giant red hot dog flapping like a dying fish on the Simco's sign, heading down Blue Hill Avenue toward Mass General to see Nana Tanks. Condemned houses hopscotched the avenue, blistering with peeling waterlogged concert promotion posters.

The golden cross spinning high above the avenue

announced Morning Star Baptist Church as we approached Norfolk Street. Riding along Blue Hill Avenue, I looked at the new Jordans plastic-wrapped in the window of Andrew G's Fashion. We drifted past Lili's Market and Nina's thirsty ass damn near broke her neck watching the dreadlocked man with no shirt on doing pull-ups in the doorway of P&R, the Jamaican beef patty spot. All I could do was shake my head.

We hit a pothole and one of our hubcaps shook loose and sparks clapped from the car's underbelly. The hubcap raced alongside the car passing Taurus Records, Fernandez Beer and Wine, Ali's Roti, and Lenny's Bakery, finally skipping across the avenue to land flat in front of the Morton Street police station.

Apartments sprouted up two, three, and four levels above the first floors of storefront churches, laundromats, tire shops, mini-marts, and mom-and-pop stores. All were stuck together on the strip like gum. Mayor Menino's slogan, "Moving Boston Forward," was pasted on green and white billboards and his posters hung everywhere eyes could see. Satellite dishes jutted out from rooftops and air conditioners drooled down on the sidewalk plants. As we passed over Morton Street, the round red and blue "Open" sign blinked at me in the window of Boston Check Cashers.

We got to the intersection of Blue Hill Avenue and Talbot Street and I focused in on a green van parked to the side, where an old Asian man wearing a wife-beater and dress pants sat cross-legged drinking a bowl of steaming soup and selling jungle-patterned rugs. He looked so peaceful amid all the chaos. We pulled past him and the truck selling discounted soon-to-expire breads and pastries on the corner near the Franklin Field projects, swarming with people. We floated past Fire Station 52 into another stoplight. A group of licorice-black West Indian women wearing blue tank tops and white pleated skirts played netball in Franklin Field as they blared calypso. Pigeons lined the top of Sun Pizza's long red awning.

A flock of geese flew overhead in a sharp V, honking off their clown horns. Ma looked up at the geese and smiled and started drumming the steering wheel as she sang along with the Kirk Franklin playing on the radio, "No more cloudy days, they're all gone away."

I sighed as the light turned green. I looked at Nina as we rode whizzing past the seagulls perched on the black steel fence outside Franklin Park Zoo like skulls on sticks. Every couple of houses, little clusters of black kids sat on their stoops hefting Bibles like suitcases, looking spit-shined and pristine in their mini-tuxes and sequined dresses, waiting their turn to get a dose of the Spirit. As we pulled into Grove Hall, a line of suited black men, all dark-shaded wearing black top hats, strolled across the crosswalk to enter the big mosque.

The number 28 bus cut us off as we pulled into a red light, coughing a trail of black smoke. Ma pumped the brakes, unbothered, and kept singing, "I feel like I can make it! The storm is over . . . now!"

The red light changed to green, and I shook my head as we took off, wishing I believed it was true.

Nana Tanks was asleep when we got to the hospital. Ma talked to the doctor as me and Nina sat quietly beside her bed. The doctor said she'd be released to a rehab facility in a few days and that she'd be able to come back home in a few weeks. After the doctor left the room Ma said a prayer and rubbed some prayer oil on Nana Tanks's forehead and we left too.

When we got home from the hospital, Ma was still acting

weird. She walked into the living room and turned on the afternoon gospel on WILD AM 1090 and sat on the couch still wearing her hat, coat, and gloves.

> We wor-ship youuuu! Hal-le-luuu-jahhhh, hal-
> lelu-jahhh!
> We wor-ship youuuu 'cause you are Goddd!

Ma sang along with the chorus and I heard a loud thud in the living room. I stood up from the kitchen table and she was on her knees, arms stretched toward the ceiling like she was outside on a cliff welcoming the rain or signaling a plane. Her earrings sparkled in the sunlight and her eyes were closed. I could hear her whispering to herself, "Yes, Lord. Yes, Lord. I receive it. I receive it."

The song faded out and the radio cut to a commercial. She snapped out of it and stood up. I didn't even look at her. Every couple of months Ma gets "born again" and charges up on some new divine crusade. She gets her mind set on an idea, any idea, and if you ask her questions about what she's doing she says, "Being led by the spirit," and walks away. When she's like this, there's no reasoning with her. It makes me want to chew off my own fingers sometimes when all I'm looking for is a straight answer.

The last time she pulled this crap, she started waking me and Nina up at five thirty in the morning to sit in the living room, drinking water and praying as a family while old tapes of Bishop Jackson preached in the background. Her crusades never last. After a few weeks, she tires out and things fizzle back down to normal. It's weird, I know, but according to her, if God said so then that's all that matters. Long story short, I could tell she was charging up. With that misty look in her eyes I knew she was about to start acting all brand-new about some life-changing idea. I just hoped it wasn't too drastic.

Everyone gets high, it don't matter the method, one way or another everyone's gotta ease up the pain some way, and Ma's fix comes every Sunday at church. I looked up the hallway and Nina rolled her eyes at me and gave me the finger. The family crisis truce from Nana Tanks's being in the hospital was officially over. We saw her and she was fine. I gave Nina the finger back and she yelled out "Ma!" and I swung my hand down and banged my wrist on the table.

"Yes, Nina?" Ma called back.

Nina laughed and stepped inside her room.

I cradled my forearm between my belly and thigh, and Nina replied, "Never mind."

Ma shrugged her shoulders. "You know what, Andre?"

"What?"

"You need Bible study, Andre."

She pointed at me and I didn't answer her.

"A Friday night Bible study. It'll be good reason to keep y'all reckless behinds off the streets causing trouble. We'll host it here in the living room."

Here she goes talking 'bout "we." I wanted to shake her. A Friday night Bible study hosted at our house? She's crazy, with the way roaches graze all over the place like lazy cows and stampede into the walls and the floorboards whenever any-one turns on the lights or steps into a room. I don't even like having company over. When the house is quiet, sometimes I can hear the mice squeaking in the walls or scurrying around playing jail tag.

I wanted to ask her if she was trying to ruin my rep at school and around the way but I already knew the answer I'd get.

"Don't worry, Andre, you'll see."

Again I didn't answer her.

She grabbed a staple gun, a stack of rainbow-colored construction paper, and a black marker and went into her room. She came back out an hour later wearing a hoodie, sweatpants, and jogging shoes. A rectangle, clearly the stack of construction paper, bulged from her stomach. She gave me a wide-mouthed drunk-on-Jesus smile and strutted into the hallway. She tilted her head down and glanced up, slowly sliding her sunglasses on all dramatic.

"Going for a walk to cover the neighborhood in prayer. Be back soon."

She flashed me the peace sign and walked out the door humming an old hymn to herself.

Maybe if our block was a warm circle cake, it would be just as easy as walking around the neighborhood humming a hymn, waving her arms in the air like magic wands, and her prayers would frost over everything and it'd be all good. The beef between me and Nina would be over. I'd be debt-free and we'd all be at peace, drinking lemonade and smiling. One big happy barbeque and nobody would get the stank-eye for wrapping a plate in tinfoil to take home to eat later. It'd be sunny and beautiful, but Ma ain't dumb, she knows shit don't work that way. She can feel the beef brewing on the block, heating up the sidewalks, she knows it's gonna be a hot summer.

After she left I rode my bike to the store to get some munchies. She walked around the neighborhood every day, I knew her route and avoided it. I peeped the first flyer for the "Battel Bible Study" as soon as I hit the parkway on my way back home from the store. Ma must have lost her goddamned mind, putting our house phone number on the flyer too. She's so corny, she even drew a little lighthouse under the words "Battel Bible Study: Coming soon . . . so tell a friend!" She wrote it all in bubble letters. I looked up the block and the flyers rainbowed at me from every telephone pole I could see up the parkway.

I could already hear the words "Church Boy" ringing in my head.

That's what everyone is going to call me, fucking "Church Boy." I ripped that sign off the pole and rode home, promising myself that the first person to clown me to my face would get an unholy beat down. There were so many signs. I wanted to pull them all down but the last thing I wanted was to run into Ma and for her to see me touching the signs.

When I got home I dropped my munchies off in the kitchen and headed out to the backyard and ducked off into my burning bush to blaze a little before Ma got home. After Papa Tanks yoked me up inside his toolshed I didn't smoke in there anymore. On the other side of our backyard there are some tall pea-green hedges, they're hollow in the middle and at the base there's smooth dirt. The bush hid me from most of the daylight. It makes a good spot to smoke and chill.

I sat in the cool dirt and rolled my blunt. I could hear the weedwhacker buzz of Reggie and the Team Seven niggas on the corner running dirt bikes and four-wheelers up and down the street, playing cat and mouse with the jakes. I was bumping to my favorite Outkast album, *ATLiens,* on my headphones. I finished rolling my blunt and "Wheelz of Steel" came on. I sparked up, inhaled, and blew my smoke up in the air. Andre 3000 sang the chorus,

> Touched by the wheelz of steel . . .
> Now show me how you feel . . .

For whatever reason the words made me think about Tun-netta. The chorus reminded me of that "Feeling Good" song she sang to me before the first time I kissed her. I still remember it's by Nina Simone, though I've never actually heard it.

No matter how loud I turned up my headphones the buzz from the corner seemed to keep getting louder. I wiggled the cord of my headphones, trying to get the full sound to come through to my right ear, and a fly started bopping in and out of my face. I swung a few times and it went away.

As I smoked, my mind started doing Hula-Hoops. With all these urges boiling up inside me it's been hard to act decent. There's so much I used to say I'd never do that I've done. Smoke weed. Smack Nina. Play bitches out like I ain't got a sister of my own. Back then I thought I'd really grow up to be one of the "good niggas" running shit, but I guess we all gotta learn to deal with regrets, don't we? It's like the urges consume me and I don't trust myself not to just act the way I feel. It's all I've been doing lately. No matter how much I tell myself I know better or I'm not going to do something, it's like in the heat of the moment the urges take over. I know it's me doing these things, not them, the urges, but sometimes I wonder who or what's to blame, 'cause what the hell is wrong with me then?

I guess all I'm saying is, I just ain't been too proud of myself these days.

It's funny, 'cause Pop and all my ain't-shit uncles been crossing my mind a lot lately. I wonder if they regret the way they all done fucked over any twinkle of brightness in their dark-ass worlds or if they really just don't give a damn. For me it's a mixture of both, because it's not like I don't know right from wrong, it's just when it really comes down to it I feel powerless over myself sometimes. In the heat of the moment

I don't think too straight and it's not like I don't know I been fucking up lately.

I blew a few smoke rings and watched them spin. The fly came back, but there were a couple of them this time, flying in circles around my head. I swung a few times and missed, but finally I smacked one to the ground and it landed in a ray of light breaking through the hedges. I watched the fly's little legs kicking up at me, begging for a mercy kill. I leaned in closer and wound up my hand to squash it. At this point it sounded like the buzz from the corner was starting to overtake the Outkast. In the little spot of daylight I looked and realized it wasn't a fly in agony, it was a pissed-off bumblebee. It turned over on its side and darted up and stung my neck. I jumped to my feet and head-butted the entire hive to the ground, gaining the whole swarm's attention. I dropped the blunt and started running away and swatting at them but they were everywhere.

I tossed my whole hoodie off as I ran through the backyard. When I got inside the bathroom I swatted at the air making sure all the bees were gone, and they were. In the mirror it looked like I was getting the chicken pox. My whole upper half throbbed. I ran some cold water and sat in the tub letting it wash over me until I didn't feel like I was sitting on a cactus.

Once I gathered myself I moved to the kitchen table with a bag of frozen peaches snugged to the back of my neck, two value-sized packs of pork chops freezing over my chest, and a family-sized bag of steak fries cooling my back.

I was about to read my favorite comic in the Sunday funny papers, *Family Circus*, when Ma got back from her walk and barged straight into the kitchen. She took off her sunglasses and tossed the staple gun on the table. She looked at me and I looked at her. She was sweating, with that look in her eye like she's not even inside of herself.

"Fix your face. What happened to you?" I looked away and didn't answer her. She laughed. "Well, the neighborhood's covered in prayer." She chuckled again. "It is done. They'll come and you will see."

I kept looking away and didn't answer.

I rustled the paper and got back into my bag of Doritos and dropped a few Skittles in my mouth. I head-nodded yes, and didn't speak. She sucked her teeth and walked off to her room. I finished my chips and opened a pack of coffee cakes. Ma called out to me from her room but I didn't hear what she said.

"Huh?"

She didn't answer me.

"Ma?"

She said something again but I couldn't hear her, so I ate the rest of my coffee cakes, then opened up a Mounds and a Twix bar. If you eat them together they taste like them caramel Girl Scout cookies in the purple box.

"Andre, get up from the table and clean your room. And take all that food off your chest and stop being ridiculous." I heard her this time but I was chewing and opening my Mountain Dew when she said it so I didn't answer her.

"Andre!" I rustled free some gummy bears.

"Huh?"

"You gon' stop ignoring me. Now get up from the table and clean your room. Your father gets home soon and we need to start keeping the house clean. And put my damn pork, peaches, and French fries away. What's wrong with you?"

I said okay and put the food back in the freezer and walked into the hallway feeling the stings pulsing on my neck and chest. Nina stepped back out of her room in a red skirt and a black tank top.

"Bye, Ma. I'm going to have dinner up at Stanley's."

She stepped out in front of me and turned on a dime so her long-weave ponytail could smack me as she walked toward the door. I wanted to snatch it off, but didn't with Ma nearby.

"Tell Miss Myra I say hello," Ma said as Nina slammed the door, yelling back, "Okay."

I walked into my room to take a nap.

That Sunday the Bible and the bees marked the start of a really bad period, only darkness to come.

12

Nothing Forgotten

Lately every day feels the same. I wake up hazy-headed, still riding last night's high with a clamp of pressure weighing down my eyes. It only takes a few seconds for the gut punch of cloudy-belly to cramp and bite at my sides, forcing me to hold still. My munchies-soured stomach burps and gurgles. It's always in this lull that I find myself wondering: Andre, who the hell are you becoming? Soon enough the cramps start to loosen and I ask God to help me. I swear to Him that once I get myself out of this mess with Smoke and Reggie I'll quit everything. I'll quit smoking, hustling, and even fucking Tunnetta behind Beezy's back. Not that I feel bad, I'm just saying. Beezy did it to himself.

Tunnetta and I ain't talked for the rest of that school year and that whole summer. In the months we stopped talking I took Reggie's advice and focused more on ball. I heard Tunnetta got around plenty over the summer. Her name was starting to ring bells with niggas in the hallways and in the locker rooms. The word was that she turned into a real community ho jump-off type. Now she don't know how to break it to Beezy that he's nothin' more than a long rebound she don't know how to drop.

After I watched Sade Fulton beat her ass, I tried to act like there was nothing between us, but I felt horrible about how I just walked away from her. As much as I distanced myself and kept away, I couldn't get her out of my head. We were pretty close and I missed talking to her on the phone. Even with all the rumbles about her gettin' around, I still felt like things weren't finished with us. So in the fall when school started back up, I slipped a note in her locker that said, "I'm having Mary & Jane over for an afterschool study session at 4:20, we need your help with math homework. We miss you."

She showed up that day after school in my backyard blushing, but she was a little awkward and standoffish at first. She told me not to get any ideas and that she didn't want to smoke inside the toolshed, so we went off into the woods behind Decker Street. We sat on a big boulder, and as we blazed I apologized for not doing something to help her. She accepted my apology but said she wasn't going to break up with Beezy because he was nice to her. Still, she agreed we could be how we were if I promised not to tell, and just like that we been creeping ever since.

They officially became boyfriend and girlfriend at the end of the summer before the school year started and I got home from a basketball tournament in New York. Since I got back, I been wanting to smack him in his big mouth. He's been stomping around the block and the hallways at school like he's King Ding-a-Ling XL and shit, looking like a damn fool. He be acting like he was shitting on somebody, bagging Tunnetta. Like he can control that cageless bird. I wasn't the only one enjoying her in her free time and I grew to accept that. She ain't my girl and I don't question her about the things I hear about her, same way she don't question me.

In school, ever since Ma made them damn flyers I been trying to lie low and blend into the scene. I sit with the other cats from the basketball team at lunch and avoid any set of eyes that lingers on me too long. I act like I don't know what they're laughing about. Beezy and Tunnetta sit across the cafeteria from the basketball players' table and I be watching this cup-caking motherfucker Beezy kissing her on the mouth, holding her hand under the table like a little bitch. He'd even buy her lunch and let her get a second slice on pizza day for an extra $1.25. It's weird watching how Beezy is for her. When he looks at her it's like she's the only person in the cafeteria, but only it's sicker than that 'cause he looks at her like in her eyes he sees the honey-sweet version of his dreams.

But I don't know what the hell he really sees when he looks at her 'cause how can't he see her flashing the fuck-me eyes to half the niggas sitting at my table? When the bell would ring and we all worked our way back to class Beezy would toss his hand over Tunnetta's shoulder and they'd stroll away, seesawing off to class together. It looked funny how Beezy would damn near be walking on his tiptoes trying to cuff her, and for whatever reason he just didn't seem to see anybody laughing at him. I just be shaking my head and wondering to myself, How do you get like that?

I don't even know why God even bothers blessing me any-more. After the high school basketball season I got ranked seventeenth out of the top twenty-five players in my class in the state of Massachusetts. So now I stay late after school doing workouts in the gym. Basketball's been the only thing that helps ease up all the pressure that's been building up inside me. It's also the only thing I can do right. The weed ain't strong enough anymore to affect how I play. It just don't get me high like it used to. I get out on the court and play off pure instinct and it works. The weed just makes me eat and want to smoke more. Well, I guess that's another reason I been doing extra workouts, 'cause I been sucking wind at practice and Coach said I'm getting bitch-tits and chipmunk cheeks, but when the summer comes I'll be ready. Talent always wins out, and bitch-tits or not I'm going to make Coach eat his words. Plus, I like the walk home better when everyone's cleared out. That way, if Smoke or anyone tries to run up at least I'll see them coming.

While I do my thing at the gym, if anyone comes around looking for trees, I get whatever bags off that I can, then I walk straight home looking at the fallen leaves on the ground while ignoring Ma's Bible study flyers. I been trying to stick close to Reggie, really getting deep on my Team Seven shit. It's starting to feel like a pressure cooker out there on the corner. Sometimes Smoke rides up the street all slow playing his music loud with his tinted windows half cracked like he's 'bout to stop and do something. I love it when Smoke pulls dumb-ass tough-guy moves like this because I ain't scared when I'm with Reggie. I never seen Reggie run from a fight in my life. He's a laid-back cat, but when he gets going he's another kind of animal. The day Reggie put me on with some work, he told me not to worry 'bout Smoke. The way Reggie called it was: me and Smoke have a low-level disagreement about some money. This is, he says, not his business. Reggie and I getting money is his business. If Smoke fucks up my getting the money, then that would force things to become Reggie's business.

I'm probably two weeks away from having this nigga Smoke's sixteen hundred dollars but I got a feeling he don't really want it no more anyway. He wanted the money a long while ago, and Reggie's trusting me on the re-ups now. I've seen Smoke plenty of times and he usually acts like I'm not there at all. He ain't the passive-aggressive type, so I think he's either plotting on me or maybe he wants blood now. Why else hasn't he caught me coming out of school? For some reason, even though Nina's moody and we don't really get along, I don't think she wants to see something happen to me. So I wonder if she's asked him to chill, because when he does acknowledge me there's a certain fire in his glare that says, "Ain't nothin' forgotten."

By the time Ma gets home from work and dinner rolls around, I'm high like I promised God that I wouldn't be. This is how it's been lately. One moment I was riding on top of the softest part of cloud nine and I was so busy looking up that I didn't notice the moment when everything evaporated. Now every day I'm just confused and constantly wondering how I got so caught up trying to be the man that I ended up drifting deeper and deeper into the storm, with the rest of the niggas who be fucking up. It burns me that Reggie was sort of right about what he said to me that day at Kelly Park. Other than hoopin' and playing hopscotch around the block trying to avoid Smoke, I don't know what the hell I'm doing anymore these days.

Pop's back living at the crib with us, which is another mind-fuck all by itself. He came home a couple of weeks ago and if anybody was styling on me it was Pop. Mr. Watson set his job up real proper and I know he's making decent money. Just two weeks after he got home and started working he sold his Bronco and bought himself a white Chrysler LeBaron, a soft-top convertible too. It's used but he cruises around the block with the top down, reggae music blaring, volume on asshole like can't nobody tell him nothing. I be wanting to run my house key up the sides of that car so bad, but I got enough drama these days, not to say that I don't get the urge.

When he first got home I was walking into my bedroom.

Nina and Ma ushered him, huggin' on him like he'd just come back from a war. I heard all the noise of him coming up the hallway, but I wasn't fast enough. Ma was on some bullshit acting like I was a little kid and she could make peace between us. Pop's always kept me at an arm's length and the issues between us run deeper than she'll ever understand. I'm off the porch now, she can play like she don't know, but the window for that man to be a father to me been opened and closed and that was his choice. I was literally inches away from closing my bedroom door when Ma called out, "Andre!" I paused and heard footsteps coming toward my room.

A boot kicked into the crack of my door and I stepped back and opened it and it was like I was looking into a broken mirror. We were face-to-face, me and Pop. My heart sped up and my knees wobbled, but I kept it cool. Never let 'em see you sweat. I looked at the floor.

"Hey, Pop," I coughed it out and didn't look up at him.

"Hi, Andre."

I turned back to close my door when I felt Ma's hand on my shoulder. "Nuh-uh, Andre, give your father a hug."

She stepped beside him and the face she made said she was serious and I looked up and over and Pop was searing a sober glow into my hazy red eyes. He reached out and bear-hugged me and started shaking me like he wanted to pick me up. He clasped his arms around my head and in the noose of his elbows it started feeling like I wanted to tap out. He squeezed my head up against his chin stubble and slowly grated it along the side of my face.

"Remember me? Your dad?" He slipped me into a headlock. "Did you miss me?"

He pulled me tighter and everything slow-motioned in front of me and it sounded like I had water in my ears. He rocked me back and forth and right before I felt like I was going to pass out I stomped on his foot and bucked my back against his ribs, threw a wild punch over my head at him, and he jumped. We looked at each other and I felt nothing for him. He flinched at me and I ran at him and we tangled like crabs in a pot and wrestled until I regained my balance and pushed him back off of me and he fell back against the front door. Nina and Ma were motionless, like statues or figurines. It felt like anything could have happened, and they'd never looked so small to me, huddled together in the kitchen door like that.

Pop stood up huffing and puffing. As I rested my weight on my knees looking up at him, Ma screamed out, "Stop it, you two! Please," and the dryness in her voice was enough to break my heart.

I can only describe the feeling that crackled up my spine as Pop hugged me with his man strength as something close to getting your eyeball crushed inside an eagle talon. He stepped toward me and I threw my fist up, ready to swing, but he could tell I wasn't really ready to throw hands with him. But I was sure pissed enough to try. He stood there looking at me, smiling and winded, and I kept my fists up and backed away, eyeing him the whole way back into my room until I closed my door.

He called out, "Ah, Andre, come on!" Like it was a joke and he can laugh all he wants. Shit ain't no movie, he was lucky Nina and Ma were around or I'd have pulled my shank on him—see how bad he was then. It's all good, though, it ain't over. In every direction I turn, it seems like there's a new person popping up who's got an issue with me, and at this point he can just add his name to the list. If he tries to come at me on some rah-rah billy-bad-ass shit again, he'll get his issue.

―――――――

Since Pop works the day shift for Mr. Watson, Ma set it up so that he takes me to AAU practice on Tuesdays and Thursdays at this fancy-ass private school called Baxter out in Weston. It's about an hour away or forty-five minutes if the highway's clear and there's no construction on Route 9. The ride is always awkward, and I listen to my headphones and act like I'm asleep until we get to the gym. We don't say much more than "hi" and "bye" to each other and around the house we stay out of each other's way. He mostly hangs out in the basement, listening to old records and drinking Heineken. With all that's gone down, you'd think we'd have something to say to each other, right? Sometimes as we ride to practice I can feel him electric-eyeing me all deep like he wants to talk, but I don't play his game.

He drops me off at the gym around seven thirty and peels rubber out of the parking lot, knowing he has two hours to be back to pick me up. He never stays to watch me play like all the other fathers sitting up in the bleachers, holding cups of coffee or straight stealing swigs from a flask. Sometimes he fucks up and comes back too early and comes inside to pee and gets caught up talking to Mr. Watson or some of my other teammates' fathers. The white fathers—businessmen types—seem to like him. I can see their inner laughter under them fake smiles. But Pop hates white people all the same, and I could see the bullshit dripping off him too.

I hated seeing him up there acting like he really had something to do with me, fronting for all the other fathers up in the stands with the sleeves of their dry-cleaner starch-creased white oxfords rolled up, their Brooks Brothers ties hanging slack around their necks. Pop's no angel, but I can't blame him for the way shit is right now. I did it all to myself. I fucked up the money and he ate a charge for me. I know. I remember. But karma and bitch-ass niggas will get you in the same way.

When Ma's not around, all the silence and tension in the house make it feel like being at the library, everybody quietly studying each other, doing their best not to talk unless it's absolutely necessary. Since I clapped Nina we don't hardly speak and when we do she's talking shit. I feel bad for smacking her, but now she's made me a bit nervous ever since, it always seems like she's up to something. She knows if she comes out on the back porch, after Ma's in bed, I'll let her blaze with me, but that don't mean I trust her, 'cause I don't. Right about now I don't trust anybody other than Reggie. Nina's too tricky. Other than the fact that she's sleeping with the enemy, or whatever she terms what she's doing with Smoke, she also be trying to hang around Pop, being all friendly and shit, acting like his spells of doing the right thing ever last. She can call me an asshole all she wants, but I'm not buying it, Pop will never change, he just gets better at hiding the shady bullshit about himself. Just the other day Nina told me she really thinks Pop reformed when he was away and that I should give him another chance. Then again, this is the same girl who believes that every bitch who tells her Smoke is creeping around is a hater. Ma and Smoke's mother, Miss Myra, are friends, and I guess they're trying to be supportive or just ignoring it, in hopes that it'll be a phase and they'll fizzle out. Nina's eighteen, they can't stop them and neither can I, but all I know is I'm sticking to my guns.

Even though Pop and I ride to and from practice together, the closest thing to quality time we share are the nights we're both in back of the house smoking in our separate slices of darkness. Him, sitting down in the backyard on a lawn chair smoking a joint, and me looking down on him from above on the second-story back porch, smoking too. And just like when I used to spy on him and Uncle Elroy, when I was younger, he has no clue I'm up there watching.

Tonight as I sat out on the back porch, midsmoke, Nina swung the back door open all slow so the hinges could squeak, just for effect, and I had the biggest urge to punch her in the nose. She tiptoed out onto the back porch, scaring me half to death, not answering when I called out, "Who's there?" She came outside smirking at me like an asshole and sat down on the recycling bin on the other side of the porch. I told her she plays too much and she snatched the blunt from me and we smoked for a short while.

It was all good until she started laughing and talking 'bout how I better pay Smoke his money before he catches me slipping around the way and airs my shit out. She enjoys fucking up my high. Like I don't know that I've been ducking him like a lil' bitch for the last however long it's been now, and it's been a while. She took a few more drags from the blunt and as she got up to go back inside, out came Pop into the backyard with a six-pack of Guinness, a joint tucked behind each ear, and one in his mouth. Nina walked over to the railing of the porch and squinted at him as he sat down in his lawn chair and sparked up. She looked back at me and whispered, "Ain't that nigga on probation? What's he doing?"

I shrugged my shoulders. "I dunno, being a changed man." I laughed and hit the blunt.

"But don't he get drug-tested?"

"You wanna know so bad? Go ask him." I was being sarcastic but she turned around and said, "I will," and walked inside.

I heard her get halfway down the basement steps before she turned back and went into our apartment. I figured she'd lost the nerve to actually go out there, but I knew she wasn't about to let it go that easily. I don't know what she wants from him, but she refuses to accept that Pop's like a steel vault, and trying to get a straight answer out of him was a waste of time. But Nina's always the one to start some bullshit, drawing unnecessary attention to herself, making shit hot. I'd seen him out there smoking plenty of times but what was I supposed to say to him? I wondered about him getting drug-tested too, but I had no legs to stand on, considering it was my weed that got him on probation in the first place. So I'd just let it be, finished smoking, and went in the house.

The next night I went outside to smoke around eleven. Pop was already on beer number three by the time I got out there. Nina wasn't home yet, it was Friday. Plus she and all her girls graduate soon, so they ride around stuffed inside Smoke's car, smoking, drinking, and generally raising hell around town. The cops let them do it, it's a town tradition for the seniors to race around blaring off their horns, toilet-papering houses, and silly-stringing the sidewalks.

As I sat down to light my blunt, I heard the loud vibration of the subwoofers in Smoke's car, and I knew Nina was home. Pop didn't pay any mind to all the commotion out front until Nina stumbled down the hill into the backyard, giggling with a bottle of Alizé in her hand. I could tell from the sway in her walk that she was drunk. I couldn't even begin to predict what was about to come out of her mouth.

Pop stood up when he heard someone coming, and sat back

down when he recognized it was Nina. Before Pop could get a word out, she started snapping.

"Look at you! Smoking like you ain't on probation and shit. If you go back to jail, what the fuck you think is gonna become of us, huh?"

Pop opened another beer and sat slouched back in his chair, looking off into the next yard like she wasn't there. She continued anyway.

"Maybe if you wasn't so busy trying not to hear me, I'da told you what your son's been up to lately."

She took a big gulp of Alizé and crossed her arms at her chest, gripping the bottle by the neck. Pop didn't look fazed. He sighed through his nose and looked up at Nina, standing in front of him. "You're a pest, you know that?" He took out a joint and lit it. "Y'all live in Milton, not Mattapan—the real hood. Look around you, it's quiet and safe. What are you so mad about?"

I walked over to the railing so I could hear them better.

"So what? You come and go from this place like a cousin from out of town, not our father. That's why I'm mad!"

She paused and took a swig from the bottle.

Nina's good at flipping the script. She can go from one to ten in the snap of a finger.

"What do you think knowing the truth about my life will do for you and your life anyway, Nina?" Pop asked.

Nina laughed, but there was nothing funny.

"What happened to you, Daddy? I at least deserve a straight answer."

She grabbed the lawn chair leaning against the side of the house and sat down in front of him. Pop took a couple drags from his joint, and I saw a burst of light in front of Nina's face as she sparked a blunt of her own, all comfortable like they'd been smoking together for years.

"Ain't no right or wrong answer, really, I just wanna know why the fuck it's so hard for your slippery ass to tell the truth about yourself, coward!"

Pop sat gazing downward and away from Nina, sort of like a little kid being yelled at, though when she said the word "coward" his whole body twitched. He turned in his seat and pointed at her as she exhaled smoke and tossed her head back, taking another big gulp from the bottle. I stood looking down on the two of them, amazed at how fast liquor removes the filter between your brain and your mouth. Before Nina could continue, Pop clapped his hands together and sat up.

"Listen, I can't save you, same way couldn't nobody save me from myself. I just hope whatever it is that's got you burning up gets out of your system with you still in one piece. Look at you, smoking and drinking. You think you're grown? Let's talk like adults then."

He reached down and grabbed another beer and bit the top off and lit another joint. The anger in his voice seemed to soften Nina. She sat quietly waiting for him to speak.

"Doesn't matter what I do in the streets when I'm gone, it's simple. Humans are creatures of habit. A drug addict does drugs, an alcoholic drinks, simply so they can know who they are. Fingers point and pass judgment, always saying, 'Look over there, and over here,' but never in the mirror. What makes you think your life's so tragic?"

Nina leaned toward him and blew a stream of smoke in his face. I almost laughed, I thought he was going to smack her but he didn't. As she sat there smoking her blunt and sipping her bottle, a part of me felt jealous that I wasn't sitting in that chair. All the nights we'd both smoked out there in silence, and she just stumbled down there drunk and got him to give up the goods.

Pop raised his voice, "I may be ignorant, selfish, hardheaded even, but I'm no fool. I've just always been sort of bored with life. I never claimed to be a good or great father. No one forced me to do anything. I've done plenty of bogus things and I've paid dearly for them all."

I don't know what set Nina off about what he'd said but she took the last swig from her bottle of Alizé and smashed it on the ground.

"Fuck that!" She stood up. "Enough jive talkin' like an old-timer. Thought we was gon' talk like adults?"

Nina picked up the broken neck of the bottle and sat back down. Pop looked a bit shocked now, as Nina went on, "You don't see what this shit's doing to Ma. She's pretty much a vegetable after she gets off work, sitting alone in the living room eating burnt popcorn, watching old videotapes of Creflo Dollar, T. D. Jakes, or any other sweaty black man jumping around on BET in the morning selling hope, promising change gon' come."

She tossed the piece of bottle she was holding.

"Dammit, Daddy! Why don't you care?"

Pop looked at her with no emotion in his face and said, "Save me the hysterics, okay? Just know that when the shit hits the fan, and trust me it will, everyone scatters and the trouble is all yours to deal with, and I carry mine! I see you riding in the car with that boy, acting like you're one of them kinda girls."

"What the hell does that mean, 'them kinda girls'?"

"It means, it ain't that hard to cop a habit or make a kid. Now shut the hell up and listen! Clearly we don't know each other very well."

For the first time, I heard something genuine in his voice. I took the last drag of my blunt and ashed it on the railing. He cleared his throat and began, "I was fourteen years old when I showed up in Boston from Jamaica, it was 1974, and Boston was a very different kind of place then. No one thought my accent was cool, people were impatient with me, and I was always fighting because of it. That fall, they desegregated the schools and the busing thing fucked up the city even more. Boston felt like it was going to explode. Shit got out of hand, quick. All the blacks started to band together because groups of white boys from South Boston had been riding around, jumping any brother in sight. Some nights me and your uncles would get loaded drinking Thunderbird and take out our father's car, doing the same thing, jumping out on any white boys in sight. I was one of the most dangerous things on the streets back then, a brother with not a thing in this world to lose."

Nina interrupted him. "Sort of like Andre?"

He laughed, waved his hand, brushing her off, and kept talking, "That kid's nothing like me."

I almost stood up and yelled, "Fuck you," but remember they didn't know I could hear them so I held my tongue and listened, I don't want to be like that nigga anyway.

"I'd do anything in those days and not think twice. Mind you, this was also around the time crack flooded the streets. It came through like daylight, wasn't a place it didn't touch. So there, you want an explanation? Crack, Nina, crack is a major part of what happened to me. When crack touched down, either you were selling it, using it, or doing both. Me and your uncles got real caught up with that stuff."

He paused and opened another beer and lit a cigarette, Nina sat quietly waiting for him to continue.

"Another thing that happened, your Uncle Edgerin, well, he didn't really die in the war like we told you he did. He overdosed on a good batch of that hard Baltimore rock. It was hardly even stepped on. It was his twenty-first birthday and I'd brought it over to his girl Gladys's spot to celebrate. I took the first hit of the night, and I'd never had a batch of rock that pure. It made my heart start kicking at my chest and I felt thumping in my earlobes. The veins in my eyes pulsed, I remember hearing a low ringing and my whole body got hot. Really, I thought I was having a heart attack, but then it all stops, and it's over. Smoking that rock with your uncle that night was one of the best and worst nights of my life. As soon as I came down, I wanted it again, but I was scared because I already loved it too much. Your uncle was already in way too deep with the stuff and he hit it extra hard that night. We all took one last blast before I went home for the night, and I guess none of us ever quite knew when enough was enough. After Edgerin took that last hit, he dropped the pipe on his chest and slouched over to the side. Me and his lady thought he'd nodded off into a dope nap, but nope, he'd expired right there in front of us and we were too happy being high to realize it in the moment."

He lowered his voice and leaned toward Nina and said, "Do you have any idea how it feels to hand your brother the rock he'll use to end his life with? Around that time I thought I'd reached the bottom, but I still had some falling to do. The morning he died, I quit cold turkey. I just stopped. It all hit too close to home. I got all righteous and shit, said I wouldn't give my life to a pipe." He finished his beer and laughed. "I was young. I started going to service on Sundays, and that's when I really started getting into music. I played the drums at church, that's where I met your mother. I was at my best then. She sang in the choir, and with her I got the rare feeling of being at home. But we married young, too young really, and I'll never marry again unless I meet a woman who can keep me in the house, truthfully. I was clean up until a little bit after you were born. I'd passed the postal exam and started working at the post office. This is when your mother still believed in my ability to overcome, but she had no idea how bad it could get with me. Somehow I confused her into believing I could beat the odds and blow the Boston reggae scene wide open, but I fell short. Me and your uncle Duval had a band and we built up enough steam to put together a little local circuit tour down in Florida. It was supposed to be our big break, but life never happens how you want it to. I asked for two weeks off from work but they laughed me out of the human resources department. So I said fuck it, told your mother the time off was approved, and me and the boys packed up the van and hopped on 93 south, heading toward Florida. And right in the back of that smelly old van, I broke. Duval had some rocks and we smoked 'em, and just like that I was sucked right back into the life. Never say never, protect yourself. It was an impulse, a disappointing impulse too. Smoking rock wasn't as great as I'd remembered. But I smoked it and I was back. I didn't like being that out of control, but I was. Once you take that blast, crack is the boss, and you do as it says. That second voice in your head starts talking to you, and you're now under its control, you're no longer yourself anymore. When you wake up, it's the first thing you think about and sometimes you hear that voice in your dreams. The voice calls for devotion and undivided attention. It's a shitty relationship, you wish you didn't love the motherfucker so much or else you'd leave it alone and never come back. And every time you find yourself back exactly where you don't want to be, you hate yourself a little more and trust yourself a little less. We only played three shows before we ran out of money and started squatting at this groupie chick's trailer. Even though I knew I was fucked, I kept telling myself it was just a treat and that I'd get back straight tomorrow, or the next day. I kept telling myself, 'Today I'm going back home,' but when you get strung out the days pass like minutes and months pass like weeks and all that voice is screaming at you is 'More! More! More!' and like I said, you listen."

He paused to light another cigarette, and I heard Nina sniffling, but I couldn't see her good enough to know if she was crying. I thought he was done talking but he dove back into his story.

"One night Duval said he wanted me to try some new shit with him, and when I saw the needle and the band around his arm I was shook. I don't like needles, but the first time I speedballed, I was in love all over again. I didn't know where I was or what was going on. I woke up six months later and called your mother one day and just cried into the receiver of the pay phone. Crack is one thing, but that heroin is the dark side of the street. Shooting up had become like a job and I was tired. Your mother kept saying, 'Baby, where are you? Baby, it's okay,' and I couldn't even make my lips form the word 'Sorry.' Your mother sent me a bus ticket back to Boston, but no cash 'cause she knew what I'd do with it. When you get strung out you end up staying somewhere a lot longer than you expect.

"See, babygirl, there was a time in my life that I turned it all around and then I went and fucked it all up, and the best I can do is believe that maybe one day I'll find the strength to do it again. All I'm saying to you, Nina, is everybody's got a bag of demons to deal with, all different kinds of stuff. So before you go blaming me for everything wrong with your life, remember we can all blame but we all gotta deal. So if you find yourself in a fucked-up spot in life, just make sure it was *you* who put you there."

I had goose bumps. It almost felt like he was talking to both of us. He leaned back in his chair and smoked his cigarette. The silence felt thick. The only sound was Nina clearly crying, and the crickets. After a short while she whimpered out, "Thanks, that's all I wanted."

In a way it's kind of what I wanted too, but he told the story to her, not me. She stood up with her arms wide like she wanted to give him a hug and I went back inside the house. With all the same neighborhood issues hanging over my head, something inside me just wasn't quite as moved.

13

Smoked Out

School let out in early June and now it's the twelfth of the month and it feels like everyone's been whispering about the "Battel Bible Study." Nobody's clowned me outright to my face about it yet but I'm waiting, and since me and Beezy been on some frenemy shit and Chucky's busy with baseball, I been kicking it over on the nicer side of town with Aldrich Watson. With the whole Smoke situation, I been wishing nighttime didn't pause for day. Every time I step out the house I feel myself sliding on the last grains of sand falling through the hourglass. If I can just make it until the fifth of July then I'll be gone hooping with my AAU team for the rest of the summer.

I got Smoke's money but I been a little too nervous to go and give it to him. I asked Nina to take it to him for me and she refused. And Reggie don't mention it, and I don't say anything to him about it because the last thing to be wearing out here is a coward-heart on your sleeve. I had a growth spurt a while back, and my size alone makes most niggas think twice. Only thing is, if that problem don't think twice, then it's indeed a big, big problem. A problem big enough to crush me. It'd be like the steam coming off the concrete after the rain: I could try and run from it but not for long.

I don't even bother talking to God anymore. With the way I be getting down, what's the point? I stay high, hazy, and all smoked out. I'm smoking more through force of habit, but

I hardly even get that high. I still be hustling, me and Pop still don't really be talking, and Nina still talks shit. Nowadays when I be getting wit' Tunnetta I be taking out all my stress on her. Sometimes I feel bad, but other times I can't help hating her for the way she carries herself and how we could never be anything. She does her bouncing around from nigga to nigga, but she always comes back to me. I tried to explain the situation to Reggie but he told me, "Some broads don't like nice guys, sometimes they needs niggas like us to come through and fuck up their worlds. Don't trip, lil' homie." So I just let it ride. I think Beezy caught wind of how Tunnetta's been getting down because he been mean-mugging me more lately and we don't speak no more. It's all hand pounds and head nods between us.

The first Bible study is still a few days away and I don't want to go. Ma doesn't know that yet. I been chilling by Aldrich Watson's crib, staying out of harm's way, acting like I'm really into *Dragon Ball Z* and going to their country club, chilling with the other high-siditty folks from Milton. I even been caddying golf there too. Don't knock the hustle, it ain't hard work. All I do is carry the bag of clubs and walk just far enough away from whichever golfer from the country club decides to take me out. If I'm hiding out, I might as well be getting paid.

All the members are some kind of important person and they always invite other important people over to the country club to golf with them. It's not what I thought it would be, I don't need to know the clubs because I put the bag down and the golfer picks his club himself. Really I'm just a tracker. They send me off a far distance to forecaddie when they're teeing off, I mark where my golfer's ball lands and wait for the group to make it up the hill and he picks his club. That's it, eighteen holes and it's done. I'm usually a shade or two darker from roasting under the sun, but golfers tip well.

Plus I like to listen to all the big-boss shit-talk them rich old cats talk to each other on the course. It's some higher-level shit-talking, not like the smack we talk on the basketball court, in the barbershop, or on the corner. Them rude old rich dudes talk shit in the form of questions and it seems like everything is fair game. It's like politics, they ask loaded questions and try calmly to answer them. Questions like "What number wife is this one?" "Is your daughter still in rehab?" "That sissy-boy of yours come out yet?" They ask each other the craziest shit with the straightest faces. Besides the boss-talk, the best part of caddying is listening to the golfers trying to one-up each other, especially when they get going about their kinky-ass fucked-up sex lives.

It seems like the minute one of them rich old bastards gets away on a business trip there is always a secretary or a waitress or a bitch from a bar that wants to fuck the money out of their pockets. They egg each other on, grinning, nodding, and winking at each other, making eyes with me to confirm that we all know these stories are a bunch of lies.

Some days I lie and say I am going to Aldrich's and walk down to Mattapan station and get on the bus, riding from avenue to avenue by myself, court-hopping or trying to sneak into the YMCA. Other than doing workouts, playing in the city is the only thing that helps me get my game up. After I got ranked I earned myself a nickname in the parks. Folks started calling me "Dreidel" because they say I be leaving cats spinning when I handle the rock. I like playing streetball in the city parks much better than organized ball; no blood, no foul is the only rule. You gotta have heart enough to hold your own playing out on the blacktop. Like when I slash across the lane and catch the ball in traffic and put it on the floor and it feels like I'm trying to bust through a gauntlet. I cup the rock to my chest like a fullback and dip my head and stutter-step through the lane, and when I see the tiniest bit of daylight I come up for air and focus, gather my weight, square my hips, and render my angle. I find the little red box and explode, teardroppin' it home.

If I make it, and most likely I will, when I land someone's getting screamed on, chest to chest, nose to nose. If I slip up and don't make it, then it was a foul, but I won't call it. Unless it's game point and when I call it, I call it like I mean it, like I'm ready to smack the mouth of anyone who feels any different, but usually there's no need to take it there. Generally in the park, the guy defending you calls foul for you, if he's got any decency. Ain't no pretty-boy shit, though. Don't fall out of bounds and grab your wrist sounding like a dog biting down on a squish toy talking 'bout a "foul." That's what causes fights. If it's really a foul, the whole court stops play because your defender's usually helping you up off the pavement. Shake hands, check ball, play on. That's the difference between hooping in Milton and playing in the city—that's where all the heart's at.

Around the way, Reggie and Smoke both stepped it up to selling coke now, and it seems like every nigga in Team Seven is clipped up and gat touting except for me. I could get my hands on a burner if I really had to go there, but I'm good with my chrome flick-knife for now. If Ma found a gun in our house, she'd probably shoot me with it. Milton's really not that kind of place. Some guys try and act hard because they know somebody in a hood in Boston, but generally it don't go too much past a fistfight, or maybe somebody getting jumped. But I can't front, though, all these guns around here are starting to make me nervous.

When I'm in the house, if it wasn't for Nana Tanks, I don't know what the hell I'd do. She's the only one who still laughs and jokes with me and treats me like a normal person. She don't know the half about me, though. If Papa Tanks told her about our little run-in inside his toolshed, she sure as hell don't act like it. She still tells me, "Andre, you're a nice boy," and pats me on the head and I smile playing along with her.

After I come in from playing ball I sit with her, rubbing my sore knees with Cofal. I'm not really sure what Cofal is, but Nana and Papa Tanks seem to use it to cure everything from muscle aches to upset stomach. It's sort of like Bengay but stronger, and sometimes Nana even puts a scoop in her tea if her cough is bad enough. Anyway, she tells me stories about all the madness and drama that went on back home in Costa Rica.

If I go upstairs and she's watching her evening *novelas* on Telemundo, I know not to say anything until a commercial break. She'll be sitting eager-faced on the edge of her seat, thinking out loud with her whole body, yelling at the TV in Spanglish. She's always trying to warn her favorite characters about what's going to happen to them, which for some reason she always knows. Nana Tanks just has a way about her, always trying to look out for somebody.

About a week ago she was sitting in her comfy chair when I walked into her room to rub my knees with Cofal. It was Saturday night and Reggie and them weren't out on the corner. I knocked on her door and she smiled at me as I walked in.

"Sit, my dear. Take off your baseball cap." She studied me

from head to toe as I hung my hat up besides Papa Tanks's. She eyed me and her nostrils puffed out and her forehead coiled up.

"Why you keep yourself rough so like Barabbas? Ya hair don't brush and you smell like sow." I sat on the edge of her bed and opened the canister of Cofal. "Why you don't cut your hair like a nice boy, Andre, ya don't see ya mudda go' start up Bible study?" She reached over and cupped my chin in her little palm and looked me in the face. I met her eyes and respectfully looked away. Her hand was warm and tender on my chin and I smirked.

"That's not it, Nana, I just haven't had ten bucks to cut my hair, but I'm sure Ma will give me ten bucks Friday when she gets paid and I'll get it cut for Bible study." I gave her a kiss on the cheek, "Okay, Nana?" I stood up and held her hand.

Nana Tanks sat back in her chair. I hadn't thought about it before Nana Tanks brought it up, and wasn't in the mood for being questioned. She looked up into my face and I could tell she wasn't mad but genuinely confused. Ma talks about us "new age kids" and how she doesn't understand us, but Nana Tanks really did come from a different place in time. But the truth is, I guess I'd been avoiding the barbershop. There's always a long wait and what better place to get caught slipping?

The week of the first Bible study we were in the middle of our first heat wave of the summer and it was officially on and poppin'. I could feel the trouble coming, it was like a cloud swelling up over my head, growing bigger and bigger. I been watching Nina super close because with the way she's always warning me about Smoke, I think she might be scheming on

me too. Sure, she called Ma and told her I hit her and h
was acting "bad" in the streets, but I know Nina, she's vici
Her, Aldrich, and Tunnetta are the wild cards in this wh
mess. They're all dumb and think they're smart, never rea
ing how close they are to real danger until the shit is actual.
in their nostrils.

Reggie and my Team Seven niggas called Aldrich a dick-
rider the last time I brought homie to the block. I should've
known that running with this petrified-black nigga was
gonna get me caught up. He's just so damn thirsty to be up
under niggas, but he's got not a drop of common sense.

All week, Smoke and his boys posted up on their end of
the street and we held down ours. The girls wore hardly any
clothing and played in front of the water spraying from the
busted water hydrant in the middle of the block. All the old
folks sat in the house watching the Maury Povich show or
whatever other talk show helped them pass the day and keep
their brains off of waiting for the other shoe to drop. The
whole block seemed on edge 'cause of the heat wave, everybody sitting around sort of aggravated like something bad
just happened, but nothing ever did except some old folks
getting heatstroke or sun poisoning. Yet everyone flocks to
the supermarket and stuffs their cabinets full of canned food,
candles, and bottled water, like there's ever really a way to
prepare for trouble or rough times.

The day the dark cloud over my head exploded, it was like
the perfect storm and felt like watching a nurse jab a needle
into my arm, nothing could ready me for the sensation. It
was the first Friday of Bible study and the eighth straight day
of ninety-five-degree-plus weather. Ma was on fire, floating
around in a trance and being led by the Lord. Nana Tanks
spent all day downstairs helping Ma clean our apartment.

They baked brownies, fried chicken wings, and made a jug of Kool-Aid. Nana Tanks got tired and sat down as Ma sprayed down the house with a can of "Country Fresh Scent" Raid roach spray, and Nana Tanks took mercy and offered up their living room and front den upstairs to host the Bible study. Nana Tanks was just like that.

After she told Ma to host the Bible study in their place, she went upstairs and called down and told me to come up to her room. I walked into her room and there was a ten-dollar bill sitting on the edge of the bed.

"Come, sit down, babylove." She smiled at me and whispered, "You need haircut."

She pushed back and looked up at me from her comfy chair.

"Woiy, you getting big so. How many girlfriends you have now?" She smiled, started shaking my wrist. "Come on, you can tell Grandma."

I laughed and said, "Other than my basketball, I don't have any girlfriends, Nana."

She looked me in the face and folded her arms. "No girlfriend?" Her lips sunk deep into her denture-free jaws, her eyes narrowed, and she turned her head and looked up at me sideways, "A big broad-chest boy like you, with jacket-shoulders and no girlfriend? You don't like boys, do you?" She pointed up at me and leaned in like she was telling me a secret, "I don't like boys that like boys." She said it low.

I shook my head, "Whoa, no, Nana. I don't like boys."

Her face loosened and she said, "Good," and perked back up and handed me the ten-dollar bill.

"Be a nice boy, Andre, and go get a haircut so you can find yourself a little girlfriend."

I took the money and my pants sagged as I stood up and the edge of my boxer shorts peeked out from under my T-shirt.

Nana Tanks grabbed the waistband of my jeans, yanked them up, and hissed. I pulled my jeans up and she let go.

"Why you sag your pants like the ruffian on the corner? Don' make Grandma have to vex now. Wear your pants on waist, like nice boy." She rested her elbow on the arm of the chair, hunched over, and gave me a look that shrank me down a few inches. Then she pointed again. "Because even when I'm dead and gone, I'll come back down from heaven and pull them back up." She broke a grin at me and I laughed.

I stood and gave her a kiss on the forehead and she hugged my upper shoulders. She looked up at me and said, "Ya know Grandma love you, right?" and squeezed my hand.

"I know, Nana. I love you too."

"Remember what I said, ya hear?" She leaned back and closed her eyes.

I said I would and gave her another kiss on the forehead and walked out the door heading downstairs. She turned up the Telemundo and shimmied herself comfortable so she could fade off into a nap.

Fifteen minutes after I got downstairs, Nana must have woke from her nap and forgotten she'd given me the money because she called downstairs and started complaining to Ma about my hair and Ma made Pop give me ten dollars to get a cut, which I gladly took.

I could tell Ma was nervous that nobody was going to show and that the whole thing would be a big divine joke and she'd look like a fanatic or a fool around the neighborhood. As I got ready to walk to the barbershop I heard Ma call Mr. Watson and set up plans for Aldrich to meet me at the barbershop and walk back to the house with me for Bible study. Ma's not dumb. I think she could tell I was up to something. Aldrich grates on my nerves, but it's not his fault his folks brought him

up so square it hurts. His parents only let him come to Mattapan when he was with me, and it was like a field trip for him.
She saw me wearing my basketball gear under my clothes, but
it wasn't going to stop me. It was smart thinking on her part,
put a snitch candidate like Aldrich with me. I'd never even
mentioned not coming back in front of her but she's tricky like
that. But she can't stop me. If I don't want to come back for
Bible study then I'm not going to. The worst she could do is
beat me, and I take harder hits at the park.

As I walked to Mattapan Square all of Ma's flyers blew in
the wind. Some of them had been tagged over by this point.
People had started drawing penises and tits and anything
else that went against the idea of a Bible study. The flyers
were faded and worn, flapping against the telephone poles
and laughing at me. I started hearing a chorus singing the
words "Church Boy" in my head and I wanted it to stop, but I
couldn't shake the thought. I'd reached the point of no return.
I had seventy dollars in my pocket, twenty of which I didn't
need in the first place, and about a half ounce of bud tucked in
my sock. I always walk with at least fifty bucks on me to make
sure I'm good for the day. I really ain't need their change.

When I got to the shop, it was empty and my barber Keon
was sitting in the chair half asleep. He wiped his face all fast
and got me in the chair and scraped me up sharp. He asked
me if I wanted a design in my hair and I said yeah and told
him to surprise me, and he carved the three-stripe Adidas
logo on the side of my head and I asked him to write my street
ball name. He wrote "Dreidel-17" in cursive. I think he tried
to carve out an actual dreidel but it ended up looking more
like a tornado.

Aldrich got to the shop a few minutes later. He kept telling
Keon how "cool" my cut was and I heard Keon ask him if he

wanted a design too and he blurted out, "Yes!" I rolled my eyes. The shop was starting to fill up and I watched ESPN on the big screen in the front. Before I knew what happened, Keon was spraying Aldrich's head down with hair sheen and as he spun Aldrich around in the chair and the spray cleared I looked at the side of Aldrich's head and the dick-rider really got the same exact haircut as me, only his said "Big Al."

It was too late to do anything. Aldrich smiled at me all stupid. I iced Keon and looked him off, shaking my head at the floor. Clippers in hand, Keon tossed his arms up and said, "Ay, youngblood." I looked at him as he dropped the clipper heads in some disinfectant cleaner and turned his back to me. "He asked me for one too. Don't look at me like that."

Aldrich grinned at me.

"What? You don't like it?" He paid Keon and got out of the chair and walked over to me. "Wanna get a slice before Bible study?" I wasn't really hungry but if the bitch-nigga was paying, why not? It'd give me a minute to figure out how to ditch his ass. I couldn't show up with the asshole having matching haircuts, that's suspect like shit. Nina does that kind of stuff with her girls. They have certain days when her and all her girls wear the same outfit in different colors. Reggie and them already think Aldrich's a nut-rider.

We walked to Mattapan House of Pizza, got a couple of slices, and sat down to eat. I'd already cemented my decision to walk over to Mattapan station so I could catch the trolley over to Ashmont and catch a bus from there and court-hop the night away. It didn't matter if I wasn't there in Nana and Papa Tanks's living room to defend myself from the whispers and name-calling that I knew was coming. In the tangle of the grapevine my name'd been steady collecting dirt.

As we sat eating our slices of pepperoni, I debated whether

I should ditch Aldrich or try to convince him not to go to Bible study and to ride out with me.

It was five thirty and Bible study started at eight. Ma wanted me home by six forty-five. Then the bells above the door jingled and I looked up and in walked Beezy with Tunnetta's bucket-head ass seesawing up to the counter all awkward, acting like they didn't see us.

Aldrich laughed and whisper-shouted, "Cupcaking," and then he put his cap to the side of his face like Beezy and Tunnetta wouldn't know which one of us said it. He was looking guiltier than O. J. Simpson. He looked at me laughing like I was supposed to laugh. See, Beezy ain't really a fighter but he'd fold Aldrich's punk ass and I really didn't want to have to explain what happened to Aldrich to his dad. Beezy turned around and flashed us a look and I could tell he was ready to start putting on and acting stupid, like he was down to fight a nigga for trying to pull his card in front of the wifey. Aldrich wiped a greasy napkin stained red with pizza sauce across his mouth and leaned in toward me, whispering, "Seriously, though, she ain't half bad, man. She's a good look for him."

I felt a jolt in my veins, tried to leave it alone, and wagged my hand at the wall. I couldn't. I sighed and said, "Man, Beezy share that girl. Who ain't been wit' her? A girl like Tunnetta is more for niggas than a nigga's girl. Ya dig what I'm saying?" I said it just loud enough for Aldrich to hear me, and his eyes lit up. He thought about it and then his lip folded down low, stretched the length of his jaw and got crowbar stiff, and he said, "Really?" He began picking at an island of pimples that covered his left temple, and then he squinted at me all skeptical. He started biting his fingernails.

"You hit it?"

I waved him off again. "C'mon, man. Don't ask damn questions."

Aldrich started laughing and leaning in, looked m the face, cackling like a fucking weirdo. He kept rep "Didya? Didya?" I moved back but he stood up lear me and when I smelled the sourness of his breath I reach and smacked him in the forehead. He yelped out "Owwww!" and held his face. Beezy and Tunnetta both turned around and I made eye contact and she smirked at me. Aldrich caught her little smirk and kept laughing. "I saw that. What was that? You hit it, didn't you? She ain't half smile at me."

I clamped my jaws and growled, "Dawg! Cut. The. Shit." He stopped laughing.

See, this is when urges start to boil up and all that "Fuck-you" in my blood begins to turn me cold and I feel like I'm the hardest motherfucker alive. I try to think of good things, and I hear Nana Tanks's little voice bouncing wall to wall in my head saying, "Andre, be a nice boy," but then them urges quiet her and something inside me screams, "What the fuck for?" Then I recall a line that Bishop Jackson said during church a couple months ago: "It's easier to ask for forgiveness than per-mission." And I added a line of my own: "Right, wrong, or in between, who defines that shit anyway?" The voice screams louder and louder until I find myself just doing what I feel. For a second I stopped and thought about me and Tunnetta, what we were and what we weren't. How things started out so sweet and simple, then how time oh-so-gracefully revealed our situation for what it really is, and regardless of our atti-tudes, what mean-mugs get exchanged or what we say and don't say. Me and Tunnetta got an understanding, and that's just how we do.

When Tunnetta walked back from the counter with her food, I belched and she looked at me. We made eyes and she smiled like she ain't already see me. She put down her food and I waved to her and like a boomerang she started to walk over to our table. And Beezy tucked his dick between his legs and watched Tunnetta walk away. Aldrich was so thirsty, giggling and looking back and forth between me and her. He damn near drooled on himself when Tunnetta said, "Hey, y'all," and put her cell phone on the table. She had a pink scrunchie around her wrist and she reached up and pulled her hair up into a ponytail. Then she smiled and picked up her cell phone.

"Y'all going to Bible study? I'm excited about it." She said it with that sweet Southern drawl and gave me one of them syrupy looks that got me caught up messing with her in the first place.

Aldrich blurted out, "Me too, I'm pumped. We're walking there right after we finish our slices. Wanna walk with us?"

Of all the shit in the world he could have said, he had to say that. She grinned and looked back at the pout on Beezy's face and sighed. She said, "Maybe," then popped her hips and poked out her ass as she walked back over to Beezy. She sat down and opened up her Pepsi and gently placed her hand on top of Beezy's and they locked eyes and he smiled. She had Beezy roped, he was her little bitch. Guess some niggas' junk really is the next nigga's treasure.

We stood up to throw our crust away and Beezy looked at me and said, "See you at Bible study, Andre." And he chuckled and then coughed and said, "Altar boy," under his breath. I heard what he said and froze. It seems he'd grown balls. I walked over to their table and Tunnetta started fidgeting with her purse. Beezy looked away, all suspect and shit, and said nothing. Aldrich must have heard it too because I could hear him chuckling behind me. I reached down and snatched Tunnetta's cell phone off the table and said, "You ready?" I picked up her Pepsi and swigged down the lump that was swelling in my throat. She looked at the floor, stood up, and the three of us started walking toward the door. And, like a true bitch, Beezy threw out the rest of his slice of pizza and trailed behind us.

We got outside and started walking back toward Milton. I looked at Aldrich and whispered, "See, he share that girl." Aldrich started laughing like a fucking idiot, jumping up and down in front of me on the sidewalk, blocking my way. I pushed him and he turned around and I looked at the back of his head and remembered the asshole got the same haircut as me.

Tunnetta looked and said, "Dang, y'all are too cute," and then said to me, "Can I have my cell phone back now?"

Beezy caught up with us and chimed in, "Yeah, nigga, give her her phone."

Beezy smiled at me and his bitch ass still thinks he can give me that smile. It irks me that after he wanna act all cute for the whole fuckin' pizza shop he still thinks our shit's sweet. Aldrich shut his mouth and stood next to Tunnetta as Beezy stepped up in my face. I remember seeing the roundness of Beezy's fat face and it's like I blinked and all the "Fuck-you" spilled over and the urges weren't just urges anymore. I swung at Beezy so fast he didn't even have a chance to put his hands up. He fell to the ground and Tunnetta screamed, "Oh my God, Andre, stop!"

She ran over to Beezy, who was splayed out on the concrete kicking his right leg and making a weird groan. Tunnetta knelt down and cradled his head in her lap and she started crying, calling all kinds of attention to herself as she shook Beezy until he started blinking. Tunnetta helped Beezy stagger up to his feet and before he could even stand he was running his mouth.

"You done fucked up now," he yelled.

Tunnetta stepped up and cried, "Andre, gimme my damn cell phone!" and charged at me like she'd lost her marbles. To avoid the crowd that was slowly starting to gather, I ran across Blue Hill Avenue into Mattapan station and waited for the next trolley leaving for Ashmont. Aldrich, Beezy, and Tunnetta chased after me the whole way there, and Beezy busted his ass and fell when him and Tunnetta made it to the platform. She helped him up and they sat hugging each other on the bench. Tunnetta pretended like she could really hold Beezy's ass back if he wanted to get up and do something, and he let her.

As the trolley pulled up Beezy yelled, "I'm telling Smoke, nigga. You watch." He kept repeating it. I turned around and looked at them both. Tunnetta was pink-faced and puffy-eyed and Beezy's left eye was already starting to swell. Aldrich stood next to me waiting for the trolley, breathing all heavy, saying, "Dawg, what happened back there?" The trolley stopped and the doors dinged open and the people flooded out. Tunnetta screamed, "Gimme my phone!" and I pushed past Aldrich, got on the trolley, and took a seat. The doors closed and the trolley's engine revved up and the driver rang the bell. As we pulled off I took one last glance at the three of them looking like bums in the station, Beezy and Tunnetta sitting on a bench and Aldrich at the edge of the platform screaming, "Where you going?"

I sat up and looked forward as the trees canopied overhead and cast a green darkness on the trolley. I didn't answer him because I didn't know the answers myself. I had no idea where I was going or what happened back there. I thought hitting Beezy would have felt different. For as long as I'd wanted to slug him for all those times he gave me that grin and all the times he tried to style on me with Tunnetta, I didn't feel too much better. It felt like I jammed every single joint on my right hand. When I saw Beezy struggling with Tunnetta in the train station and heard her scream, I felt like a monster.

I'd also never felt more alone. Beezy knows better than to jump up in my face like an idiot. There's no way I could show my face inside that Bible study now. I just wanted to go somewhere and smoke some bud—someplace where nobody knew anything about me, not even my name. The last thing I heard Aldrich yell before the trolley got completely out of the station was, "Man . . . Dre! What am I supposed to tell your mama?" He was asking all the right questions. I just didn't have answers. Big vines, shrubs, and weeds overgrew the rusty metal fence running alongside the track. The driver touched the brakes and the trolley's wheels screeched a hiss of metal kissing metal.

The driver slowed down and rolled through the Capen Street stop, a request-only stop. As we picked up speed it sounded like the power went out or something. There was this stillness in the car. Nobody was talking louder than a whisper and for some reason as I sat breathing the musty trolley air it felt like someone had just died. Everybody looked tired, defeated, and unfriendly, like they'd really rather be elsewhere.

Someone pulled the line to request a stop and I flinched when I heard the ringer go off. I squeezed Tunnetta's cell phone with my right hand and it felt like a bunch of little needles were rolling around inside my knuckles. I tucked my hurt hand in my lap as the trolley powered down and we swayed into the Valley Road stop.

I kept flexing my hand and balling it into a fist, but the pain only got worse and my wrist felt stiffer. I started trying to figure out how to work Tunnetta's phone so I could read her text messages when an old brass-skinned coolie man limped up to me with his cane and stopped. He smelled like something fried and curried with a hint of mothballs and I looked away, but he tapped my shoulder.

"Can I beg you a seat, my youth?"

I didn't answer him, I just stood up and let the little man into the seat beside me. I heard a loud sports muffler burn rubber and a car cut off the trolley as we began to pull out into the busy intersection on Central Avenue and Eliot Street. The trolley driver tooted his horn and pumped the brakes, and the whole car stutter-stepped and everyone jolted forward. I reached for the bar on the chair in front of me but I grabbed with my hurt hand and lost my grip. My weight shifted and I wobbled onto the old brass-skinned white-haired coolie man sitting next to me. The old man's cane clacked against the wall and then he sighed like I'd crushed all the wind out of him.

The trolley straightened out and I still had my arm snugged around the old man's shoulder as I regained my balance. I looked down at his little trembling body and I held the man's bony frame still, like I was steadying a bag of golf clubs.

"Sorry, sir," I said, looking down at all the sharp silvery white hair growing out of the old man's ears. He flapped his elbows and slithered out of my grip and gave me a strange look, like I was trying to do something funny to him. He looked me off and cleared his throat as he shrugged his shoulder, tossing up a hand to acknowledge my apology. Tunnetta's phone vibrated in my lap and I used my good hand to click open a new text message from Beezy.

> You done fucked up now. Nigga you know you shouldn't of did that. You know that's coming right back around.

I closed the text message.

I looked across the trolley at a woman with bald-headed twins sitting on her lap. They were both letting out the sound of pure baby joy. They weren't angry or tired, they were both intrigued, the boy trying to steal the keys from his mother's red leather purse and the little girl completely consumed with trying to get the cap off of her mother's green bottle of Mountain Dew. Both of their big bald doughy heads bobbled in different directions as we trolley-chugged along. They looked at each other as they played, almost like they were racing to something, but it was a friendly race because they were giggling with their unformed wiggly slack baby smiles.

The phone vibrated again, and again it was Beezy.

> . . . and MY girl wants her phone back, dickface.

At first I chuckled 'cause he called me a dickface. Who says that? Beezy's always been a clown, since we was kids. But Smoke's a live wire, and then I thought the only reason Beezy be acting tough is 'cause this only pours fuel on the fire I already had with Smoke.

As the trolley rolled along I looked out at the thick patches of pine trees whizzing past in the window and I sat wondering to myself, What would Reggie do? Reggie's the realest cat

I know. He always has the right answers even when I don't want to hear them. He always holds me down. He could've tripped on me 'bout how I starting dealing with Smoke before him, but instead he held me down and blew a cloud of smoke in my face and said, "Hardheaded niggas learn the hard way," and he tossed me the product.

The driver rang the bell and the overhead speakers scratched and squealed PA fuzz as the driver announced, "Butler station. Please exit to the right."

The trolley doors stayed open, letting in all the hot air as the trolley driver got out to help an old man get his wheelchair onto the handicap lift. I watched the overweight white man slowly rise into the car. The trolley began to vibrate as we pulled away from the Butler Street stop. I'd seen the cemetery on the trolley ride between Butler and the Cedar Grove stop before, but now it gave me a bad feeling as I looked at all them tombstones.

We pulled into Cedar Grove and the trolley idled a second without the doors opening. The trolley's engine let out a big sneeze and then the doors opened. I don't know how the fuck he'd pulled it off, but when them doors opened I saw Beezy standing there with his swollen eye turning all kinds of weird colors. He was standing next to Smoke. His boy Kendrick and Tunnetta and Aldrich were all standing there behind them.

There was no games. It was straight business. Smoke hopped up in the doorway of the trolley and looked at me like we'd never met. I flinched back against my chair and looked side to side. There was nowhere to go. I caught eyes with the old man sitting next to me, and he shifted his body away from me and looked out the window, two hands on his cane.

"If you wanted trouble you picked the right one, playa. Bring yo dumb ass on." Smoke flashed me an evil smile and motioned his arm out the door as he stepped up into the car. I looked at the woman holding the twins and in her eyes I saw fear. The boy and the little girl were now both playing tug-of-war with her keys that had been pulled from her purse. I could tell she was scared for me and she was scared for her babies. She kept sneaking glances at me and Smoke. He jumped into a defensive stance and said, "You gonna run? Motherfucker, you think shit's sweet. Fucking bitches in other niggas' beds? Playing a nigga like you don't owe me?" He motioned out the door.

His hands were shaking, but I don't think he was nervous. He stood there and I sat looking at his shaking hands and I didn't answer him. The baby boy was laughing with the set of keys in his hand while the baby girl was deep in a cry. The mother grabbed the boy's chubby cheeks and said, "Listen, everything is not yours. You need to share."

I was caught, there was nothing to say, no way to escape. Smoke stepped toward me and knelt down so we were eye level as I sat. He looked me in the face, elbowed me in the mouth, and snatched me up out of my seat by the collar and walked me down off the trolley. As he did, the crying baby pointed at us and screamed out. The mother snatched the keys from the baby boy.

The doors closed. The trolley pulled off.

Smoke pushed me into the back of his boy Kendrick's gold Chevy Caprice. Beezy was in the back with me and Smoke. Tunnetta and Aldrich were up front with Kendrick, looking scared as shit. There was no music playing, all I could hear was the car squeaking with the bumps and turns in the road and an occasional siren. Nobody said anything. I could feel the sting from my busted lip and Smoke kept his arm around me like we were buddies. Beezy kept smiling at me with his bubbled-up eye, looking proud of himself, like I wouldn't slump his punk ass again if Smoke wasn't breathing down my neck. Tunnetta looked at us in the rearview mirror and this was when Beezy started to get cute.

"Fuck you looking at, nigga?"

Then Beezy cocked his fist and punched me right in the eye.

"Sucker!" He laughed and smacked me again in the back of the head. I lunged at him and Smoke tightened his grip and laughed, "I wouldn't do that."

I looked at Aldrich and he looked like he wanted to cry as we pulled into the parking lot of Kelly Field and Kendrick tossed the car into park. We all got out and started walking off and once we made it behind the track, I knew they were taking me into the woods. I wanted to shit myself or scream out for someone to help me, but I didn't. In a weird way I felt a certain peace about being in no-man's-land as we walked into the brush. We followed a hiking trail until we made it onto a clearing and we all stopped. Smoke pushed me and I stumbled but kept my balance. I turned around and everything went Christmas Eve silent as everyone scattered away from me. I looked at Smoke and he had his pistol pointed right at me. I felt lightning in my blood. I couldn't run or do anything. All I said was, "I got your money. If you just take me home I can give you your money."

Smoke shook his head. "I'da took the money a while ago, but that's before you decided to fuck a bitch in my bed, lose my money on some ol' humbug shit, then punch my brother. Nigga, I oughta shoot your stupid ass."

I farted a few times as I stood there and everyone else tried not to call attention to themselves. Smoke lowered the pistol and jogged at me and all I remember was seeing him swing and a flash of blue steel, I felt a sharp thump and everything went dark. I opened my eyes and I was down on the ground and I was leaking blood from somewhere on my face. Tunnetta was screaming and I heard Smoke yell, "Shut that bitch the fuck up."

I saw Aldrich's black Adidas try to run away, but Kendrick grabbed him. He said, "Slow down, brah, we 'bout to dip," and Aldrich didn't try to fight him at all.

A black and a blue pair of Timberlands walked toward me and I looked up a bit. It was Beezy and Smoke. Beezy leaned down and started patting at my pockets. I rolled over and put my bloody hands out in front of me. Then Smoke kicked me in the ribs.

"Move and I'll pistol-whip ya ass again. Say anything. Say one motherfucking word about this and I'll fucking kill you. I try to put you on. Teach you some game and this is how you cut. You lucky today, I'm feeling led by God's shining light. I'm 'bout to hit Bible study, nigga. Mama can't always save ya lil' ass."

He kicked me again, and then Kendrick grabbed Tunnetta, who wouldn't stop screaming, and started walking her and Aldrich back toward the car. I swung my arms trying to fight, but I felt like I was underwater and I wasn't moving fast enough. Beezy found the weed in my sock as Smoke took out a joint of his own and sparked it. Beezy handed my weed to Smoke and Smoke said, "Oh, you got work now? Guess we'll call it even then, buster. See ya at Bible study."

Smoke and Beezy walked back toward the car and I stayed on the ground. It felt safer there. I closed my eyes and heard footsteps again. I looked, and it was Beezy patting me down.

"And gimme my girl's phone."

Again, I stayed down.

It was just my luck to stumble out of the woods and see

Reggie shooting around at the basketball courts as I tried to regain my balance. He was the only person I wanted to see until I actually saw him. I had dirt all over me. My face got hot and I put my head down and limped toward the courts. All bloodied up like I was, there was no way of denying something had just happened to me, but I didn't feel like explaining myself. My right hand felt full of loose glass shards. The skin under my left eye was puffy like a ketchup packet when I touched it and the swelling made it hard to see. My whole body felt road-rashed and everything was either tingling or warm and numb. The cut on my forehead was beginning to feel like a glob of Jell-O and the blowing wind made it sting. I glanced up at Reggie and he stared me down as I limped over, but he didn't say anything. He met me at the picnic table and sat down across from me. Sweat-burning water ran from my eyes, but I wasn't crying.

I sat sideways on the bench of the picnic table with my body facing the basketball courts away from Reggie. In the corner of my eye I could see the sides of his lips wiggling. I could see his bunched-up cheeks restraining that smile, that I-told-you-so expression. I looked down at the grass trying to stare at the brown dirt.

I tried to sneak a glance at him and he saw me and looked me off, shifting his gaze onto the empty basketball courts.

"So is that what's been having you hiding out? An ass whooping? I just seen them all pull away. Might as well just come on with it."

I turned around in my seat, my back to Reggie. I was still stuck on that initial grin I saw on his face. Somewhere inside of himself he thinks this shit's funny. He's been all over me about tightening up and cleaning up my act, and I been telling him I got my shit under control and not to worry. But the blood in my mouth, on my hands, face, and shirt tells a very different story. All I wanted was some ice and a blunt, I wasn't in the mood for a Reggie-sermon but I felt one coming on anyway. He took a joint from his pocket, sparked up, and passed it to me.

"So what happened, Dre? How is it I see Kendrick and Smoke and them dipping out of the parking lot and a few minutes later you come out the woods looking like a basket of bruised berries. They jumped you?"

I tossed my hand up. "Nah, they ain't jumped me. Smoke gun-butted me across the face and then Beezy bitch-ass-punched me in the eye and ran my weed while I was on the ground. It's all good, though. Smoke said we even for that old debt. So I got off, kinda. I took the whooping and I got the money to pay you for the bud they up took off me. They only got me for half an ounce."

I looked over at Reggie and he stood up. His nostrils belled out and his narrow cheeks flexed. He had on a white wife-beater and it looked a size too small for him. He looked down at me and balled his fists and his muscles bulged. A large vein wiggled across his forehead.

"Wait. That nigga took something up off you that belonged to me. No bet. Ain't no letting that shit slide, Andre. Especially when it comes to Smoke. Fuck the money, he ain't 'bout to be running around here bumping his lips, 'bout blazing up my trees or anything else. Cool fucking haircut too, nigga." He giggled but didn't smile. "I been waiting for a reason to ride."

Reggie shook his head at me and turned around and started walking away toward the parking lot. He called back, "Let's go."

14

Aftermath

We stormed off and got inside Reggie's Jeep and as we rode there was a glazy red distance in his eyes, his mind was made up. I thought we were 'bout to flash on the block, jump out, and roll on Smoke and his crew, and I was down for the action, but instead he took me over to some apartment off River Street in Mattapan.

We didn't knock. Reggie had a key.

"Who?" called a mousy voice as Reggie turned the key, pushed the door open, and we walked into the dark hallway of the shotgun apartment.

"Fuck else gotta key, Jasmine?" Reggie said as we walked up the hallway to the living room.

"Nigga, you need to knock. Scarin' a bitch half to death." Reggie flicked on the lights and he pointed at her.

"Andre, this is Jasmine, and she talk too fuckin' much." He gave her one of those charged-up glares and she sat up on the couch, took off her head wrap, and started brushing down her hair. It smelled like she'd freshly cocoa-buttered her long rum-brown legs. She looked at me and her forehead twisted into a puzzle of wrinkles. She tossed her hand over her mouth and kicked her feet into her slippers.

"Eww, nigga! What happened to your friend?"

"Lil' tussle . . . nothing that concerns your business. Now stop asking questions." She gazed down at the floor and looked away. Reggie walked into the living room and sat on the couch, put his pistol on the glass coffee table, and started unleafing a Backwood. I stood in the doorway watching. He tossed the tobacco in the little bin beside the couch and paused to look at Jasmine.

"Do me a solid—clean him up." He opened the bottle of Johnnie Walker Red that Jasmine had sitting at the shiny gold foot of the coffee table. She groaned like she was annoyed, stomped toward me, and grabbed my good hand and pulled me toward the hallway. Reggie didn't look at her, he just started breaking down a neon green bud.

"Rude-ass nigga," she snapped under her breath as we walked down the dark hallway of closed doors.

Even though Reggie talked to her like she wasn't shit, I knew he didn't feel that way. Reggie never seemed impressed by a bad bitch, he had a gang of 'em, but Jasmine still intimidated the fuck outta me. She was one of the fat-booty flat-stomach broads—way out of my league. I stood in the doorway and slick-eyed Jasmine. She stood there in the mirror, tiptoeing around the bathroom looking for something, giving me a moment to glance her up and down, acting like she ain't seen me watching her donkey-stiff booty until she finished braiding her long jet-black hair into a ponytail. In the good light I could see that she had green contact lenses in her eyes. Her hair looked soft and wavy. I wondered if she was one of them stuck-up black girls that claim she got Cherokee or some other kind of Indian in her blood. She opened the medicine cabinet and the mirror swung out and I caught a good look at myself. The white part of my right eye was pepper red and underneath bulged up plum purple. My forehead looked bad. The blood was crusting, but I could tell the cut was deep and very much still open.

She slammed the cabinet closed and turned on the faucet and let it run until I saw steam coming off the water. My upper lip was all swollen. It didn't really hurt, it mostly felt fat and numb.

"Sit down, lil' nigga." She shifted her juicy hips to the side, reached up into a closet, and pulled out a washcloth. She tossed it into the steaming soap water and came over and knelt down in front of me. She rung out the rag and swiped the cloth over my face. My entire head throbbed and burned. I winced and balled my fists, scrunching my eyes and clamping down my jaws, trying not to squirm or look like a bitch. I opened my eyes and she smiled at me with her round spaced-out dolphin teeth.

She held my chin. "So you at least whoop the niggas you was beefing wit'?" She grinned.

"Yeah," I mumbled as she paintbrushed the rag over my face.

"Mmmm hhhmmm." She bunched her lips to one side of her face. "If that's true, I bet you left 'em wishing they never messed wit' you." It wasn't until she laughed and smacked a handful of Vaseline onto the cut on my forehead that I realized she was being sarcastic, playing me out completely. "You gonna need some stitches for this gash up here."

I shrugged my shoulders and said, "Nothing a few Band-Aids won't fix." I looked away as sharp pains lightning-streaked across my face.

I heard boots stomping up the hallway and Reggie appeared in the doorway smoking a blunt.

"Is he gonna make it? Shit, you doing surgery back here?"

Jasmine rolled her eyes and pouted her lips.

"Yes. He's fine, but that cut on his head is big. Butterfly strips ain't fixing that. Take him to a hospital."

Reggie took a long drag from his blunt and blew a few smoke circles.

"Just put some tape and gauze on it and get him one of my old T-shirts."

She looked away from him, jilted. She stood up and walked out of the bathroom and Reggie smacked her ass, and Jasmine smacked Reggie's hand away and they both laughed as she walked off. It was like watching a magician at work the way Reggie had mind control over Jasmine. Even though she acted like she was aggravated about all of his demands, it didn't stop her from listening and doing exactly what he said.

"Here." Reggie handed me the blunt and the bottle of Johnnie Walker and I took a gulp and coughed. My chest burned as I swallowed and took a drag from the blunt. Jasmine came back with a gray V-neck T-shirt and handed it to me. I put it on and held still as she put a few butterfly strips and some gauze and tape on my cuts. I sniffed her fruity perfume as she bandaged my face. Reggie tapped his hands on the top of the door frame as Jasmine finished cleaning me up. He passed the bottle back and I took another swig and heard a baby start crying. She stood up and arm-barred Reggie out of her way and swaggered up the hallway.

"Y'all loud-asses woke up your son," she called back to us.

Reggie looked at me as I stood up, he chuckled and shook his head, but I could tell he wasn't amused. He took a big gulp from the bottle as we walked back to the living room. My head was beginning to spin and my vision bounced a bit whenever I moved too fast. I heard a door slowly squeal open and then I heard little feet smacking against the hardwood floor and I froze. I looked behind me and saw a little boy in just a diaper baby-waddling toward us, his arms in the air, the light from the bathroom glowing through his little baby-thin 'fro.

"Da-da, Da-da, Da-da, Da-da." Reggie stopped and turned around. He smirked at the little boy and knelt down and the boy fell into his arms. He picked him up and suctioned his little body against his chest. He walked past me into the living room and sat the little boy on his lap and took the pack of Backwoods out and tossed 'em to me. I took one out and started to unleaf it. He picked up the little boy and placed him one cushion away on the three-seater and I sat on the love seat on the other side of the room. The little boy sat grinning at Reggie and he took another swig and pushed his pistol out to the side and started breaking up some green. I heard Jasmine's slippers sliding up the floor and she popped into the doorway, hand on hip, neck crooked to the side, in her meanest ghetto-girl pose with the screw face on heavy.

"Umm, no. Y'all ain't 'bout to sit here smoking in front of my son."

Reggie tossed his hands in the air like he was innocent and opened his eyes all wide, waving at me, mocking her, "Andre, I think she wants me to put away my gateway drugs."

Reggie busted out laughing and swigged down the last sips of Johnnie Walker. I grinned, but didn't really think it was my place to be cracking up like Reggie was. I figured she wasn't wrong and put the leaf back inside the pack of Backwoods. Reggie's eyebrows arched at me and his broad nose scrunched in and his forehead wrinkled up stiff. His eyes narrowed to slits and he growled, "Gimme the bag." No questions asked, I slid it over to him.

He opened the bag and took out the leaf and started rolling a blunt and Jasmine stood in the doorway watching him. I glanced at a neutral spot between Reggie, the floor, and the coffee table, and we all watched him. I don't know how babies can tell when something's up, but the baby boy stayed put and watched Reggie with us too, until the tension got too stiff and his little lips started to ripple and his eyes pinked up as tears wiggled down his cheeks. The little boy's face twisted like he'd tasted something sour, and he reached out for Jasmine and bawled out.

"Ma-ma, Ma-ma, Ma-ma." The little boy bounced on his butt. "Up. Up. Up. Pick . . . up."

Jasmine glared at him.

"Dammit, Reece, stop it!" She groaned again and stomped over to the little boy. His fingers waved out for Jasmine. "What! Reece, your little ass should be in the bed anyway." She picked him up and walked back over to the doorway, balancing Reece on her hip. I looked at Reggie and he flicked his lighter and inhaled the blunt and blew the smoke right at Jasmine. She shrieked like a hawk about to attack and tossed Reece on the couch next to me and charged at Reggie. Reggie stood up and stopped her charge, snatching her by the throat and shoving her back in the direction she came from.

Reece crawled over and grabbed onto my arm and started wailing, "Ma-ma, Ma-ma." He alternated loud moans and screams and drooled all over my arm but I didn't have it in me to push him away. Jasmine popped back up off the wall.

"You ain't shit-ass nigga, you gon' hit me? You gon' die by that."

I looked at Reggie and maybe it was the Johnnie Walker but from where I was sitting on the couch Reggie looked like he'd grown an entire foot. He took two big stomps across the room and swung his open palm at her face.

"Shut up, bitch." It sounded like he'd popped a can of rolls.

"Mmmmmm," Jasmine sighed deep. He'd hit her so hard

she could only hum and hold her face as she rested on the floor balled up like a fetus, Reggie standing over her. "You need to get yo ass in the motherfuckin' bed."

Images of Reggie jumping my father back on that Christmas Eve seven years ago flashed in my head. I don't know if it was the liquor, the shock, or hearing screams and cries, but as I sat watching Reggie and Jasmine fighting, and as Reece clung to me screaming, drooling, and nibbling away at my arm, my heart broke for him. I reached out and hugged him to my side and patted the top of his head until Reggie walked back to his seat. Jasmine wasn't behind him. Reece whimpered into my shirt and Reggie looked up and his face softened. He lit the blunt back up and hit it a few times, then he stood up to pass it to me and snatched Reece up and sat him on his lap. He kissed him on the forehead and bounced him on his knee.

"Mama hurt, Dada. Mama hurt." Reece tugged at his sleeve.

"No, Mama bitch. Mama bitch, baby," he said in a baby voice as he laughed and bounced him on his knee.

I could hear Jasmine in the kitchen tearing through the pots and pans, clanking glass together. It sounded like she was looking for something or just breaking things. I smoked the blunt and watched Reggie as he bounced his son on his knee. In all the days I'd kicked it with him I'd never heard him mention having a son. I'd never even seen Jasmine riding in his car, and for whatever reason, knowing Reggie was somebody's daddy made me realize what responsibilities he was talking about that day at Kelly Park. It's like I'd drifted off into a trance and forgot what had just happened. I just sat watching Reece bouncing on his knee until I heard fast footsteps up the hall and Reggie bounced his knee up extra high and shoved Reece to the side and hopped to his feet. I thought he was about to hit me for some reason, so I tossed my hands over my face but he wasn't worried about me. He grabbed the empty Johnnie Walker bottle from the table and flung it into the doorway. I heard the glass shatter. He lunged at the door and I stayed in my seat, looking at Reece reaching out at the door.

"Bitch, you lost your fuckin' mind. I'll fuckin' kill you dead before you cut me."

"Get . . . the . . . fuck . . . off . . . of . . . me," Jasmine struggled out the words as I could hear the skidding squeal of her skin dragging up the hallway. She screamed until he tossed her in a room and shut the door behind them. The walls were thin but they muffled their words and all I could hear were muted bumps and thuds. Reece howled with his eyes closed, kicking and screaming up at the ceiling. I stood up and walked over to him and picked him up as he sobbed and balled his hands into my shirt, shaking his little fists, gnawing at my upper arm.

"It's okay," I told him, even though I knew it wasn't. I bounced him side to side and hushed him until the swaying became too much and I started to feel sick and I put him down. He rolled back and forth on the couch, shrieking out to nobody. I sat as he maneuvered himself off the couch and started crawling toward me as I heard a hallway door open and slam shut.

Reggie's hand waved in the door to the living room, "Let's go."

I looked into the little boy's tender face, stood up, walked into the unlit hallway, and left the apartment without saying anything to Jasmine. The lock clicked behind us, but then the door creaked open a crack and I looked back into the dark slit but I couldn't see Jasmine. Reggie tossed his hands out at his sides. "In the fuckin' bed," he said matter-of-factly and the door slammed shut. I followed behind him outside. He never looked back.

When we got out to the street I could feel the liquor swaying my steps. Reggie was a few steps ahead of me and he wasn't walking too straight either. In my head, all I could see was that little boy's crying face, and all of them Team Seven niggas huddled up stomping out my pops. It's like I was fading in and out. We got to the Jeep and I gripped the door handle and thought to myself that it probably wasn't the best idea to drive anywhere. But then I remembered that it was about nine thirty and Bible study was probably in full swing and I had to be somewhere. Where really didn't matter.

I got in the car and figured maybe a little more weed would mellow Reggie out. Plus, after the way he just did Jasmine, I wasn't really trying to get in his way. I ain't have a clue what he was thinking or where we were going. He stomped the gas as the tires burned rubber and we pulled off down River Street.

We cruised over to ODB Liquors, he hopped out and left the Jeep running, then came back with an eight-pack of the sweet-flavored Backwoods and a fifth of Johnnie Walker Black. I really didn't think I could take any more drink, but we sat outside the liquor store and Reggie rolled a blunt and when he passed me the Johnnie Walker, I drank it and passed it back.

The blunt burned slow and at first the Johnnie Walker went down warm and smooth but it gradually began twisting my stomach up more and more with every sip. I hit the blunt a few times but Reggie mostly smoked it and I slouched in my seat feeling wavy as hell, hardly able to sit up straight. I closed my eyes and wondered what exactly had him tripping. As we sat in silence, I began to doze off when Reggie started the Jeep and tossed the roach out the window. He popped the clutch and the Jeep lurched forward and started rolling backward into traffic. He shifted into first gear and we roared out onto River Street as he rolled down all the windows and the breeze howled through the Jeep.

I looked over at him and there was electricity in his narrow glare at the road that felt unwrapped and very dangerous.

"So what are we going to do about this shit?" He didn't look at me.

"What, the trees? I told you I got the money to pay you for the trees."

Reggie giggled real high-pitched like a baby playing.

"Try again, pussyboy, this time answer me like a man with a dick between his legs. I mean what the fuck are you going to do about getting robbed and beat like a bitch in your own neighborhood?" He swung his fist at me and I flinched back but he didn't hit me. Instead he held his fist in front of my mouth like an announcer holding a postgame interview.

"I'm saying we can go see him." I looked over his way.

His eyes were pasta-sauce red, and mine were probably worse. He turned on Jam'n 94.5 and the *Friday Night Throw-down* was on. The DJ was taking requests, and some girl from South Boston called in and requested Notorious B.I.G.'s "Mo Money Mo Problems." He turned it all the way up as we pulled up to a red light. He glared at me.

"You fuckin' right we gon' see that nigga. Nobody takes Reggie's shit. Reggie's shit is Reggie's shit."

"I gotchu. I gotchu." I nodded my head.

"See, I told you to stop fuckin' around. I told you to tighten the fuck up, and now look at this shit. Ain't no bag of money big enough for me to let Smoke walk around talking 'bout them Team Seven niggas is soft. I'm on the verge of greatness, Andre. I'm not to be fucked with. 'Cause see, I don't give a fuck. I come from a long line of pimps and hustlers, and my mama was a sorry ho. It's all gravy, I beat the game when I graduated high school. Get it? I can't lose. I'll cash it all in right fuckin' now and I'd still die a winner."

The light turned green and we pulled off. I kept my eyes locked on the road as Reggie started speeding up and slowing down right before we almost rear-ended the car in front of us. I grabbed the overhead handle and put on my seat belt.

"Aww, you scared—you want me to take your punk ass home?"

I sat up and rubbed my hands over my face as I asked, "I'm saying ain't you tryin'a go see Smoke and Beezy and them niggas?"

"Say it like you ain't about to take a shit on yourself."

"Let's go see them niggas." I clamped my jaws.

"Real recognize real, and I was wrong about you." He smacked me in the chest and grabbed a handful of my shirt and pulled me toward him. "You afraid to die, nigga?" I looked into the yellowy-red glaze in his eyes. "Fucking answer me!"

He punched the dashboard and yanked the steering wheel as I braced down on my hurt hand and fell against the passenger-side door as the Jeep swerved on two wheels across River Street into oncoming traffic. He jerked the wheel back and we bounced back down onto four wheels and a horn blared and brakes squealed and I tossed my arms over my face as the bright white headlights fogged my vision.

"Yeee-haaaa," Reggie screamed as he jerked the wheel back again and we swerved back onto our side of the road and hopped the curb.

"You scared?" he asked me as he stomped the brakes. "You scared, nigga? I said, are you afraid to fuckin' die?"

My heart was beating so fast I thought I would yack on myself if I said anything more than "Nah" and shook my head.

He tossed his head back and began laughing again, his Adam's apple pulsing up and down. He grabbed a joint from his pocket, sparked up, and gulped at it a few times, "'Ight, 'ight," he coughed and we pulled off. "We'll see."

He passed me the joint and his face went no-bullshit stiff. He mashed the gas and we sped off the sidewalk. He kept asking me if I was afraid to die and swerving in and out of the right lane. I was pouring sweat and felt on the verge of puking.

We got to the intersection of River Street and Blue Hill Avenue, and I looked at the bridge to Milton. We stopped for a moment, letting the radio play. Then he peeled off and we rolled up over the bridge into Milton and he swerved the car a few more times and I tossed my hand in the air like I was at school and Reggie was my teacher.

"Stop the car," I waved my hand. "I wanna get out—stop the car," I said.

He pulled off to the side of the parkway, stopped, and smiled at me.

"I knew you was a pussy, just like that nigga Smoke. Get the fuck out."

I stepped out of the Jeep and wobbled a bit but gained my balance, Reggie swerved off and it felt good to be alone on the sidewalk. I started limping home. I felt no pain. Johnnie Walker had me feeling warm and ready for war with whoever was in my way when I made it to the block. Can't be a bitch forever. I started muttering "Fuck it" to myself as I walked up the parkway toward Verndale. I began playing out fight scenarios in my head, and they all went the same way, I walked up onto the block and coldcocked the first asshole to say some dumb shit. Smoke, Reggie, Beezy, Pop, Aldrich, I ran through 'em all. But when I actually got to the corner of Verndale, I sobered up quick. The block was thumping, I heard bass, I could hear girls laughing. I couldn't see in a straight line but I could tell there was a lot of people chillin' on the corner of Lothrop.

I gathered myself a bit, then started walking as regular as I could manage. The first person that laid eyes on me had to be Sade Fulton's bucket-head ass. The trickin' ho was all leaned up on Big Maal against the side of my front porch, and there was kids from school everywhere. From the corner my crib looked like the community YMCA more than it looked like there was any type of Bible study going on. Smoke was bold. After him and Beezy jumped me and took Reggie's weed, instead of trying to get lost for the night, him, Kendrick, Tunnetta, and Aldrich actually showed up for Bible study. The story was, I'd never shown up at the barbershop and Beezy was sick in bed fighting off a cold. According to those in attendance, my mother worried herself sick, not because I wasn't at Bible study but because Smoke coached Aldrich and Tunnetta into keeping straight faces as they told my mother that they hadn't seen me that afternoon.

It was a plan as flawed as my ability to hustle. I later heard that my mother got to the end of her opening prayer when Miss Myra rolled up into Bible study, drag-walking Beezy behind her, and she was pissed, and Beezy was bruised. I've heard many versions of what happened next and the only consistencies among the accounts I've heard are that Miss Myra walked into Bible study and tried to hem up Smoke.

He restrained her—everyone makes certain to mention that he did not hit her—he held her wrists and kept her from punching him. Fights scare away the girls, fighting always scares away the girls, so they ran outside and the dudes stuck around to see what was about to happen, which made some of the girls come back inside. At some point Beezy admitted that I punched him in the face, and he coaxed Tunnetta's simple ass into telling my mother I took her cell phone but that I gave it back before I ran off into the train station, which was the last place anyone saw me. This is where, I've pieced together, I reenter the equation. Sade Fulton peeped me walking around the corner and I saw her run inside my house, and knew she was about to go up there and dry-snitch, but she did me one better and straight up ratted me out. Sold a nigga upstate. She walked into the middle of the chaos and yelled, "Andre's limping up the street looking fucked up like shit. I mean messed up. Sorry, Miss Battel." And everyone stampeded back out of our house and Nina was one of the first to make it outside. She looked at me and when our eyes met and she sprinted off the porch toward me the liquor probably made my limp look worse. She got to me and looked like she was going to cry.

"What the hell happened to you? You look a whole mess."

I didn't answer her. I looked up on the front porch and saw Smoke, Tunnetta, and Aldrich standing there, and I locked in and started walking toward them. Smoke smiled at me and I could tell he wasn't scared at all. Out came my mother, Miss Myra, and Beezy from the door behind him and I stopped. The three of them started walking toward me and Nina. The five of us formed a pentagon huddle. Nobody was smiling.

"You punched Beezy in the face and stole some young lady's cell phone," my mother accused more than asked me.

"Did Beezy tell y'all he punched me in my eye too? Did Smoke tell you what he did? Everybody snitching tonight, huh?"

I blame the Johnnie Walker—I should've stopped talking then, but I didn't.

"How you gon' be hugged up with the same nigga that split my head open, literally?" I said to Nina. Her face hung loose and then she cupped my chin.

"Smoke hit you?" she asked me.

I nodded my head. "I ain't do this all to myself." I looked past Nina up at our front porch. Aldrich and Tunnetta were walking toward us with a crowd of who's who from the hallways trailing behind them, everybody had come out for Bible study. I think it was the Kool-Aid and the chicken that roped niggas initially, but that's beside the point. Aldrich and Tunnetta got to where we were all standing, and my mother and Miss Myra stood next to each other arms folded wearing Grinch faces. I made eye contact with my mother and I remember feeling consumed with embarrassment, shriveled by her glare. I looked around and Sade Fulton and Keyona Lawson and the whole Hot Girls crew were looking at me, Big Maal and Tito and them BRC cats were standing behind them. Mr. Watson pulled up in his Range Rover and hopped out, looking confused. I looked off past him and saw Smoke and Kendrick slinking their way back up the street. They strolled together until they passed Chucky Taft's house and Kendrick cut down a side alley heading toward Blue Hills Parkway and I watched Smoke as he walked by himself.

D-roc and Buggy were posted up, blasting their music and spitting game to the girls surrounding them on the corner until they saw Mr. Watson pacing around and asking everybody questions. They turned down their music, I could tell they smelled the trouble in the air because they all piled into Buggy's car and pulled off. As they rounded the corner I heard tires squeal and I looked up the street and saw Reggie peeling rubber over the hill. Him and Smoke were heading right at each other. Reggie pulled his Jeep to the side of the road and hopped out and walked up on Smoke and a stillness fell over everyone as we just watched as they stood face-to-face.

Mr. Watson called to my mother, "Ruby, I don't know what's going on but it looks out of hand. I'm calling the police." No one responded to him as he took out his cell phone, dialed, and held it to his ear. We all watched, frozen and breathless, as Reggie and Smoke stood exchanging quiet words that none of us will ever know. It wasn't until they started yelling that everyone started squirming. Reggie pulled his pistol first and Smoke yelled, "Fuck you gon' do with that?" and pulled out his pistol too. Reggie held his pistol with his finger on the trigger with his arms folded, Smoke held his by the handle down at his waist like it was a nightstick. Again, not looking very nervous.

Reggie took a step closer and gangsta-growled, "You got five seconds to pay me my money and say you sorry or I'ma start letting off out this bitch." Smoke didn't seem moved. Instead he took a step back and said, "Nigga, put your little toy gun away."

My mother and Miss Myra couldn't hold still any longer. They started running off up the street toward them and we all hurried behind them.

Reggie laughed a long evil laugh and said, "Toy?" then took a step back, raised the pistol to chin level, and pulled the trigger. I remember seeing a flame leave the gun and in the night it shot a party popper of sparks into Smoke's face and exploded mounds of skull and strands of brain out the back of his head. One of Smoke's feet stomped forward and the other one fell back as his body jerked to the side and dropped to the ground. Everyone started screaming and running toward them. My mother and Miss Myra got there first. Miss Myra fell on top of Smoke screaming out "No!" over and over again. My mother fell next to her and Miss Myra held Smoke's bleeding head in her lap and my mother hugged her shoulders. Smoke's blood was all over both of them.

Reggie ran back to his Jeep and cleared everyone from the street when he sped off pedal to the metal, daring anyone to stand in his way. I couldn't run anymore. I fell to my knees and started throwing up violently all over myself and all I could hear was the commotion. I heard Nina crying, and it didn't occur to me until she wiped the blood leaking from my forehead that she'd been standing right beside me the whole time. I crawled to the curb and sat down and the entire block was awake and outside. I could see the suntan ladies already huddled up, gossiping as ambulances arrived and the jakes slowly started to filter onto the block. I didn't know where Reggie had sped off to, but I could tell he was in the area, I could hear his bass thumping. I heard male voices off in the distance yelling, "Hey, hey, sir, please drop the gun. Sir, please drop your weapon."

Then I heard an eruption of gunshots, and for some reason I didn't have to run back onto Decker Street to see, to know Reggie had held his ground and shot it out with the cops. It felt so simple, so easy, finger-snap fast, that that bullet could have exploded out of Reggie's pistol and a few seconds later everyone was running back onto Decker Street to see Reggie's crime scene.

I stayed where I was. I'd seen him do enough.

Nina sat beside me on the curb bawling as my father pulled up to the house, drunk himself, and staggered over to us. He saw the vomit all over my shirt, all the flashing lights, and Nina crying. He kept asking us, "What happened?" Nina was so upset she couldn't even make words and he knelt down beside her and rubbed her shoulder and she slouched over and sobbed into his chest. He hugged her and kept asking me, "What happened?" I ignored him and looked away as the ambulance pulled off with Smoke inside. I could hear that he was still trying to talk to me but something inside of myself just wouldn't allow me to say a word to him. Some things just get left wrong.

Ma and Mr. Watson walked up to me with an EMT, and Ma told Mr. Watson she had it under control, and him and Aldrich hopped inside the Range Rover and that was the last time I saw Aldrich that summer.

The EMT took off my bandages and walked me over to an ambulance and took me down to the hospital. On the ride over, the EMT told me and Ma that whoever tried to patch up my cut had used masking tape to keep the gauze pads in place. I got stitched up and rejoined Beezy, my mother, Miss Myra, and Nina in the waiting room of the hospital because Smoke didn't die immediately. They said he still had a pulse. They also said that even if he came out of the coma, he would've been a vegetable at best. We waited.

When the news came, hearing Miss Myra crying shook the tears out of all of us. Beezy hugged her and my mother hugged them and me and Nina hugged her. Death is a permanent parking spot, no coming back from it. Done is done. I don't understand what it was between them two that made it have to be like that and I'll never get the chance to ask Reggie why he went to jail but I believed him when he said he was never going back. I don't know if Reggie or the cops fired first, but at this point it doesn't matter. It was headline news:

> *Two dead bodies, and a whole neighborhood's worth of traumatized children after a rare shooting in Milton leads police to use lethal force on the gunman. No obvious motives.*

The pigs sniffed around the block for a few days, questioning anybody who would talk as they tried to piece some kind of story together. News camera crews hovered the block for the next couple days too and the suntan ladies were all over it, telling any camera that would listen that "this is a good neighborhood" and "Milton's just not that kind of town" and how they knew "those boys on the corner were up to no good," carrying on all dramatic for the cameras. Anybody that really knew anything about it stayed low and wasn't talking about it for damn sure. The next day I called Aldrich and he answered his house phone and told me he wasn't allowed to hang out or talk to me anymore. He told me not to worry, his father didn't know he had been late for Bible study, so he just let him believe what he did and that I'd never made it to the barbershop and left it at that. It's all I really wanted to know anyway.

Nina was so broken up about Smoke she just stayed in bed all day crying and listening to Mary J. Blige and Aaliyah. Between consoling her and going back and forth to Miss Myra's house, Ma was so busy she hadn't really gotten a chance to properly press me about what *really* happened that night. Me and Beezy agreed that our story was that we'd got into a fight but

that Smoke and Reggie's issues were all theirs and that's all
we knew about it. After the proper authorities arrived and
cleaned up the crime scene, people came and put down teddy
bears and baskets of flowers in the spot where Reggie killed
Smoke and in the spot where the cops killed Reggie. I did my
best to stay out of the way. Word around the block was that
the cops had been calling people in for questioning, and it
took a few days but I knew they'd get around to wanting to
talk to me. They were calling everybody down to the station
like there was anything left to solve. What and why it happened and the motives matter very little at this point. Both of
them are dead, there's no justice to be had. When the police
came to the house asking for me they rang Nana and Papa
Tanks's doorbell instead of ours. They asked Papa Tanks if I
was home and he told them that I wasn't even though I was.
He was so angry he didn't even summon me himself, he told
Nana Tanks and she called downstairs and told me to come
up to her room.

When I walked into her room she was sitting in her comfy
chair, wiping tears from her face and shaking her head. I sat
down and she looked me in the eyes.

"Your grandfather tells me police just come a'yawd, saying
dem have some questions to chat wit' you." She rubbed her
hands together like she was cold and sat up in her chair and
gave me a razor-sharp glare. "What type of devilment you
mix up in to make police wan' chat you?"

She blew her nose and I felt a lump swelling in my throat as
I watched her cry. I didn't know what to say to her and when
I tried to speak she waved a hand in the air halting me, "Your
grandfather tells me him seen you run wit' the two boys who
just get killed shooting guns . . . Look on the big bandage on
your head and now police looking for you."

I looked at the floor and didn't answer.

"I thought you was a nice boy, Andre." She closed her eyes and shook her head, "Nana loves you, but go 'way. Come out of me room, me cy-an't look 'pun you right now."

I didn't argue, I just said, "Sorry," and left. By the time I got back downstairs Ma was waiting for me in the kitchen, and she too had spoken with Papa Tanks. We wasted no time getting in the car to ride over to the station. I knew it had to do with Smoke and Reggie, but I didn't know what exactly they wanted to know. I'd thought about that night inside and out and there wasn't anybody other than Jasmine that could say I was with Reggie that night, and I knew she wasn't going to tell the cops anything productive if they ever caught up with her. I had my story straight, I missed Bible study and rode the train all night until I came home and everything went down and other than that I don't know nothing 'bout nothing.

Ma was so pissed off she didn't say a word to me as we drove down to the police station. The cops asked me if I knew anything about the Smoke and Reggie stuff and I told them I didn't. They asked how I cut my head and I told them I was wrestling with a friend. I generally played dumb and I could tell they knew that I knew a lot more than I was saying, but without anything to charge, or a case pending, they eventually had to let me go.

Ma waited until we pulled up to the house and parked the car out front to address me, she grabbed my shoulder and said, "I've been down this road with your father. Let this be the last time I ever drive you home from a police station. You understand me? You're supposed to be a cut above the rest, now act like it."

She rolled her eyes at me, got out of the car, and slammed the door behind her. I followed her into the house and she went into her room and I was looking forward to just having some alone time by myself until I opened my bedroom door and found Papa Tanks sitting in my room on my bed. At first I jumped back, I wasn't expecting him to be there, and when I saw the anger and disappointment coiled up in his face I wanted to run away, but I knew better. He stood up and I took a few steps into the room but stayed back in case he tried to hit me. He took one giant step at me across the room and I jumped on my bed and then he stood in front of me and said, "I dash away everything me know and love to come a'foreign to America and I worked hard, every day, until I retired, so me family could have a better chance, not so me grandson could run wit' the vagabonds and turn a'derelict himself. Now I soon dead and it cy-an't work so, you mus' turn this aroun'. I see you running wit' the corner boys dem even if you nah' do enough for the police dem to keep you. You head all bust up, I know somehow you mix up in it?"

He paused. I looked down and away and didn't say anything.

"Tell me you had nothing to do wit' it."

I shook my head at the floor and said, "I didn't."

He chuckled and said, "Just 'cause you deny it don't mek it less true. Show me your company and I'll tell you who you are, remember, you can shake a man hand but ya cy-an't shake him heart. Even if a hog hide unda sheep wool, him grunt always betray him. Champion, you mus' turn this around." And as quick as he appeared he turned around and walked out of my room and closed the door behind him and I stretched out on my bed and closed my eyes.

At the end of a fall, if there is nothing else there is relief. Even in their absence, Reggie and Smoke sent the entire town into a frenzy. When death comes around it puts a certain perspective on things. Maybe I'm sick in the head or something but I still have that gray V-neck from the night it all went down. I don't know why I still have it, I just do.

It felt like the whole town came out to Smoke's funeral, and I doubt they cared about him as much as people simply despised how he died and what happened that night. Reggie's funeral wasn't as big as Smoke's but a lot of people still came out to pay their final respects. I saw Jasmine during the funeral service but we didn't speak. The sermon from the pastor focused on how no one moment can truly define a man, and he told everyone not to judge Reggie, because we're all God's children. Jasmine held Reece the whole service and I sat with all the Team Seven cats. Reece kept sneaking glances at me over Jasmine's shoulder but I don't think he recognized me. Jasmine just ignored my stares.

After the funerals and the camera crews stopped coming around it felt like something else was going to happen, but things have been pretty quiet. The next Friday came around and Ma was sure nobody would show, but it's like everyone needed somewhere to talk that shit out because I was shocked as I saw the who's who of the hallways packing into Papa and Nana Tanks's living room. At first there was a tense vibe in the air, it was the first time everyone had been together since the funerals and things around the way had begun to settle down.

Ma walked into the center of the room looking around and smiling at everyone. As she thumbed through her Bible she said, "Before I fall back and give you all the floor, I'd like to give you a little Scripture to think about before we all talk." The room was silent as she put on her reading glasses and touched her index finger to the open page of her Bible and cleared her throat, "I'm reading from the sixth chapter in the book of Luke, verses thirty-six through -eight, 'Be merciful, just as your Father is merciful. Do not judge, and you will not be judged. Do not condemn, and you will not be condemned. Forgive, and you will be forgiven. Give, and it will be given to you. A good measure, pressed down, shaken together and running over, will be poured into your lap. For with the measure you use, it will be measured to you.' "

She closed her Bible and everyone was still quiet and she continued, "There's no avoiding the lingering feelings after the tragic loss of two of our own and I'd like to thank God you all found it in your hearts to return to Bible study tonight. I'd like to open up the dialogue, but bear in mind that right now we all need some healing, and judgment and vengeance won't do us any good. There are times that we will disagree in here, but never is there a time that disrespect will be tolerated. Okay!"

She stared around at everybody and walked back to her seat. The room was cemetery silent. The energy turned from tense to just strong. I looked across the room at Sade Fulton as we all stewed in our own thoughts, and it almost felt like a moment of silence until a smile bounced across her face and she raised her hand and said, "So I think I sort of understand the Bible stuff you was talking, so like, every day that I don't say nothing to ugly people, I'm getting points in heaven sort of, right?"

We all busted out laughing and Ma waved her hand laughing and said, "Child, please."

It was a random but fitting comment from a girl so conceited, but we needed something light and the little joke switched the mood and the conversation rolled on from there. Really, Bible study's more like group therapy for neighborhood kids than it's actually Bible talk. Like today, Ma usually opens things up with a little parable from the Bible and a topic and sits back and gives us the floor to talk, and it turns into one big clusterfuck of a conversation, but it's fun. It caught on like lighter fluid, and other than hanging with Chucky Taft sometimes, Friday nights have been the only day of the week that I've kicked it with people this summer.

Without Reggie being around with the crew, it fell apart. I'd see them dudes around sometimes and they'd be in groups of two or three but it seemed like they didn't really run together much anymore. I at least know they stopped hanging on the corner. When all the dust settled, the only thing I hadn't completely ruined was basketball, but with a severely sprained wrist I wasn't allowed to travel with the team, so it's been a lonely summer. But it's sort of better that way. Most days I just try to keep busy. I ain't touched or talked to Tunnetta since the night it all went down and I stopped hustling too. It feels good to finally keep some of the promises I keep making to God.

Me and Beezy are arm's-length-cool, and I don't give two fucks, he can have Tunnetta. After it all went down, I still had a good amount of weed at the house and about two thousand dollars in cash, and I didn't really know what to do with it, so I signed up for a basketball camp in Honesdale, Pennsylvania. From what I heard the best players in the nation always attend this camp, at least that's what Coach Fulton told me.

It was like the plug got pulled and the block felt stale and old, sort of like ruins. I still wake up and scramble my eggs and watch *American Gladiators* on ESPN Classic but nothing seems to feel the same anymore.

I finally got my cast off my right hand and it feels weak as hell and my jump shot's pretty sorry, but it'll all come back slow. At least I got my body back in shape. I make layups in my sleep—it's like riding a bike. I can still hoop. I work out late at night, two or three in the morning when the whole town's asleep, seven days a week. I sprint between the telephone poles and dribble around the sewer caps, even after Bible study.

I'm slowly starting to accept the block's new version of normal, but I know I have to get outta here. Sometimes I sit on the front porch half expecting to hear bass thumping out of the trunk of Reggie's Jeep or to look up the street and see Smoke and his boys blazing up, posted on top of the hill, playing music of their own, but I don't and never will again. The sun-tan ladies still oil-fry under the sun, sipping their liquor-mugs, gossiping about each other to each other, and the old folks still perch on their high porches reading books or magazines, slowly watching the days passing them by. Now the crows line up single file across the telephone wires, cackling cries that echo out bouncing around the block and ruining the other birds' songs.

These days the only thumping on the block is my basketball against the concrete. The neighborhood feels so empty now, the stillness is a silent reverence, the block's testament to the fact that the streets can turn a cool cat into a killer in a matter of seconds, and what's done is done. It's hard to know what's on someone else's mind or what the next man is willing to do to silence the voice that gnaws away and hammers at the back of his head.

Knowing what I know now, I realize I understood very little about both of them cats and it's not about the wrong and the right or the good or the bad of the situation. I fired no shots but I know my role facilitated things. I got caught up and didn't realize the gravity of the moment. Reggie always told me to stop fucking around and now I see what he meant. Regardless of my intentions, some things just can't be taken back, and nothing can be done against the truth, regardless of how long it takes to see through the initial onsets of denial. It went down how it did and bottom line I learned from both of them.

So now that I've finished packing my bags, I'm leaving. I told Ma that I was going to a basketball tournament in New York and she didn't question me too hard about it. Before Ma can wake up and prod me any further about it, I'm going.

As I tiptoe out of the house with my backpack on and my duffel bag in my hands, Papa Tanks is outside bright and early, his whole upper half under his red Dodge Neon. He slides out from under the car and looks at me with confusion in his face, "Champion, where you going wit' bags all packed up?"

"To a basketball camp, Pa-Paw. I'm taking a bus, it stops in New York first."

"I sure hope you're going where you say." He fixes me with a serious look and sort of shakes his head at me.

"I am, I promise."

He shrugs his shoulders and slides back under the car and I start walking toward Mattapan station. I signed myself up for the camp and paid for it with my own money too. I got a pair of new basketball sneakers, and after spreading the money around a little bit I'm leaving town with fifteen hundred dollars in my pocket.

As I walk away from town, I start thinking about Jasmine and Reece. Since the night I first met them, I've wanted to reach out and visit little Reece, but I didn't really think Jasmine would have cared to hear from me. As I cross the bridge carrying my bags into Mattapan, I walk down River Street and ring Jasmine's bell. She answers the door in sweatpants and a mesh head wrap.

"Yes?" She blinks at me all fast like I'm stupid or something.

"Well, I—I . . . I know that there's nothing I can say that could really help change what happened. I just been wondering if you two were okay, and so I know Reggie was close to my mother and I know you're a mother and I just thought maybe this could help toward something someway somehow." I hand her a stack Reggie-style, ten hundred-dollar bills, leaving myself with five hundred. Jasmine takes the money out of my hand and drops it on the floor.

"What did you have to do to get this money? Bet I wouldn't wanna know. All of your kind make me sick." I kneel down and start picking up the bills off the floor when I hear a man's voice coming from inside the apartment. I can't make out what he is saying but she calls back, "It's nothing, babe." She steps to the side and slides her body half behind the door. "That's got to be dirty money in your hands—is it burning a hole in your pockets? You watched that man self-destruct in this place and you just rode along for the ride. Reggie didn't need people like you yes-men in his life. Get the hell from 'round here, lil' nigga." She slams the door.

I want to say, "Hey, but that's not me," but I don't respond. Clearly I showed her different. I just turn around and walk back toward Mattapan station and I stand alone, ready to prove to myself that I can still hoop.

I think I am going crazy as I start to get on the trolley and hear two older voices yelling "Champion" over and over again, like they are calling someone. Papa Tanks calls me that sometimes and the only other person who calls me that is my father. I step into the car and sit down with my bags in front of me and turn to look and, sure enough, it's him, my father in his convertible, and one of my strung-out halfway-house-looking uncles hopping in the passenger seat. They're waving me to come over to the car but I nod my head at them, look away, and put on my headphones. The doors ding closed and the engine sneezes on and the train rattles a bit as we take off. I look at them one last time, now it seems like they are cursing me, until a few cars behind them start blowing their horns. They speed off, and I watch the backs of their heads fade as the trolley rumbles and clacks away.

Acknowledgments

I would first like to thank God without whom none of this would be possible. I am eternally thankful to my mother, Jean Burke, faithful partner in the trenches, and the strongest person I know. To my sisters, Xandria and Ayana Burke, for always looking out for me and setting such a great example. Proper respect and thanks to my grandparents, Lloyd and Ruby Sharp, two trailblazers ahead of their time, and to whose memory this novel is dedicated. I couldn't imagine what my life would be like without Mary Coats, thanks for everything, my dear, it's just the beginning! To Robert and Shari Coats, thank you for believing in our dreams.

Much love and respect to Charlie Tufts and Brian Atkinson, my two day-one Lothrop-Ave. brothers, I couldn't have asked for two better best friends. Much thanks to Carmen and Al Atkinson, for letting me eat up all your food and somewhat live at your home for most of my teenage years and anytime I'm in town. To Robert Badwah, my surrogate older brother, I cherish the times we shared, I think of you often. Thanks to Dave, Ann, and Paul Eder-Mulhane for allowing me to play basketball in their driveway at all hours and for their continued friendship and encouragement over the years.

I'd like to thank the teachers and faculty who helped and encouraged me during my high school years: Michael Langlois, Katherine Lanson, Emily Lucket, Mr. Young,

ACKNOWLEDGMENTS

Mr. Collier, Ms. Star, Mrs. Wilson, Christian Huizenga, Mr. Blute, Nancy Bradley, Maria Gupta, Paul Murry, Cecilia Pan, Landon Rose, and Donna Williams.

I owe a huge debt of gratitude to the teachers and faculty who took the time to help me realize my value in the classroom. Special thanks to Anne Reenstierna for taking a chance on me while I was slightly rough around the edges seventeen-year-old and welcoming me into the Brimmer and May Community. To Nancy Drourr, for being a great teacher, adviser, and friend. Your encouragement and support over the years have been instrumental. To Janita Robinson, for listening to my earliest writing, before I had the courage to show it to anybody else, and for urging me to continue. To Amanda Lombardo, for introducing me to the work of Zora Neale Hurston and changing the way I thought about literature.

I owe a huge thank-you to my agent, David McCormick, for believing in this project before it was finished and for his unwavering support, patience, and editorial insight while we worked on the manuscript. I'd also like to thank Bridget McCarthy and the staff at McCormick & Williams. Another huge thank-you to my editor, Gerry Howard, at Doubleday, for also believing in this project and helping make this a much better novel. Thanks also to Jeremy Medina and the staff at Doubleday. I couldn't have asked for a better team to introduce me to the game.

The Iowa Writers' Workshop changed the course of my life forever and I will always be grateful. Thank you to Lan Samantha Chang and Connie Brothers, for bringing me out to Iowa, treating me great, and giving me the time, resources, and space to write. I'd like to thank the Maytag Fellowship, the Iowa Arts Fellowship, and the MacArthur Foundation for the financial support that allowed me to complete this novel.

Thanks also to Deb West and Jan Zenisek, for all the laughs and helping me stay on schedule while I was a student at the Workshop. I'd also like to thank the amazing cast of fiction writers and professors who have taken the time to read my work, and have knowingly or unknowingly offered meaningful conversation and encouragement. Many thanks to: James Alan McPherson, Marilynne Robinson, Peter Orner, Benjamin Percy, Allan Gurganus, Paul Harding, Tom Grimes, Silas Zobal, Gary Fincke, Karla Kelsey, and Tom and Sarah Bailey for their generosity. I'd also like to thank Lisa Scott, Phil Winger, Dr. Lucien T. Winegar, Dan Olivetti, and Dr. Dave Ramsaran.

Here's the part where I give a few shouts to some old teammates and friends:

Special shout to my SU homies: Josh Robinson, Donta Phillips, Bryan "B.Maj" Majors, Erich Majors, Kenny Anyanwu, Jose D'Oleo, EJ Duncan, Big Rob Cosgrove, Harvey Pannel, Daryl Augustus (gone too soon), Zac Smith, Katie Peters, and Yvonne Donovan.

To my college basketball teammates: Hunter McKain; Fran Brzyski; Jason Dawson; Frank Marcinek, Jr.; Matt McDevit; Joel Patch; Spenser Spencer; and Chad Cohle. Thanks to Coach Frank Marcinek, it may have taken a bit but I'm glad we found common ground.

To Khailia Williams, Jason England, Ayana Mathis, and Nikki Terry, thank you for your generosity when I first arrived in Iowa City.

To my great friend, colleague, and sparring partner Nick Butler, the Workshop wouldn't have been the same without those nights around the starlight. To my sister from another mother, A. Naomi Jackson, for all the laughs and good conversation, I can't wait for your book. To the first friend I made in Iowa City, Scott Butterfield, much respect and thanks for always keeping it 100. To Dr. Lisa Kim, you are an amazing person and I'm thankful I've had the pleasure of working with you. To Ken Duerre and Susan Hazen-Hammond, for your continued friendship, thank you.

Last but not least I'd like to give the biggest shout-out to all the underdogs out there who are misunderstood and underestimated, and yet continue to overcome . . . keep on pushin'.

God bless,
Marcus Burke, September 25, 2013
Iowa City, Iowa

Printed in the United States
by Baker & Taylor Publisher Services